I set my glass on the counter and gently caressed her cheek. "It's healing nicely," I said. "Not even tender to the touch."

"Hey," she said. "What's all this about?"

She tried to pull away, but I held her close. After a moment, she pressed into me.

"Who took a poke at you?" I asked. "Sal?"

She leaned back and studied me intently. I helped her take another drink. The effect was beginning to show in her eyes.

"You're one of Sal's girls, aren't you?"

"Who are you?" she asked.

"Name's Rossi," I said. "Max Rossi."

"Ummm, the sax player," she said.

"That's right. And your name is Evelyn. You're one of Sal's girls. Isn't that right?"

She took another drink, then laid her head against my chest. "Does it make a difference?" she asked.

"It does to Sal," I said.

ROSSI'S RISK

A Max Rosssi Crime Noir

by

Paul W. Papa

ROSSI'S RISK
Published by HPD Publishing
Las Vegas, NV 89105

Published in the United States by:
HPD Publishing (A division of STACGroup llc)
PO Box 230093
Las Vegas, NV 89105

ISBN (pbk): 978-1-953482-06-8; (10-digit) 1-953482-06-6
ISBN (ebk): 978-1-953482-05-1; (10-digit) 1-953482-05-8

Cover design by Elizabeth Mackay Graphic Design
Cover Photo: Deposit Photos

Printed in the United States of America.

HPD Publishing and the HPD logo are trademarks of STACGroup llc.

Keep up with Paul W. Papa's books at www.paulwpapa.com

6 9 1 5 8 2 3 7 6 10

ROSSI'S RISK

ONE

THE PLACE HAD barely been open for a month. It was an experiment really. A test to see how it would do in a town often labeled "the Mississippi of the West." It was called the Moulin Rouge, after the famed Parisian cabaret, birthplace of the raunchy dance known as the Cancan. It was to be the first interracial casino in Las Vegas—welcoming whites, coloreds, and anyone else eager to separate themselves from their hard-earned scratch.

Our purpose for going there was to take in the Tropi Can Can revue, or more specifically, to hear the young colored sax player who was making a name for himself as part of Benny Carter's band. Jimmy Five of the Five and Dimes arranged tickets to the show, and we were to meet him and his gal, Nancy Williams—a Dice Girl—at the casino.

Virginia made me wait three days before she agreed to go with me, a penance I was paying for having pressed my lips where they didn't belong. I'd seen the error of my ways and my Copa Girl had somehow managed to forgive me for the deed; or maybe she just wanted to see her show's competition. Of course, my having almost died in the process helped.

As I pulled my bright red Roadmaster into the porte cochère, a colored valet attendant—the first of his kind in Las Vegas—greeted us. I didn't mind. He took a piece of paper from his jacket pocket, tore it in two, and handed me one half. Then he placed the other under my wiper blade, the same as the white valet attendants did at the Sands. I tossed him a couple of nuggets from my pocket.

He opened the passenger door and let out my leggy companion. She wore a light blue sheath dress with matching kitten heels and a white bolero jacket. Crystals dangled from each ear and a matching piece adorned her very lovely neck. Her gloves were white, her purse clutch, and her eyes brown. Her brunette locks, parted to the side, swept behind her right ear and cascaded down the left side of her face in an abundance of curls. She was simply marvelous, and I told her so.

She kissed me on the cheek, and my knees buckled a bit.

Other than the name, Las Vegas' version of the French landmark looked nothing like its Paris counterpart. The front was demure, except for the larger than life, googie-style lettering designed by neon sign artist Betty Willis, that rested atop the main building. The same words accompanied a 60-foot high neon Eiffel Tower, which was also designed by Willis. I thought it strange that there wasn't a red windmill in sight.

The original Moulin Rouge burned down some thirty years prior. I hoped Will Max Schwartz's version fared better.

I gave Virginia my arm, and she took it. A hint of lavender filled the air as we headed inside. A doorman greeted us, opening the door just fine for us as we entered. I handed him another couple of nuggets.

Though booked as the "Resort Wonder of the World," the inside resembled every other casino in town: dim lights, busy carpets, no windows or clocks, the distinct sound of coins dropping into metal trays. There was, of course, one exception: people of all shades and colors, dressed to the nines, filled the place—and there were a lot of them. All enjoying themselves, gambling, drinking, and having a gay old time. Just like every other casino in Las Vegas, only busier.

We found Jimmy and Nancy near the entrance to the theater, talking to a large man with a cauliflower ear. I recognized him right away.

Jimmy lit up when he saw us. "Hey, glad you two could make it," he said.

We shook hands. Virginia leaned in and rubbed cheeks with Nancy. I kept my distance. Nancy and I had an encounter once, and not a good one, but it wasn't what you think. She had, in my opinion, trouble keeping her petit nose in her own beeswax.

Jimmy turned to the man standing next to him. "This is..."

"Joe Louis," I said, finishing his sentence. "The Brown Bomber. I am very pleased to meet you."

The boxer held out his hand. It dwarfed mine, but I took it anyway. It was firm, but light, as if he was intentionally holding back. Like how a giant might shake hands with a child. Joe Louis was an idol of mine. I'd done a little boxing back in Boston. My father thought I should be able to defend myself and took me to a gym. It was a good gym, and I learned quite a bit about the sport of pugilism. Even had a couple fights of my own.

"Joe's part owner of the Moulin Rouge," Jimmy offered.

The big man tried a smile, but it didn't work. There was something melancholy about him. He had one of those faces that always seemed to be holding a secret—a painful secret, something he wanted to share but knew he couldn't. He became the heavyweight champion on June 22, 1937, when he knocked out James J. Braddock in eight rounds. My father took me to Chicago to see the fight. I was just a young kid, but the man had an impact on me.

"I watched you fight in '37," I said. "Saw you knock out Braddock in eight and Schmeling in one."

One side of the man's mouth raised. It was probably as close to a genuine smile as he ever got. "That was some fight," he admitted.

I assumed he was referring to the Schmeling fight. Having lost to the man in '36, Louis would likely never have considered himself a true champion until he beat the German-born Schmeling—something he did handily, much to Hitler's chagrin.

"You a fighter?" he asked.

"I've dabbled," I said.

"You ought to come to Johnny Tocco's," he offered. "Show us what you got."

My mouth formed a silly grin, like a kid offered a pony. "I'd like that," I said.

He told me to come by anytime, then excused himself, turning to the line that was forming behind him. We headed into the showroom and were shown to our seats. The ladies seemed impressed, especially with the stage. I didn't blame them. The room was larger than I expected it to be. Complete with a full stage that rivaled the Copa Room and huge, draping curtains. Tables, some round, some square, laid out in rows before the stage. The back wall showcased a painting of fancy women dancing the Cancan on the streets of Paris, a large windmill in the background. It was the first place I saw one.

We'd missed the dinner show—both ladies had dancing to do—but were just in time for the 2:30 am late show; or early show, depending on how you looked at it. Jimmy had done very well, getting us seats in the front, adjacent to the band, where we could easily hear the sax player.

A cocktail waitress came to our seats, and we ordered our two-drink minimums. The ladies each chose a tom collins, Jimmy a sloe gin fizz, and I my typical manhattan. The room filled quickly and there were just as many coloreds as anyone else. As the band took to their instruments, the stage came alive with dancers in bright, pleated dresses, scandalously lifting their ebony, garter-clad legs high in the air, revealing their ruffled drawers, plumed hats strapped to their heads.

The music was fast paced, as was the dancing, and just as Jimmy had implied, the kid on the alto saxophone stood out. He was young, dressed in the suit coat and tie that was the band's uniform. As he played, I directed my attention away from the dancers and focused on him. His fingers flew effortlessly on the keys and he played long stretches with little breath. I was both mesmerized and impressed.

At one point in the show, a young colored woman by the name of Ann Weldon took the stage and began singing the blues. She had a smooth, deep voice that flowed effortlessly, filling the room with a velvet sound that defied her age.

Jimmy leaned over to me. "She just got a record deal," he said. "She's gonna be big."

It wasn't hard to believe.

The barefoot dancers returned to the stage dressed

in grass skirts and coconut bras, gyrating to a jungle beat as they did the Watutsi, while a witch doctor juggled a pair of squawking chickens. They were only partway into their routine, when the doors at the back of the room flung open, and bluebottles came pouring in. O'Malley, a detective with the Las Vegas PD, was at the lead. The music stopped, as did the dancing, and all heads turned. O'Malley and several of the bluebottles headed directly to the band. He stood right in front of the sax player.

The man's eyes widened.

"Casper Moses Jones," O'Malley said. "You're under arrest for the murder of Margaret Lee Paige."

One of the dancers fainted.

TWO

THE ARREST OF the sax player put a definite damper on things. Two stagehands dressed in attire as dark as their complexion assisted the lightheaded dancer offstage, while the rest of the group followed the old adage and continued on with the show. I tried my best to enjoy the spectacle—the manhattan I'd ordered helped—but my mind was elsewhere, and, it seemed, Jimmy's was as well.

When the show was over, we followed the crowd to the casino and, eventually, the front door, where I handed my half of the torn ticket to the attendant. We would have stayed longer, but it was late and the girls each had an early call along with three shows to perform the next day. Besides, the bitters in my manhattan had smacked me in the kisser, and I was in no mood to gamble.

The attendant brought Jimmy's car up first—a Montclair, convertible, white on the top, navy on the bottom, with thick whitewalls and a bumper that meant business. It was clean and shiny. Like it had just come off the showroom floor.

I let out a long whistle, then followed it with a compliment on his choice of wheels.

"Thanks," Jimmy said, as the attendant opened the door for Nancy. "Just brought it home today."

"It suits you."

Jimmy smiled and made his way to the driver's seat as Nancy wrapped a scarf around her head. The girls said their goodbyes and before Jimmy hit the gas, he swung his arm over the seat and turned to me. "You coming to practice tomorrow?" he asked.

"I'll be there," I confirmed.

"You'd better," he said, and sped off.

When the Roadmaster appeared, Virgina and I followed our companions' lead even down to the scarf. The top was still down, and I left it there. I enjoyed having it down at night. It let me see the blanket of twinkling stars, feel the desert breeze on my face, and contemplate my own existence. I turned left on Bonanza and headed down the road, going underneath the railroad tracks, past Main, and down to Fifth Street. From there, I took another right and then a left on Clark, arriving at Virginia's apartment building. I slid into the open spot next to her Thunderbird and was just about to put up the top when a soft hand on my arm stopped me.

"Not tonight," she said. "I have an early call and you kept me up way past my bedtime. A girl's gotta get her beauty sleep."

I forced a grin, but wondered if it had been O'Malley who ruined more than just the sax player's evening, or my own past indiscretion coming back to haunt me. Virginia leaned in for a kiss. I didn't mind, and I proved it by kissing her right back. It was good to have her in my arms again, and I didn't care who knew it. Once the heat between us cooled a bit, Virginia turned toward the seat and pressed herself against me.

"Got plans for tomorrow?" I asked, gazing down at my brown-haired beauty. "I could come by and we could make a night of it."

"Not a chance," she said. "Tomorrow's a three show night. The only date I have when it's all over is with my pillow."

Lucky pillow.

We sat there for a moment, enjoying the silence. Just the two of us—she tracing the patterns on my tie with a forefinger, and me musing over opportunities lost. Then she patted my chest, kissed me quick, and slipped out the passenger door. I started to open mine, but she stopped me a second time.

"I'll be all right," she said. "You just go home and get some rest."

I mounted a protest. After all, what would my Italian mother say if I left a lady without an escort?

"I know what you're thinking," Virginia said, quickly, "but I'm a big girl and can find my own front door all by my lonesome."

I never doubted it.

"What have you got planned for tomorrow?" she asked.

"Practice with the band and a gig that night."

"And then?"

"Nuts," I admitted. "I'll probably nibble one and put some Bees in my hand for spending money."

"Sands?"

I nodded.

"Maybe I'll see you during the break," she said.

"Maybe," I countered.

She paused and eyed me intently. "Can I trust you to be good?" she asked, a little more sincerely than I expected.

I crossed my heart.

"Promise?"

"On a dime," I said.

She pursed her lips, tapped the car door twice with a delicate hand, then turned and left.

I watched her walk—her lovely hips swaying back and forth as she glided down the walkway—and she knew it. Just before she disappeared into the darkness, she paused, winked at me, and skirted away. It's a good thing the car was in park.

I should have gone home. After all, the house I was renting was only a few blocks away. But I didn't. Instead, I went to this little diner I knew and ordered a cup of joe, buttered toast, two poached eggs, crisp bacon, and a hooker of hollandaise sauce to spread over the top. I had just been served and was busy minding my own business when a man who could make the Pope reevaluate his stance on forgiveness interrupted my early morning feast.

"Well, if it isn't Max Rossi," the man said. "I thought you were dead."

His name was Salvatore Manella, Sal to his friends, of which I was not one. Sal was a hard man. A mobster tried and true of the New York variety, though now he conducted his ill-begotten affairs here in Las Vegas. He had a grip on the pro skirts—a firm grip at that—but was open for anything that put cabbage in his pockets. Sal and I had history—the kind that'd make a man want to rewrite the books. Sal cast two shadows, one the size of a mountain, the other a molehill.

"Sorry to disappoint you, Sal, but as you can see, I'm very much alive."

"For now," he said, adjusting the cufflinks on his sleeves. Sal was the type who dressed to the nines, probably hoping to be named Best Dressed Mobster of the Year by *Cosmopolitan Magazine*. Tonight, instead of his typical sack suit, he wore one much more loose fitting. A single-breasted style with vents, notched lapels, and three buttons up the front—his square matching his tie.

"Going casual?" I asked.

Sal let out a quick humph. I glanced at the Mountain. "You've got something of mine." I said to him. "And I'm going to want it back."

Sal turned to the Mountain. "You got something that belongs to Rossi?" he asked.

The Mountain shook his oversized head. "I ain't got no idea what he's talkin' about," he said with a grin. "The man likes to flap his gums, but it don't mean nothing."

Although I'm embarrassed to admit it, my last encounter with the Mountain didn't go so well. He caught me by surprise and before I could make a move, he'd gotten the better of me. The boys in the gym would've been terribly disappointed in my performance—so too would've been my father. It made us even though, one apiece. Except in this encounter, the Mountain had walked away with more than just my pride; he'd also gotten my gat—something of which I had grown very fond.

"Maybe I should just take it from you," I said, my bravado getting the better of me.

It was a bonehead thing to say. After all, I was sitting in a booth and they were standing, but I was in a bonehead mood, so I said it anyway. I tried to accompany it by standing, but the Molehill caught me by the shoulder and shoved me back down.

"You should've left when you were told to," Sal said. "Vegas doesn't like you, kid. The sooner you get that into your thick head, the better off you'll be." He jerked his head to the side, then turned to leave. His shadows followed.

I looked down at my eggs. They had somehow lost their appeal, so I pushed them across the table. It wasn't the first time Sal had soured my meal.

THREE

AFTER PAYING THE tab, I climbed back into my Roadmaster and headed home. It was a lonely drive, made more so by the thought of my own stupidity. My father had always admonished me to control my temper. I tried but mostly failed, as the morning's actions attested.

When I arrived home, I took a quick nap, freshened up, then slipped on a pair of flecked navy blue Pincord trousers, the type with a continuous waistband, and secured them with a thin brown leather belt. I paired the trousers to a plaid Gaberdine shirt with a high button collar and a matching button down flap over the pocket, two-tone loafers, and argyle socks. If I didn't look like a jazz musician, I didn't know who did.

I donned my walking lid (the one my grandfather had given me), grabbed my Selmer Mark VI, and headed for the Bootlegger to meet up with the rest of the birds who made up the jazz group known as the Five and Dimes.

Jimmy Five, the man who had procured our seats at the Tropi Can Can the night before, headed the ten-piece band. I'd met Jimmy after an encounter with another man named Vinny "Keys" Collins—an encounter which, had it not been for Keys, would surely have cost me my life. However, besides having saved my neck, Keys also reignited my passion for the alto saxophone, getting me to purchase not only the Mark VI sax I was currently getting ready to play, but also setting me up to sit in with Jimmy's band—for a time, anyway.

I opened the case, put the neck on my horn, and placed the Vandoren reed in my mouth to soften it up. I was attaching the reed to the mouthpiece of the same make when Jimmy approached.

"Great to see you, Max," he said, extending his hand. "I'm so pleased you came." From the moment I took Jimmy's hand, I knew something was amiss. His skin was moist, his grip far too firm, and he moved my hand up and down in a succession of short, jerky motions.

"I'm going to need that hand for later," I said.

Jimmy quickly let go, giving me an awkward grin, then rubbed his hand up and down the leg of his pants.

"You all right?" I asked.

He tried to smile, but it didn't stick. "I've got some exciting news," he said.

"Spill it."

"Benny arranged for Maxine Weldon to sing with us."

The name didn't register. "I'm afraid you have me at something of a loss," I admitted.

"Maxine Weldon is Ann Weldon's sister." When my blank look persisted, he continued. "Ann Weldon from the Tropi Can Can?"

"The dame with the velvet voice?" I asked.

"The very one. The pair sing as a duo off and on, and with Ann at the Moulin Rouge, Maxine is free to sing here with us. She'll be coming in a bit later."

I was more than a little impressed. "This is good news," I said. "So what's the catch?"

Jimmy looked at me strangely. "What do you mean?"

"You don't look like someone with good news," I said. He was all clammy, like a man who had a hit put out on him and knew it.

"Do you know what this could mean for us?" Jimmy asked. "This could be all we need to launch us, to bring us the notoriety it takes to get somewhere. This could be our chance, Max! Our ticket to the big time."

"Well, we'd better razz her berries then."

Jimmy smiled brightly. "That's the spirit," he said and scooted off.

I finished assembling my horn, putting the mouthpiece in position, and strapping the thing around my neck. Then I took my place on stage next to Johnny Boy—the bari sax player—and slapped the hand of each of my newfound bandmates. We played the same set they had the night I'd seen them here, starting with Take Five, then moving on to *Doodlin'*, *Rhumba*, and *'Round Midnight*. We had just finished up *On the Sunny Side of the Street* when Maxine arrived.

I'm not sure what I was expecting, but it wasn't what walked into the room. Maxine Weldon was a beautiful colored girl with high cheekbones, sparkling eyes, and updo hair. She wore beige pedal pushers, a black blouse with pintuck pleating and a large white bow at the neckline. Thought she seemed every bit a woman, she was no more than a teenager really, much younger than I expected. Accompanying her was a white man in a long coat and brown fedora. He arrived with a colored goon that towered over him.

An uneasy nervousness filled the room. Jimmy was like a faint-hearted child on Christmas morning, almost reluctant to peek around the corner, hoping against hope that Santa left that oh so important gift in the living room, by the tree. Then running with full might when he spotted it there.

He jumped from the stage, nearly tripping over himself to get to her. After an awkward introduction, he brought Maxine to meet the rest of the band, naming each one of us in turn. Maxine smiled politely, extending her hand when introduced and expressing her pleasure to meet us.

"Let's get this going, shall we?" the fedora said, looking at his timepiece.

Jimmy nodded, then brought Maxine to the microphone and adjusted it clumsily for her height. "What do you want to sing first?" he asked.

"How about *That Man*?"

"Perfect!" Jimmy said, as we all pulled out our music. He turned, started the band, then stepped aside, tripping over the mic cord in the process. If he was going to make a go of this, he'd have to get rid of those nerves.

As I looked over the sheet music on the stand in front of me, the drummer started the down beat. The piano player joined in, followed by the bari. Then Maxine.

"*I'm in a little bit of trouble,*" she sang. "*And I'm in real deep. From the beginning to the end, he was no more than a friend to me.*"

Maxine's pipes were clear and strong, and as the song continued, she easily demonstrated her ample range. She had a theatrical bent to her singing, which brought the song to life. Jimmy was all smiles. The man in the fedora remained stone-faced.

"*Ooh, that man is like a flame, and ooh, that man plays me like a game. My only sin is I can't win. Ooh, I*

16

wanna love that man!"

She followed it up with *All that Glitters, Pack the Louie,* and *Tongue Tied.* Each song better than the last. I was beginning to understand Jimmy's apprehensive excitement at the prospect of performing with this young woman. Her talent was evident—even to the unenlightened.

We were playing along on all eights when I caught sight of a man I knew slide into a booth at the back of the room. Jimmy saw him too and nodded. It was Garwood Van, a bit of a legend in the local music scene, having run a band at both the EL Rancho and the Last Frontier. He now owned a little music store in San Francisco Square, across from the Sahara, called Garwood Van's Music Land. It was at that same music store that I met the man and it was at that same music store that Garwood sold me the Mark VI I was currently playing.

When it was all said and done, Jimmy and the band cooed over Maxine, and rightly so, until the man in the fedora decided it was time to leave. He took Maxine gently by the arm and led her to the door, stopping only briefly at the table where Garwood sat before taking their leave, the goon trailing behind.

I didn't like the man in the fedora. Not that I could tell you why, not that there was anything to hang my hat on. I just didn't like the guy, that's all. He made my big toe itch. It's a free country and I can dislike who I want.

As I packed up my sax, Jimmy came over again. "Man, that went about as good as it could've gone," he said, pressing his hands together.

I had to agree.

"You think something'll come of it?" I asked.

"We'll see, but I'm hopeful. This could be the break we need," he repeated.

"Wonderful," I said. "I hope it works out for you."

"For us, you mean. You're one of us now."

"Oh no," I protested. "I'm happy to sit in on gigs and the like, but the musician's life is not for me. Give me a crisp deck of cards and a fresh manhattan any day. If you make the big time, more power to you, but don't expect me to tag along for the ride."

Jimmy looked like a kid who'd just had his puppy taken away. He nodded solemnly, then turned to go. "Oh, by the by," he said, "Garwood wants to see you before you leave."

FOUR

AFTER PACKING AWAY my instrument, I stepped off the stage and headed over to Garwood's booth. He was sitting there framed in red leather, waiting patiently, nursing what I expected was a soda, seeing the time of day, but what did I know?

"You wanted to see me?"

He offered me a seat, and I took it, setting the sax on the floor beside me.

"It's good to see you, Max," he said in his low, scratchy voice. "You're good on that horn. Seems you made the right choice with that Selmer."

I thanked him and said it was good to see him too, but I had the uneasy feeling this wasn't a social call; that he wasn't here to see how the sax was working out for me. "That what you came here for?" I asked. "To complement my playing?"

Garwood turned sheepish. "I guess it's not," he said.

"Though I meant what I said about that."

I nodded my appreciation.

He took his time, sipping his drink thoughtfully. I waited.

"You still working at the Sands?" he finally asked.

It was a left field question. "As far as I know," I said. "You lookin' for an in?"

He shook his head. "I hear you went to the show the other night at the Rouge."

"That's right. Jimmy got us tickets. I went there with him and his gal pal, Nancy. But you already know that, don't you? Look, Garwood, I don't have the temperament for pussyfooting. I doubt you came here to inquire about my social life. If you've got something to say, then I'd prefer you just get to saying it."

He took another drink. I was beginning to crave a manhattan myself. "Moses Jones," he said.

"The sax player who got pinched?"

He nodded. "He's in quite a jam, Max, and I'd like you to look into it. On the hush, of course."

"Me?" I asked, more than a bit surprised. "What have I got to do with any of this? Best let O'Malley and the bluebottles handle it. Besides, what's there to look into?" I asked. "Seems like the police already got their man."

"And if their man didn't do it?"

"You know he's innocent?"

"Well, no," he admitted. "I just . . ."

"Best let the bluebottles handle it," I repeated, interrupting.

Garwood pushed his glass aimlessly across the table, looking down at nothing at all. He clearly needed time to choose his words, and I gave it to him. Finally, he looked up at me. "He's a colored boy accused of killing a white woman, Max. How do you think this is going to play out?"

"I'm no detective," I protested, "just a card player."

"Who sees things others miss."

"I pay attention," I said. "That's all." I stood and took hold of the handle on the sax case. "I'm the Sands' man and this didn't happen at the Sands. I'm sorry, Garwood, but you've got the wrong guy."

"I know what you did for Keys," he said quickly. "And I know you stopped the Highwaymen."

"And almost got myself iced in the process," I offered.

He looked at me with a kind of quiet desperation, the eyes of a man who had nowhere to go, no one to turn to. That's how he looked. So why did it feel as if I was holding court with Lanski or Luciano—given a task I had little choice but to accept?

"He may very well have done it, you know," I continued. "I learned a long time ago not to try to guess what a man will and will not do."

Garwood shook his head. "It's not in is nature," he said.

"Oh? How's that? You know this kid personally?"

"I know of him," Garwood admitted. "Benny brought him here from Detroit specifically to play with the show at the Rouge."

"That where he's from?"

"Not originally. Moses was born in Oklahoma, but moved with his family to Detroit. He played with the Earl Hines Orchestra and became the featured soloist."

"I've heard of Hines," I said. "Dizzy and Charlie Parker came out of that group."

Garwood grinned and nodded. "He moved to LA and did some recording. You ever hear of *Easy Swing* or *The Man I Love?*"

FIVE

I LEFT THE Bootlegger, sax case in hand, and headed for my car. Once inside, I pointed it to the police station. I doubted they had released Moses on his own recognizance, and if he was anything like most musicians, he wouldn't have money for bail, even if it was granted. When I arrived at the station, I put the Roadmaster in the spot marked "Visitor" and headed up to the third floor—the one the homicide detectives called home. I should have gone to O'Malley's desk right away, but wasn't sure I could face the man without the courage of a manhattan, so I went to the only office in the place, the one with "Lieutenant Conner McQueeney" painted on the door.

I found the man sitting behind a desk, at least as much of him as could fit behind it. The linebacker-sized homicide detective made every piece of furniture appear to have been removed from a child's dollhouse and placed in his office as a gag. He sat in a chair that positioned his knees up to his chin and hovered over a desk that he made look no bigger than an end table.

He glanced up from his paperwork, what passed for a pen in his gigantic mitt, a smoke burning in the ashtray to his side. His sleeves were rolled up to his elbows, his tie loosened, and the top button of his shirt undone—a man not expecting company.

"You got that fifty?" he asked in his Boston-Irish brogue.

The fifty to which he referred was the fee to be paid for a private detective's license. Queeney had shoved the paperwork at me on a previous occasion and ordered me to fill it out—he wanting to rid me of my sordid past—something with which he himself was well acquainted.

"Not quite," I said.

"Then why are you here?" he demanded, more than asked.

"It's good to see you too, Queeney," I said.

"Look, I ain't got no time to bump gums with the likes of you, Rossi," Queeney said, returning to his paperwork, "so spill the beans or shove off."

It was always good to speak with Queeney. So uplifting. Such a boost to one's confidence. "I'd like to speak with Moses Jones," I said casually.

The name caught Queeney's attention. He took a deliberate pause, placed his writing utensil purposefully on the desk, and shot me the same irritated look my father had often given me in my youth. I think I saw the hairs bristle on the back of his neck. "What does Casper Moses Jones have to do with you?" he asked.

"Nothing right now," I said. "I'd just like to speak with the man is all."

Queeney's eyes tightened. "Why is it you're always so chummy with murderers?"

"Well, murderesses to be clear," I corrected.

Queeney did not appreciate the correction.

I pulled at my collar and tried again. "I was at the show when he got pinched. Some friends of mine are also friends of his and they asked me to check up on him."

"So you're a lawyer now as well?" Queeney asked. "I thought that was your gal pal's gig."

"Only on Sundays."

"Still a pistol, ain't ya?" He paused before continuing. "This ain't none of your business, Rossi. You're a Sands man. This didn't happen at the Sands. Take my advice, don't put your beezer where it don't belong. It ain't gonna end well for you mixin' up with the . . . what does your kind call them? Mulignan?"

I hated that word. Slang Italian. Calabrese for colored people. Heard it as a kid. It wasn't a kind word. "Look, are you going to let me see him or not?"

Queeney did nothing to hide his disapproval. "Ain't none of my affair," he said, turning his attention once again to the papers on his desk. "This one's O'Malley's case. You want to speak with Jones, ask him," he said and scooted me off with a wave of the hand.

That was definitely not the answer I wanted to hear. I'd just as soon have a seven course dinner with Salvatore Manella and both of his goons than speak with Detective O'Malley for even five minutes. I had a run-in with the man once before when he decided to redecorate a room I was renting. I offered to blacken his eye. He declined.

But what choice did I have?

O'Malley's personal abode rested in a sea of worn-out wooden desks, crammed together edge to edge. He looked like every other suit in the room—white shirt, dark tie, gray flannel suit, dark shoes, no display handkerchief, Stacy Adams resting on the desk to his right, a smoke burning in the ashtray. Though his name suggested otherwise, O'Malley looked no more Irish than I did. He had a mop of dark hair; two dark, beady eyes; a nose sharp enough to shave by; and not even a hint of the ruddiness that so defined his boss' mug. While Queeney was the poster boy for the Irish Social Club of Boston, O'Malley would have looked right at home at any spaghetti social or back of the house get together.

He looked over and saw me coming, but pretended he didn't just for fun.

"I'd like to see Moses Jones," I said to him.

"And I'd like two weeks on the shore with Rita Haywood," he countered without addressing me.

"Funny," I said. "I figured you more for a Diana Dors man."

"What do you want, Rossi?"

"I already told you. I want to speak with Moses Jones."

O'Malley turned in his swivel chair. "You're serious?"

"Of course I'm serious. I'm inquiring about the Margaret Lee Paige murder."

"What business is it of yours?" O'Malley asked. "You got skin in the game?"

"We have friends in common. I was hoping you'd let me see the file."

"And I was hoping you'd drop dead."

My fist clenched into a tight hammer, ready to pound. If anyone deserved a good sock in the beak, it was O'Malley. But then I remembered my father's frequent admonition to control my temper and thought better of it. Besides, this was O'Malley's turf and, like it or not, he called the shots.

I tried a pleasant smile instead. "Well, if I can't see the file, can I at least see Moses?" I asked.

O'Malley looked at me with a pitiless grin. "What's my end of it?" he asked.

I could feel my face flush and my ears burn. I knew my fist. It had a mind of its own, and it didn't pay no mind to whose turf it was on. If it wanted to bend a guy's nose, who was I to stop it? I was just about to let it follow its own path when a voice called out from across the room.

"Let him see the kid, O'Malley," Queeney said. "It ain't gonna hurt nothin'."

Detective O'Malley let out a sigh. He stood. He wasn't as tall or as large as Queeney, but who was? "Sure, what business is it of mine?" he said, then walked me out of the office and down the hall, stopping at a thick metal door with a built-in window, a bluebottle on the other side.

"What side you on anyway, Rossi?" he asked, before pressing the buzzer. His knuckles were reddened and stained. Telltale signs of a rumpus.

"I didn't realize there were sides," I said.

"There's always sides. A white lady's been murdered and now you want to speak with the darkie who wacked her? You got a fine habit of sticking yer nose where it don't belong, don't cha?"

From inside, the officer pressed a buzzer of his own, unlatching the door. We entered.

"You got any leads?" I asked O'Malley. "Or are you content to pin it on the first sap you come across?"

"I got a dead body, ain't I?" O'Malley asked. He turned to the officer guarding the cages that housed prisoners awaiting trial. "Let this one see Jones, but keep an eye on him, and bounce him if he gets out a line."

"So that's all it takes nowadays, a dead body?" I asked.

"It's a start," O'Malley countered. "Add a witness and it's all nice and clean, ready for the chair."

"You got a witness?"

O'Malley grinned that canary-eating grin of his, then turned and headed back down the hall without saying another word.

The bluebottle eyed me sharply as he opened the first door to the cages, using the ring of keys entrusted to him. I stepped inside. I'd been here once before, only that time as a guest of the city. I didn't like being here then, and liked it even less now.

We made our way down the narrow gray hall, separating the cages on both sides. Moses' little slice of heaven was at the back on the left. The officer slid his key into the slot, turned it, then pulled open the door.

I entered the cell. It looked just like the one I had once occupied: metal cot with a thin slice of cheese that passed for a mattress, no sheets, metal commode and a matching sink. Above the sink hung a polished hunk of metal meant to show one's reflection and doing a right poor job of it. All the comforts of home.

"Call when you want out," the bluebottle said dismissively, then closed and locked the door behind me.

At first, Moses was oblivious to my entrance. He didn't greet me in any way, or even look up. He simply rocked back and forth on his bunk, picking at his fingernails, hunched over his knees.

"You Moses Jones?" I asked.

He looked up, startled. "Who are you?"

"Name's Rossi. I came here to see how you're getting along."

"How you think I'm gettin' along?" he countered quickly.

It was a fair point; one made more compelling by the bruises that painted his face.

"They rough you up in here?"

"No sir, not in here," he said. "I got these beauties on the way to the station. Resisting arrest, they called it." He scraped a hand through his hair, then rubbed the back of his neck. Beads of sweat rested on his forehead. "You my lawyer?"

I shook my head.

"Can you get me out of here?" he asked with pleading eyes.

I gave him the same response.

"Why'd you get the pinch?" I asked.

"How should I know? One minute I'm blowin' my axe and the next I'm being accused of murder," he said, raking his nails across his arm. "Beat the livin' hell out of me when they got me outside."

"You know Miss Paige?"

"Of course I know Miss Paige. Everybody knows Margaret Paige. She's a singer in the lounge. We're her back-up band."

"That your only tie to her?"

Moses eyed me cautiously. "Who'd you say you were?"

"Rossi. Max Rossi. I'm a friend of Garwood Van's," I explained and repeated my question.

"We jammed together a time or two," he admitted. "She was set to wax a disc and asked me to play a lick."

"And did you?"

"Nah, it didn't work out."

"Why not?"

He took his nails to his arm once again and returned to rocking. "It just didn't work out is all. She chose that moldy fig Freeman instead."

"Freeman?" I questioned.

He stopped scratching and sat still. "Grafton Freeman," he said, spitting out the name. "Blows the horn next to me."

"Not a fan?" I asked.

"That jive dude's always got his glasses on. He thinks he's the straw boss, but he ain't doin' nuthin' but noodlin'." Moses suddenly clutched himself, like a woman in cold weather. "Can't you get me out of here?" he asked.

"I'm afraid I can't," I said.

"Then what the hell good are ya?"

"Indeed," I said and called for the key, leaving Moses to his rocking. The bluebottle let me out, and I was happy for it. Moses wasn't as much help as I hoped he'd be. A nervous kid in a bad fix. He'd already been on the receiving end of a nightstick or two and his prospects weren't bright. I didn't have much to go on, but knew where I needed to go next. The only problem was, I had no idea how to get there.

SIX

NOT BEING A fan of elevators, I decided to take the stairs. It's not that I'm afraid of tiny metal boxes that spend their days precariously gliding up and down on taut cables and pulleys, I just don't like tight spaces—or falls to my death.

When I got outside, O'Malley was smoking a gasper and jawing with a couple of uniforms. "Get what you came for?" he asked when he saw me.

"They going to be posting bail soon?"

O'Malley laughed. "On a Saturday? You're joking, right?" He dropped the gasper and crushed it out with the toe of his snap jack. "Judge won't be in till Monday morning. Your boy'll be lucky if he sees a judge before Tuesday or Wednesday. Maybe Thursday by the time I get the paperwork done."

He said the last part with one of those grins that needed to be slapped off his face, but this wasn't the time nor the place, so instead I headed over to Main Street to this little newsstand I knew. Seeing as how the arrest was still fresh, I figured the Review-Journal or the Morning Sun would have a piece in it by now and they didn't disappoint. The arrest made the front page on both papers. Headlines read: *Murder and Mayhem at the Moulin Rouge* and *Murder Suspect Apprehended*. I flipped the vendor a dime, folded the papers under my arm, and headed for my Roadmaster.

I pointed it southward, heading first down Main Street, then taking a left on Bonanza, and slipping under the railroad tracks. When I pulled into the valet of the Moulin Rouge, just like the night before, the attendant tore a ticket and handed me half, then he parked my boiler as I went inside.

I made my way to the front desk, found an open blower and when the PBX girl answered, asked to be connected to Garwood Van's Music Land on San Francisco. Then I waited for the pickup. He answered on the third ring.

"Garwood Van's Music Land," he said.

"It's Max. I saw your boy."

"How's he look?"

"Nervous," I said. "Took a beating from the bluebottles."

"I was afraid of something like that. He all right?"

"He'll make it," I said, "but he wasn't much help."

"He can be a little abrasive," Garwood admitted, "but don't hold it against him."

"His neck's on the line. He needs to be a little more cooperative," I said. "But that isn't why I called. I could use your help. I need to speak with Benny Carter."

"Sure, I can arrange that. Where are you now?"

"I'm at the Moulin Rouge's front desk."

I heard a chuckle on the other end. "Don't waste time, do you?" Garwood asked.

"I was taught not to put things off."

"I'll make a quick call. Benny should be in the theater, practicing for the show. You still got your horn with you?"

I told him it was in the car.

"Great, go get it, then wait there. Someone'll be by to escort you in."

I did as I was told, retrieving my horn and heading back inside. As I waited, I had a look around the place. Even though it was nowhere near any other casino, it was still quite full of people for a Saturday morning, just as busy as the Sands, the Last Frontier, the EL Rancho, or any other hotel casino on Hiway 91. The only difference being the shade of the crowd. But it wasn't just colored folk, like the night before. A scan of the room found nearly as many white faces as black.

I was impressed. The experiment seemed to be working.

It took about ten minutes for my escort to arrive. I was expecting a bellman, steward, or even a showgirl. What I wasn't expecting was Joe Louis. I had thought Garwood wanted to keep this on the down low. Having the ex-heavyweight champion of the world escort me through the casino was hardly keeping it hush-hush.

"You Rossi?" he said, extending his hand.

I took it, and just as it had the night before, it engulfed mine. "I am," I assured him.

"Benny says you're tryin' out for the show. Says you got good chops."

I grinned. Garwood knew what he was doing, after all. "I guess that remains to be seen," I said and followed the champ through the casino to the showroom. "Nice place you got here."

"Sure is," the big man said with a proud grin. "Gonna be even better when we get the golf course and tennis courts up and running. You play?"

"No, but I have dabbled a little in boxing."

Louis' face lit. "Really?" he asked. "Then you should come by the gym. Jonny Tocco's over on Charleston."

He had already invited me to the gym the night before, but it was clear he didn't recall the invitation. It didn't surprise me. By the looks of this place, he probably greeted several hundred people a night. There was nothing about me that would stick out.

"You know that show you're auditionin' for, the Tropi Can Can, was created in honor of Josephine Baker."

"Is that so?"

"Sure is. She was the first colored star in France, you know."

"I think I heard that somewhere."

"It's the best show in town, but not only that, we got the best broads in the whole city of Las Vegas working here."

"The Sands has some pretty good lookers too," I offered.

"Look, pal. I ain't never seen the gals out there, but we got the best lookin' broads in town right here in this place."

I thought it best not to argue.

We entered the theater. It looked just as it had the night before, except with no sign of the police barging in and arresting someone for murder.

"Benny's up there on stage, just to the right," the champ said, pointing. "After the audition, if you're hungry, you should try the Deauville Room. Shares the same kitchen as the Café Rouge. You can't go wrong."

He wished me luck, then turned and left. I watched him walk out of the room for a few minutes before I went on stage. I wondered how he'd gotten himself here. The mostly white men who bankrolled the place must have known their skin was the wrong color for any of them to be the front man. For that, they needed a face—one everybody knew. What, I wondered, had they promised him? What would make a man who once owned the world agree to be little more than a freak in a sideshow act? I couldn't help but feel sorry for him.

I placed my horn on stage, then jumped up after it. Benny was just finishing a tune when he caught sight of me out of the corner of his eye. He made a few minor corrections, then sent the band on a ten-minute break.

"Max Rossi," I said, offering my hand. Benny was a handsome man with short-cut hair and a well-groomed mustache. The kind of man who, under different circumstances, could have made it big time on the silver screen. He wore a white shirt and brown trousers with matching loafers. His tie, which had a paisley design, hung loosely around his neck.

He took my hand. "Garwood said you wanted to speak with me."

"I'd like to ask you some questions about Moses Jones."

His face hardened ever so slightly. "You some kind of cop?" he asked.

"No," I assured him. "Just a concerned citizen."

He looked me up and down, eyeing me cautiously. Probably deciding what he was and was not willing to tell me. "What's in the case?" he asked.

"Selmer Mark VI," I said. I would have just told him it was a saxophone, but Benny was a sax man himself. He would have already known by the shape of the case what lay inside. When he asked me his question, he wanted to know the type of horn I chose—the type of player I was.

"You play?"

"More like flirt with it."

"Well, open the case and sit in, then maybe we'll talk."

After I recovered from the initial shock, I opened my case and prepared my instrument. I'd heard of playing for your meal, but never for information. It made sense though, the more I thought about it. When I wanted to take the measure of a man, I played cards with him. I could always tell the cut of one's jib by the way he played the Bees. I guess Benny had his own way of taking the measure of a man.

I wet the reed, attached it to the mouthpiece, and then secured the assembly to the horn. Then I blew air into the thing, while running my fingers up and down the keys to warm them up. Coming off a morning jam session, I was very much worried my chops wouldn't hold up and that I would lay down some clams or hit a clinker in front of one of the greatest jazz alto saxophonists of our time.

Benny Carter was a heavy in the industry, coming out of New York with the ability to not only blow the sax, but the licorice stick and trumpet, as well as tickle the ivories. He played internationally with the likes of June Clark, Billy Paige, and Earl Hines, but playing wasn't his only gig. By his forties, Beny was composing music for greats like Satchmo, Ella Fitzgerald, and Sarah Vaughan, before starting and leading his own band. Benny was quite the catch for the Moulin Rouge. It meant they weren't fooling around.

When the band returned from break, Benny handed me sheet music for a tune called *Take the 'A' Train*, along with a few minutes to review. I didn't much like just jumping in—especially when there wasn't a dame to impress—but what was a guy to do? I needed answers, and this seemed the quickest, if not the only, way to get them.

When Benny returned, he had an alto strapped to his neck. No pressure at all. "Let's do *Take the 'A' Train*," he said to the band. Then he introduced me as being on loan from Jimmy Five and admonished the group not to take it too fast. "Let's give the kid a chance to stay with us," he said.

I'd heard Ellington's ode to the train that ran from 207th Street in New York under the East River to Brooklyn many times, but had never attempted to play it. I enjoyed the upbeat rhythm of the 32-bar tune done in the AABA sequence. Now all I had to do was get through the thing without making a fool of myself.

Benny waved his hand, and the piano started a rhythm that sounded like a train beginning its run. Then Benny brought the horn to his lips, and the band joined in. I, of course, jumped in a little late, but quickly caught up. The sax section echoed the trumpets as the tune rolled along, leading to a trumpet solo. My fingers seemed to be set on autopilot, gliding up and down the keys with ease. After my initial faux pas, I didn't miss a beat, or a key, and was feeling pretty good, that was, until Benny pointed at me to follow up the trumpet solo with one of my own.

I never was great at improvisation. I enjoyed playing— the feeling of being a small part of a larger whole. You put three, four, or even twenty guys in a room together, each with their own instruments, each with their own parts, each concentrating on only the notes they have to play and when to play them. And when it all comes together, when it's all done right, the very air glistens with the spell of music—the most beautiful sound you've ever heard. It was magic to me. Lightning in a bottle.

I wish I could tell you that when I stood and improvised I caught that lightning, but that would be a lie and my mother, and the nuns, taught me not to lie. But I played, and I didn't make a fool of myself in the process, so at least there was that.

When it was all said and done, Benny thanked the band, then sent them on a lunch break. Several of them shook my hand or slapped me on the shoulder. "You can sit in with us any time," one of them said. I thanked them graciously and was packing up my horn when Benny approached.

SEVEN

"GARWOOD WAS RIGHT," Benny said. "You got chops. Course you ain't worth a tinker's dam on improvisation, but you got some chops."

I smiled. "That get me a few questions answered?"

"I suppose it does," he said.

"What can you tell me about Moses?"

Benny took hold of the alto still resting around his neck. "Now there's a kid with chops," he said. "I recruited him specifically for this show. I needed a strong sax player; one with enough drive to get the job done. Moses' style is fluid and clean. Boy oh boy, that kid can break it down. He's probably better 'n me," he said, sporting a wide grin, then added, "though I'd never admit it."

"So you brought him here just to play for the show?"

"Yep, stole him from Basie, but he deserved it. He stole one of my trumpeters a while back."

"And it didn't bother you?" I asked.

"Bother me? I don't get what you mean."

"It didn't bother you that he bounces around so much from group to group? That he doesn't seem to stay in any one place for too long? Weren't you afraid he'd do the same to you?"

Benny fingered the keys on his saxophone. "You ever spend any time on the road?" he asked.

I shook my head.

"Life on the road is hard. Everyone struggling to make a name for themselves. I suppose you could say that about any of us," he said. "Any of us could jump, at any time, to the next big thing. Moses was no different. He's a good kid, Mr. Rossi. He's got just what you need to make it big in this business."

"Talent?"

"Instinct."

"What's the connection between Moses and Margaret Paige?"

"Strictly professional, far as I know." He said it, but I didn't buy he believed it.

"She sings in the show," he added quickly.

"I thought Ann Weldon was the show's star."

"Oh she is, but Margaret has a few opening numbers, right before the Hines Kids, and she also sings in the Lucky Pierre between shows. Moses is part of the combo that backs her up. She took an interest in him, liked his style, the easy way he blew the horn. She was going to bake a biscuit and wanted Moses to play on a couple of the songs. But it was more than that. She was working with the boy, trying to get him his own recording gig."

"Oh? How do you know that?"

"She told me," Benny admitted. "Said she didn't want to ruin anything I had here and asked if it was okay with me."

"And you said?"

"I said 'sure,' of course it was okay with me. I would never stand in the way of anyone's shot at the big time. Lord knows I got mine."

"So she put him on the album?"

Benny shook his head. "No. One day she comes to me and says, 'Moses is out,' and asks for Grafton instead. No reason. No explanation. Just Moses is out and Grafton is in."

"That's Grafton Freeman?" I asked.

Benny nodded. "Plays second chair to Moses."

"Was there a rivalry between the two?" I asked.

Benny grinned. "Course there was. You ever see a first and second chair without one?" he asked. "If there ain't no rivalry, there ain't no hunger, and if there ain't no hunger . . . well, why even play?"

It was a strong point. "How did Moses take the news?" I asked.

Benny rubbed his bare chin. "Not well," he said. "Set the poor kid back a bit. He started missing practices and when he was here, he was hittin' more clinkers than notes. I almost had to let him go."

"What stopped you?"

"Well, I felt sorry for him. He'd just had the rug pulled out from under him, and I guess we all know how that feels. But, at that age, you think the world's come to an end. You know?"

Yeah, I knew.

"Plus, Meriday asked me to give him another chance."

"Meriday?" I asked.

"Meriday Edgefield," Benny said. "Moses' girl. She's a dancer in the show."

"You think I could speak with her?"

"I don't see why not, but I don't control that part of the show, so I can't really speak for anyone else. I'd be happy to ask Clarence for you."

"What about Grafton? You think I could speak with him?"

"I'm sure you could. If you could find him. He hasn't shown for rehearsal, doesn't answer his phone, and ain't no one seen hide nor hair of him since yesterday. He's all smoke."

"You know where I can find him?"

"Far as I know, he's staying over at the Harrison House. On the corner of Adams and F Street." Benny fixed on me. "You gonna help Moses?"

"I promised Garwood I'd ask a few questions. Can't commit to more than that."

"I understand. Jim Crow and all. I guess we haven't come far enough out of them black codes after all."

"It's not that," I protested. "My cabbage comes from the Sands and I've grown very fond of that cabbage. Wouldn't want to see it go away. What can you tell me about Margaret Paige?"

"Sad thing," he said. "She's a real up and comer, got angels in her voice."

"What's she like to work with?"

He paused long enough that I could sense the gears moving in his head. This was a man giving a great deal of thought to his next words. "She's an artist," he said. "All artists are temperamental. It's what makes them good. But she did her job, and she did it well. She's a very talented young woman."

"Was," I said.

He nodded slowly.

I wondered if Benny was protecting her or himself. I decided to throw out a curve ball. "You think Moses did it?" I asked.

I studied his face, looking for the clues words rarely provide. "I don't know," he said dolefully, studying his shoes. "I just don't see how he could."

"The dame done him wrong," I said. "Ain't that motive enough?"

He looked up quickly. "Plenty of Joe's been wronged by dames. Doesn't make them murderers."

"No, it doesn't," I agreed. "But sometimes . . ." I let the words fall.

Benny didn't answer for a few moments. He just looked past me, fingering the keys on his sax. Finally, he glanced at his watch. "Time's up," he said. "Wait here and I'll see what Clarence says about Meriday."

I thanked him, and as he walked offstage, three thoughts filled my head. Why, if Margaret Paige was helping Moses with his career, did he play it off when he spoke to me in the jail cell? Why, after trying to help him with his career, did Margaret call it off? And why would Grafton not take advantage of the situation with Moses gone to show what he's got and take a shot at first chair, remind the big boss why he's here and what he can do?

I put my sax away, then sat there for quite a while, long enough to think that Benny may have forgotten about me, or that he decided he didn't care for the cut of my jib after all. I was about to leave when a young woman in a tight black top, black stockings, sporting dancer's shorts and shoes snuck around the curtains. She was beautiful, younger than I expected, with legs that could rival my Virginia's—black hair pulled tight behind her head. Even without the stage makeup, I recognized her as the woman who fainted when Moses got pinched.

"Meriday?" I asked.

She nodded and slid over to me the way dancers do, but took her time doing it. "You wanted to speak with me about Moses?"

"Feeling better?"

She looked puzzled at first, then it came to her. "Yes. Much," she said in a voice as light as her walk. "Thank you for asking. Are you going to help Moses?" she asked, clutching an arm across her chest and anchoring it to her other arm.

It was a popular question. I ignored it. "How long have you known Moses?" I asked.

"Only a little while," she said, perhaps to a person behind the curtain. Certainly not to me. "Just since we started here."

"You didn't know him before?"

She shook her head.

"And how does Margaret Lee Paige figure into all of this?"

That caught her attention. She turned and looked directly at me, her eyes tight. "My Moses did not kill that woman," she said forcefully.

"The police seem to think he did," I countered.

"What do the police know?" she asked.

"Enough to arrest him," I said.

She turned her attention back to the curtain.

"Did you know Miss Paige was helping Moses with his career?" I asked.

She laughed. It was an ugly laugh. One that didn't suit her. "Hmph, some help she was," Meriday said, crossing both arms over her chest. A color from something other than stage rouge filled her cheeks. "She didn't help him. Not one stich. No way, no how."

"Weren't they to play together on her album?"

"Oh, she wanted to play all right. She certainly wanted to play. But she was more interested in backseat bingo than recording an album and when my Moses turned her down, what did she do? The floozie pulled him off and put that lousy dope peddler Grafton Freeman in his place," she said with a whip of her hand. "My Moses can play the alto, tenor, and bari. What can that crumb Freeman do? He don't play nuttin' but clams or cornball jazz. He was always jealous of my Moses."

"I gather you're not a fan."

She didn't answer.

"So Margaret made a play for Moses?"

"Sure did, and she's lucky my Moses turned her down, or I'd have scratched her devil eyes out!"

"If Moses didn't kill Miss Paige, then who do you think did?"

She shifted her weight onto one hip. "Well, ain't that your job to find out?"

"Not my job," I assured her. "That's one for the police and they've already got their man. Tell me, where was Moses on the night of the murder? I'm guessing that since he's in jail, he wasn't with you."

That got me a glare and a pair of tight lips to match. "You ought to be ashamed of yourself," she said.

"Oh? Why's that?"

"You come here all casual. Like you're one of us—some kind of hep cat in your fancy shirt and slacks," she said while waving a pointed finger. "But you aren't, are you? You act like you're doing us some kind of favor by askin' questions that have already been asked. Playing the house dick." A vein in her long, slender neck pulsed. "But you don't care one lick about Moses or any of the rest of us. Do you? You're just some pretender, some skid rogue. Why don't you just take that axe, the one you swing like a rusty gate, and screw on out of here? Just leave us poor colored folk alone. We'll be just fine without the likes of you."

And with that, she stormed off, as only a dancer could, and disappeared behind the very curtain from which she arrived, while I waited for someone to snap my gaping jaw closed.

EIGHT

I STOOD THERE like a right rube for the longest time, wondering what had just happened. Once I regained my senses, I reached down, took hold of my axe, the one I swung like a rusty gate, and jumped off the stage. I wasn't sure what hurt more: having my playing insulted or my integrity called into question. Both sat like a rock in my gut.

I blew through the casino to valet, handed the man my half of torn ticket and waited for my Roadmaster. When it arrived, I slipped the sax into the trunk and was about to get in when the newspapers resting on the front seat caught my attention. It was at that same moment my father's voice filled my head. I was used to it being there; it had taken up residency years ago without asking permission and it seemed unwilling to leave—always spouting out wisdom willy-nilly without being asked. On this particular occasion, it reminded me to take a few deep breaths and to think before I acted. 'Don't go off half-cocked,' my father always said.

I pulled the papers from the seat, informed the attendant I had changed my mind, received another half of torn ticket, and headed back inside for a spot of lunch. It wasn't hard to find the Deauville Room, seeing as it was the only open restaurant in the entire casino. Plus, it wasn't a restaurant as much as a coffee shop. In fact, the place seemed more of an afterthought than an actual designated spot for people to consume food. Glass-top, terrace-style tables and matching chairs with removable pads occupied the open-air cement patio framed on one side by what appeared to be the building's brick exterior walls—though they weren't. Plate-glass windows provided visual access to either the pool or the casino, depending on how one positioned oneself.

An array of people filled each setup. White folk sat in the same place with colored folk, some even at the same tables, and the world didn't come to an end. The hostess escorted me to a setup of my own, and, after I took my seat, handed me a small menu with but eight options. Luckily, one of them was a clubhouse sandwich. The chefs in the Deauville Room were very fond of their version of the New York epicurean creation, much more so than their counterparts at the Sands' Garden Room. While the Garden Room chefs priced their offering at an immoderate buck seventy-five, the chefs at the Deauville Room priced that same offering at a downright outrageous four berries! I was hesitant to inquire as to the cost of a manhattan, afraid I would have to take out a small loan just to afford lunch. Still, when the waiter arrived, I threw caution to the wind and ordered both the sandwich and the drink.

While the waiter was busy doing what waiters do, I picked up the first newspaper—the *Las Vegas Review-Journal*—and opened it to see what I could find. I didn't have to look any further than the front page. It was just next to a piece on opium running rampant on the west side of town.

The Moulin Rouge, a great experiment in resort hotels in Las Vegas, opened its doors to what should have been an immediate success. Built far, far away from the Strip section which has become known all over the nation as the glamour spot of America, the Moulin Rouge has been set up as an inter-racial hotel which presents the same type of entertainment, with a Harlem flavor, to the patrons who are expected to flock unto the establishment.

Not a stone has been left unturned to make the Moulin Rouge one of the most exacting and unique hotels ever to grace the desert of Southern Nevada. The entire spot is a big addition to the city of Las Vegas and should prove itself popular to local residents and visitors alike. The management of the establishment expressed itself well pleased with opening night and predicted great success for the newest hostelry in the city.

Unfortunately, that success was marred with the death of one of its rising stars—Margaret Lee Paige— who was found dead in her apartment at the Quinzel Building on the fourteenth block of Ogden Avenue. The blonde-haired, blue-eyed Paige was a singer in both the Tropi Can Can review and at the Lucky Pierre Bar. Paige, RCA Victor's newest recording find, was discovered dead at her home by police responding to a call from a neighbor.

The death put a mark on the spectacular opening of the Moulin Rouge as the prime suspect in the murder turned out to be saxophone player Casper Moses Jones, part of the orchestra that backs up Miss Paige in both the show and the bar. Jones was arrested on Friday night, as police entered the Café

Rouge and took Jones into custody just as the show was in full swing.

Inside the same paper was a review of the Tropi Can Can show, as well as the casino itself.

The Moulin Rouge, although far from the Strip section, has all the plush appointments of the swank establishments which preceded it, and serves some of the finest food in the city.

The floor show was well staged, presenting a variety of entertainment from comedy to nonsense, with beautiful costuming for the Can Can girls. The music of Benny Carter and his men of music backgrounded the show with excellent rhythm and hot music.

There was even a quote from Mayor C. D. Baker that said, "The opening of the Moulin Rouge marked a great step forward in the history and expansion of the city of Las Vegas." And an advertisement promising that Joe Louis "will be on hand to give you the welcome of champions." Columnist Les Devor added his glad tidings to the long list of the show's accolades.

From the opening welcome to the finale, there is a furious pace. To a satiated hotel opener, the thought occurred that this would be another one of "those things" . . . a palace of pleasure. It is that, too, but the Moulin Rouge is also different. The settings are handsome, but not massive. There are plush backgrounds and attractive costumes, but they are not heavy-handed.

It is difficult to describe the dinner, suffice it to say that it was a very bright feature which conceived to be a receptive mood for the show. Cleverly integrated into the bill are Stump and Stumpy, Margaret Lee Paige, Teddy Hale, The Honeytones, and Ann Weldon. Bob Baily is master of ceremonies, and credibly doubles in the vocal department.

Outstanding, and deserving of special note is the music of Benny Carter and his orchestra. A company of 20 dancers exhaustively perform, winning solid applause. The dancers provide the show with a rapid pace which brings the audience, at times, close to exhaustion just from watching them. There could be no more dancing for a while after one of their numbers . . . it was that furious.

Coupled with the article was a photo of the dancers in thick makeup and heavy plumage, arms at shoulder height, legs spread, moving in ways no dancers had ever moved on a Las Vegas stage. It was shocking and thrilling at the same time, and, if one could believe the words written on the page, it would appear that the Moulin Rouge and its Tropi Can Can had taken Las Vegas by storm—outshining all the other casinos that had opened this year.

I wondered how the small town could sustain the growth. The week that saw the opening of the Moulin Rouge had also seen the Royal Nevada, the Dunes, and the Riviera open their doors, as well as the newly remodeled Hotel Last Frontier, which reopened as the New Frontier. By my count, there were now sixteen resort-style hotels, and that didn't include the ones downtown.

I was about to delve into another article when the waiter came to my table with my clubhouse and manhattan. Dying to know what a four-dollar sandwich tasted like, I dove right in. The sandwich was excellent, I have to admit, and the manhattan, stiff. The turkey was moist, the bacon crisp, and the lettuce fresh, with just the right amount of mayonnaise, all piled three layers high. It was a pleasure to eat, and I took my time doing just that.

As I ate, I had a look about the place. Security wore the uniform of the Gendarmerie, right down to the flat-

topped kepi. Cocktail waitresses, dressed to titillate, rushed drinks to guests, while change ladies made change and dealers dealt. And although most of those dealers were colored, the same couldn't be said for the pit bosses—almost all of whom were a noticeably lighter shade of pale.

Just to the left of one of the twenty-one tables, I saw the heavyweight champ engaged in conversation with another man, one I recognized. His name was Booker Percy. He was a local light heavyweight who had been making a name for himself in the boxing world—that was until he started losing. I wondered what business he had with Louis. Whatever it was, the champ didn't seem too happy to see the man. His face was stern and the finger he pointed at the lighter man was rigid. After what appeared to be several angry exchanges, Percy stormed off.

I was watching the man leave when a black-haired beauty with big dark eyes approached. She wore a tight, black turtleneck and dancer's shorts of the same color. A thick belt finished the ensemble. Her legs were long and her cheekbones high. There was enough there to make a man want more, and I was beginning to understand Louis' claim of having the most beautiful women in town.

"May I sit?" she asked.

I pointed to the seat across from me and she took it, sliding one long, full leg over the other.

"Are you the one they call Rossi?"

"Guilty as charged," I said.

She fiddled with a jeweled bracelet around her wrist. "I heard you spoke to Meriday," she said.

"News travels fast, Miss . . ."

"Boyd," she said easily, "but you can call me Theo. Everybody does."

"Theo?" I asked.

"It's short for Theodora."

"Nice to meet you, Theo." She smiled politely, but kept her focus on the bracelet. "Didn't I see you on stage the other night?" I asked.

"I'm a dancer in the show, if that's what you mean."

"What can I do for you, Theo?"

She shifted in her seat, then shifted again. After several attempts to find just the right position, she spoke. "Did Meriday tell you Grafton killed Miss Paige?"

"Did he?" I asked.

"Of course he didn't," she said with conviction. "Moses did."

"Oh, and how did you come by that little jewel of information?"

She pursed her lips. "Everybody knows Moses was getting it on the side with Margaret. Meriday knew it too; she just wouldn't let herself believe it. She fell for him but hard, and Moses did her wrong."

"That may be true," I said. "But it doesn't mean he knocked the singer off."

"Did you know Margaret had a recording contract?"

"Do tell," I said.

"Well, she was supposed to have Moses play on her record. At least that was the line he gave Meriday. And she was going to speak to the people at RCA to see if she couldn't get Moses his own contract."

"Oh?" I feigned surprise.

"Then one day at rehearsal, Moses and Margaret get into this huge row. They were yellin' and screamin' at each other. Callin' each other the worst of names. 'You this and that' and 'you so and so.' Stuff like that. Right in front of everyone. The next day, Benny pulls Moses aside

and tells him he's out and Grafton's in. Benny did it, but everyone knew it came from Margaret."

"And how do you know this?"

"Grafton told me."

"You his girl?"

She smiled. The kind of smile a kid gets with a hand caught in a cookie jar. "Does that matter?" she asked.

"It does to Grafton," I said, and had no sooner gotten the words out of my mouth when a man with two shadows—one larger than the other—caught my eye. He strolled through the casino like he owned the place, fiddling with his cuffs as he walked past the tables toward the back of the house. A straight line to his destination, no detours.

"You know that man?" Theo asked.

I returned my attention to the dancer. "Arguments happen all the time," I said. "Doesn't mean murder is afoot."

"No, but Moses was hoppin' mad. He gets into it with Grafton one day after rehearsals."

"Rumpus?" I asked.

She nodded. "Moses took the first swing, but Grafton finished it. Benny almost kicked Moses out of the band."

"For the fight?"

"That and other things," she said, dropping her gaze to the floor.

"Care to elaborate?" I asked. It was at that moment that I noticed the champ stop what he was doing and rush to the back of the house. Another man, one almost as large as the champ himself and dressed like a French Gendarmerie, rushed there as well. After a moment, they came back out into the casino, only now they were escorting Sal and his companions toward the front entrance.

NINE

KNOWING WHEN I wasn't wanted, I finished my drink, tipped the waiter, then put an egg in my shoe and beat it. Waiting for me right outside the front door was my Roadmaster—the engine running. It seemed just as eager to leave the place as I was. Suddenly, the Moulin Rouge didn't feel as welcoming as it had only hours before. The same felt true for the assignment Garwood had tasked me with.

Benny admitted to a rivalry between the two men. Theodora filled in the bit about the argument between Miss Paige and Moses—the one that likely cost him his record deal, if not more. Then Grafton enters stage left to pick up the pieces. Nice recipe for a murder. I'd seen it go down for much less.

Only one thing didn't fit. In my experience, when a man gets his nose bent out of shape because his gal pal has taken up with another, he usually takes his frustration out on the goose, not the dame. If Moses was a murderer, why hadn't he killed Grafton, especially after having received a beat down at Grafton's hand? There was certainly something going on between Moses and Margaret—whether professional or otherwise—but I wasn't buying it leading to murder. It wasn't Grafton Freeman lying on a slab in the morgue; it was Margaret Lee Paige, and what woman wouldn't go after the skirt who took her man?

But there was yet another thing that stuck in my craw. Why, I wondered, had Theodora pointed her finger, the one with the polished nail, at Meriday with a question of accusation. Meriday was standing by her man, that's for sure, but she hadn't accused Grafton of anything—except being a crumb with no chops. She also seemed unwilling to see what was apparently plain to those around her—if Theo was telling the truth. I knew all too well to be weary of a woman scorned. What I didn't know was how Margaret Lee Paige met her maker. Did it carry all the trappings of a man . . . or a woman?

My next stop took me back across the railroad tracks to the fourteenth block of Ogden, just past the hospital. Resting on the corner, the two-story Diplomat Apartments was a local haven for dancers, entertainers, and the like. Virginia told me Nancy had a short-lived residency there before getting her own place on Charleston.

I parked in front of the building and got out, not knowing at all which path led to the singer's apartment. I doubted O'Malley and his crew would still have the place cordoned off, on the hunt for clues, so I was left to my own devices, as slight as they were. Apartment buildings in Las Vegas were not like the ones back East. Here all doors opened to the outside air, not to a stuffy interior hallway or foyer. A common balcony connected every apartment on the second level, making the place look more like a hotel than a residential building. I climbed up the first set of stairs I saw, figuring I could work my way down.

As I examined each door, waiting for the right apartment to announce itself, I noticed a gap appear in what was otherwise a very orderly set of blinds. A pair of delicate fingers caused the gap, and eyes, which I assumed belonged to said fingers, snuck a peek from the darkness inside. I ignored both the gap and the peeking eyes and continued down the balcony. I don't know why I thought the apartment was on the second floor, but my big toe seemed to think it was, and who was I to argue?

When I reached the end of the balcony, having no clue announce itself, I turned and headed back the way I came. As I approached the peeping Tomasina, the fingers returned, only this time the gap closed as quickly as it had opened. I passed the window and was about to curse my big toe and head back down the stairs when a voice called out from behind me.

"You lost, handsome?"

The voice belonged to a busty blonde with an angled chin and sultry eyes clothed in what passed for a robe— one a bit sheerer than it should have been, with frills covering all the nasty bits . . . well, almost.

"Aren't you cold?" I asked.

Her hair swept the left side of her face, ending with a provocative curl under her chin, giving me visions of Joi Lansing. Only Joi lacked the puffiness, the hint of bruising around the eyes and neck, and the keen, probing nose that was likely stuck where it didn't belong. She batted those very eyes at me.

"You offering to warm a girl up?"

"Not me," I said, holding my hands up high.

"Too bad," she said. "You're a cute one, aren't you?"

"My mother thinks so."

The blonde eyed me up and down. I returned the favor. She had all the right parts in all the right places but was heavily made up with enough face paint to pass as a Vegas showgirl—eyelashes and all—but as a wise woman once told me: *A girl knows how to cover up imperfections.* It made me wonder who had taken a poke at her.

She took in my hipster getup. "You play?" she asked as she lit a gasper.

"I dabble."

She opened the door a little wider and leaned herself against the frame in a position that almost covered a series of small cracks near the strike plate. Her robe stopped slightly above her thighs and climbed even higher as she brought a cigarette to her ruby lips. The seamstress was apparently low on material the day she made that particular piece. My new friend took a long, slow drag, and I suddenly understood why gaspers were called Luckys.

She exhaled a mixture of smoke and scotch, then inhaled like the French girls do, taking in the plume of smoke up through the nose as it escaped her mouth. "Let me guess," she said, "trumpet?"

I shook my head. "Saxophone."

"Hmm, a woodwind man. What can I do for you, Mr. Sax Man?"

Many things came to mind at that moment, but I was a good Catholic boy and simply let them pass on by without notice or comment. No Hail Mary's for me. Besides, I'd been in Dutch before and wasn't any too eager to get back there. It was, in fact, the reason my Virginia was currently opting for a tight leash, not that I could blame her.

"I don't suppose you know which one of these domiciles belonged to Margaret Lee Paige?" I asked.

That got me a raised eyebrow. "Lookie-loo?" she asked.

"Concerned citizen," I countered.

"You a flatfoot?"

"Something like that."

The blonde took another drag and did the French thing again. My knees might have buckled, I wasn't sure. My Italian Catholic mother would have called her a floozy, a *scivezza*, but I didn't think such crass language necessary.

"It just so happens you are standing right in front of the place," she said, then pointed at a door with Lucky-clad fingers. "Room 211."

I turned to the door behind me, twisted the knob and, finding it locked, returned to my eager companion. "I don't suppose you have a key?" I asked.

She raised her arms in a grand gesture. "Would you like to search me?"

And how! I thought, but let the thought pass as quickly as it came. "What do you know about Miss Paige?" I asked instead.

"Well, I know it's been a lot quieter since she's been gone."

"Oh? How's that?"

"No more parties," she said. "Maggie liked her parties; can't say I blamed her. It was fun, a constant stream of musicians coming in and out of the place all night long. The house was rocking, if you know what I mean."

"She have a steady fella?" I asked.

She smiled coyly. "Fellas," she said.

"Oh?"

"Maggie had a penchant for musicians. A certain

type of musician."

"Do tell."

"You know the kind."

"Do I?"

"Well, let me put it this way: you've got the right church, but the wrong pew. It's not for me to say, mind you, but Maggie took her men the way she took her coffee."

"I see. Any names come to mind?"

"Maybe," she said, then shifted her weight, and as she did, she let the robe fall open to reveal a body that'd even Joi would envy.

My open collar had suddenly become very tight. "I believe it's time for me to go," I said. "Better hop it on out of here."

"You sure, handsome? I feel a wave of remembrance coming on. It only needs a little . . . coaxing."

"Oh, I'm sure," I said. "Best to leave while I'm still able."

"You're kind of a stick in the mud, aren't you?"

"The stickiest," I assured her.

She took a final drag. "Your loss," she said sharply, then stepped back inside and slammed the door.

I'd found O'Malley's witness.

TEN

I HEADED DOWN the stairs and around the corner, where I hoped to find the office of the Landlady. I wasn't disappointed. Inside, awaiting my arrival, was a stern-looking woman in a stern-looking chair, positioned behind a high counter taking a drag from an unfiltered gasper. Resting at the corner of the desk was a rocks glass with a finger or two of amber liquid. I would have put a ten spot on a handle of whisky hiding in the bottom left drawer.

I removed my lid and entered at my own peril.

She looked up at me with eyes as hard as steel. "We don't rent to men," she barked.

"I'm not looking for an apartment," I assured her. "Just a bit of information."

"You a cop?"

I assured her I wasn't.

"Well then, you can just move it along down the

block," she said. "We don't have no information here."

I hazarded a step closer. "Now, that's not very friendly."

"I'm not paid to be friendly, Mister."

"Perhaps we should start over," I said, flashing my best forty-watter. "My name is Max Rossi and I am part of the advance team looking for a place to house our dancers for an upcoming show."

She eyed me suspiciously. "And what show would that be?"

"I'm not really at liberty to announce the name at this juncture. We're mostly in the planning phase."

"You're kind of dressed all casual for a businessman, ain't ya'?"

"As I intimated, we're trying to keep this on the hush-hush for now. But I have it on good authority that this is the best place in town to house our dancers until we can finalize our arrangements."

She pressed the butt of her cigarette into a mound of similar butts overflowing an already over-burdened ash tray. Then she moved from her chair to the counter and asked: "How many apartments will you be needing?"

"Well, I'm guessing you go two to a room?"

She nodded and pulled a logbook from under the counter.

"So, I'd say ten."

That caught her attention. "What'd you say your name was? Rossie?" she asked, opening the book.

"Rossi," I corrected with a smile. "Long O. Tell me, is this place quiet?"

She hesitated. "Quiet enough," she said.

"I see. So no loud parties?"

The Landlady folded her arms tight across her chest.

She glared at me with scornful indignation. "You're not really with a troupe, are you?"

"Not really," I admitted. I could've gone on with the ruse, but what good would it have done me? It was clear a change of tactics was in order, so I opened my wallet, took out six five-dollar bills and arranged them on the counter in a nice, neat, orderly row.

Her eyes sparkled a bit as she watched me lay out the bills.

"But I'm not a cop either," I said. "Just a concerned citizen, doing a favor for a friend. Speaking of friends, my six here have some questions. Easy questions. Ones, if answered honestly, might persuade them to become friends of yours."

She reached into the pocket of her housecoat for another gasper, bringing the thing quickly to her lips. I picked up the heavy brass lighter resting on the counter and brought it to the cigarette. She lit the end and nodded her appreciation.

"Go on," she said cautiously.

I handed her one of the bills. "What can you tell me about Margaret Lee Paige?"

She took the offering, then deposited it into the bank of her ample bosom, where it quickly disappeared. "Had the voice of an angel," she said, then added, "for all the good it did her."

I fingered the next bill but didn't pick it up. The landlady rubbed a cigarette-clenched hand across her cheek and licked her lips.

"What do you mean by that?" I asked.

She studied me a moment. "Maggie was a wild child. Liked to have her fun."

"And what kind of fun would that be? She the partying type?"

"This place is full of artists, Mr. Rossi, and artists are prone to celebrations at times."

She reached for the bill, but I pulled it back. "Come now, you can do better than that."

I could see the hesitation in her eyes. She wanted the cabbage, but something was keeping her mouth sealed. Perhaps a little lubrication could help her find the right words. "You have two of those?' I asked, eyeing the glass on her desk.

The landlady took a long drag, then made her way to the desk, blowing the smoke out the side of her mouth. She dropped the butt into the ashtray, opened the desk drawer, took out a bottle of whisky that was old enough to vote and another glass, then brought them, and the rocks glass, over to the counter. I poured a couple of fingers of the Old Smuggler into our glasses, being sure to pour more into hers than mine. She didn't look the type who took ice or a couple of splashes of water with her drink. No, she was a dame who took her rotgut straight, the way ol' Lucifer intended.

She took little time or effort in downing her elixir. Mine did not go down as easy. Personally, If I were going to drink an "Old," I would have preferred Old Forester, or even Old Overholt, but, being a beggar, I could, as they say, not be a chooser. I poured her another hit, then slid the next bill over to her and watched it disappear.

"Tell me about these parties," I said.

"She liked to have her band come over, they played long into the night."

"It didn't bother the other residents?"

"Oh, it bothered them all right. Got lots of complaints. People work all sorts of different hours here, you know." She took another snort. "Course, just as many seemed to flock there and joined in."

"And you let it happen? Didn't shut them down?"

She smiled coyly, like a snake addressing a mouse. "She made it worth my while."

"I see."

"Why you asking so many questions? The same kind them hammers and saws asked."

"They ask you about parties?"

She nodded.

"And what did you tell them?"

"Same thing I told you."

I handed her another bill. "You tell them about the drugs?"

She tried to hide it, but her body betrayed her. The eyes widened, the brows lifted, and she tensed a bit. It was brief, no more than a moment, but it was enough to show her surprise at the question. She recovered quickly, sliding the bill into her bosom.

"They're jazz musicians, Mr. Rossi, there's always drugs involved."

"What kind of drugs?"

"I couldn't tell you," she said. "All's I knew was the reefer. Can't stand that stuff. Always smelled like skunk to me."

"What kind of people were at these parties?"

"Already told you. Musicians."

"Colored musicians?"

"Some. Some were white too."

"You didn't have any problem with them mixing?"

"Why would I? Don't make no difference to me."

"Anything queer about these parties?"

She looked at me strangely. "I don't get what you mean."

"You know, Diana Dors style."

She studied me for a moment, then the understanding kicked in. Her mouth fell open and her lashes began batting away flies. "You mean, was they having orgies? Mister, we allow quite a bit of leeway here, but we don't go that far."

I tried not to grin at her uneasiness. After all, it wasn't very gentlemanly of me to even ask the question, but I didn't let that stop me. Just for kicks, I threw another one at her. "She make it with any of them?"

She frowned. "Mister, you sure do ask a lot of unseemly questions."

I picked up another bill and handed it to her. She put it with the others. It was getting crowded in there.

"You referrin' to that colored boy that got popped for her murder?"

I nodded.

"Yeah, they played house."

"Just him?"

She didn't answer at first, just took a puff on her filter-less gasper. After a moment, she spoke. "Maggie was the kind to flirt, if you know what I mean."

"Just flirt?"

She hesitated. "That's not for me to say."

I poured a bit more into her glass.

She looked at the glass, then at me, then took a strong snort. "Maggie liked to spread the honey around," she said. "I don't think it went any further than flirting. You know how some women are. They like to make their man jealous."

"A peculiar way to make love," I said. "Who'd she have a dalliance with?"

The landlady leaned in. "You use awful fancy words, Mr. Rossi," she said, the hooch setting in.

"Who was the target of her flirtations?" I asked.

She grinned. "There was another sax player. Usually brought the reefer. Wasn't as good as Maggie's Moses. Least didn't seem that way to me, but I ain't no music critic. He didn't take much to her flirtations, so she switched to another. Big guy, muscles to spare." she leaned in even farther, then said: "Wouldn't mind having a piece of that one myself."

"This big guy, he have a name?"

"Never caught his name."

"What instrument did he play?"

She scrunched her face in thought, then shook her head. "Come to think of it, I don't recall he ever playing an instrument. He was just there."

"And the night of the murder, who was with Margaret?"

She hesitated.

"Moses?"

She shook her head. "I couldn't tell you."

"Look, if it was Moses, I really . . ."

She stiffened. "I said I couldn't tell you."

I picked up the remaining bills, tapped them together, and was about to place them back in my wallet, when I caught the sadness in her eyes. I folded the bills, slipped them between my first and second fingers, held them up, and asked: "One more question?"

She nodded.

"Mind if I take a look-see into Maggie's apartment?"

Her eyes turned back to steel, and she seemed suddenly quite sober. "What do you want with that place?"

"I just want to look around," I said, and moved the two bills a bit closer to her eager hand.

She studied them. Maybe she was recording the serial numbers; maybe she wasn't. What did I know? But there was clearly something rolling around in her head—something that caused her to seriously weigh the request against the consequences of filling said request. I wondered what they might be, those consequences.

"Can't do it," she finally said.

"You sure?" I asked.

She nodded, but I could tell it grieved her to do it. I flipped the bills back, pulled out my wallet, and stuffed them back inside. Then I finished my hooch and turned to leave, but before I disappeared, I stopped and turned back. "Margaret's neighbor? Blond doll. Doesn't wear many clothes."

"Evelyn?"

"Seems right," I said. "What does Evelyn do for a living?"

"She's a pro skirt, but don't go sniffin' around; you couldn't afford her, even with all your fives."

"Is that so?"

The Landlady nodded with a smile. I left the same way I'd come in and had just turned the corner when I saw a familiar figure making his way down the stairs, his two shadows in tow. I pulled back, not wanting to be noticed. The Diplomat Apartments were a busy place. I watched as Sal got into his car and headed down the road. I would've thought my timing perfect, that is, had Sal's car not slowed to a crawl when he came to mine.

ELEVEN

AFTER HEADING TO my car, I was left to wonder what the Landlady hadn't been willing to tell me. I also wondered if it was something she hadn't been willing to tell O'Malley as well. Though I was pretty sure it had something to do with that bottle of hooch in her desk drawer. There was also the question of why she wasn't willing to let me into Paige's apartment. Was there something in there she didn't want me to see? Perhaps Evelyn wasn't the witness after all. But if the landlady fingered Moses, why was she so hush-hush about that particular fact, after having been so willing to squeal about everything else?

At this point, I was sure of only two things. One, it was high time my part in this whole thing was over and done with. And two, it was going to be a late night, and I needed a bit of shuteye if I was going to be worth the price of admission at the gig tonight. So I drove home, dropped my sax and the newspapers on the couch, then stripped down to my skivvies, climbed into bed, and grabbed twenty or so winks, while visions of sugarplums danced in my head.

The house was dark when I awoke. Dark and quiet. Peaceful, like a winter's night in the cemetery. I laid there for the longest time, not wanting to disturb the silence, running the music over and over in my head, fingering the keys absent mindedly. It was to be a big night for Jimmy and the rest of his dimes and I very much did not want to be the architect of their demise. I was worried that it might have been better to let me take a seat in the audience on this one, sipping a manhattan and enjoying the show, but I doubted Jimmy would go for that.

I showered, shaved, and shined, then pulled on the same trousers I had originally, but opted for a fresh shirt—a madras with an open neck collar. Then I slipped on the two-tone loafers and argyle socks I had on before, and topped it all with my walking lid—the one my grandfather gave me. I was ready for a spot in any jazz ensemble and I didn't care who knew it. If I couldn't play the part, I sure the heck was going to look it.

I climbed into my Roadmaster, placing my horn in the back. It was, I decided, a perfect night to leave the top down and I did just that, enjoying the breeze as I headed out into the Vegas night. I loved my Roadmaster. Likely because it was the first car I ever bought with my own scratch—just like a big boy. The beast was a beauty with sleek, smooth lines and curves enough to make a priest blush. I wasn't really into red, but when Frank Scarpini pulled that car around from the side of the dealership, I have to admit, my little loathsome heart skipped a beat and my face, having a mind of its own, painted itself with a full, wide smile.

She came complete with two-tone bench seats, red with tan highlights, the top bench split to afford easy access to her matching back seat—in case anyone had a hankering for a little bingo. Tan mats hugged the floorboards like a belt around a woman's waist, and padded panels of the same color adorned the doors on either side, separated from the top by a thin chrome strip. Her handles were chrome, and her steering wheel black with a chrome insert that brought the horn to life— the center decorated with her regal emblem. The shifter was on the column, allowing a bird to keep his right arm around his gal pal and his left on both the steering wheel and the shifter to operate as needed. Frank and I negotiated for quite some time before I signed on the dotted line and took her home—there were no fools at all in the Rossi household. She's been with me ever since.

She's a pleasure to drive. Handles like a dream as she glides down the road on a cushion of air. At least she was this night, as I drove to the Bootlegger with the sweltering desert breeze drifting up from the over-heated desert sand, slapping me in the face like a scorned lover. Vegas is a different town at night. Awash in neon and blinking bulbs, it's a beacon of radiance in an otherwise vast darkness, attracting innocents like moths to a flame. How could anyone resist or survive?

When I arrived at the Bootlegger, I pulled around the back and found a spot to settle my Roadmaster into, then I pulled my horn from the backseat and headed inside, hoping Matteo was busy cooking something that would alight my Italian nona's heart. As I opened the door, an aroma ticked my nose—one that instantly let me know I was not to be disappointed.

"Ciao Massimo," Matteo said as soon as I entered. "Vieni qui!"

When a chef the caliber of Matteo beckons you to come, you come.

"Assagia questo," he said, holding a spoon up to my mouth that contained the most aromatic sauce I have ever had the pleasure of allowing into my nostrils.

I went to taste, but he pulled back slightly. "È caldo. Soffiaci sopra."

I blew on the sauce, thankful that Matteo had saved my tastebuds from a possible scorching. He stared at me in anticipation as I blew and eventually tasted the sauce. It was good . . . very good. Good enough that I began to feel I was cheating on Virginia. "È Perfetto!" I said. "Veramente perfecto!"

He pulled the spoon back with a satisfied grin. My critique bought me a bowl of pasta and a fork to eat it with. I took it, and my horn, into the dining room, finding it a buzz with waiters and waitresses preparing for the evening show and feast. I set the horn down near the stage and concentrated on the treat that awaited me.

I was about halfway through my meal when Jimmy approached, clad in his gold broadcloth jacket, the one with the narrow lapels and chain motif. He'd chosen a black shirt to wear underneath with a thin black tie that wrapped around his equally thin neck like a noose. His pants and square matched the shirt, but his shoes were gold wingtips. He'd teased his hair into a mile-high pompadour, shellacked with enough Brylcreem to make sure it didn't go anywhere without him—apparently a little dab did not do 'em.

"You ready for tonight, Max?" he asked as he adjusted his tie, looking about as comfortable as a mouse in a pit of vipers.

"The better question is, are you ready for tonight?"

"It's going to be a big night," he said, without answering me.

"That it is," I agreed. "Maxine here yet?"

He nodded. "She's in the back getting ready." The snake around his neck must have been causing him fits, because he couldn't seem to keep his hands off the thing.

"Her butter and egg man with her?"

"Yah, he's with her," he said with a quick smirk, still messing with the tie.

"You look like a man about to take the long walk. Maybe you should nibble one to calm those nerves."

"Yah, yah, that's a good idea. I'll do that."

He turned and left, leaving me to resume my affair with the bowl of pasta. I finished it, savoring every delicious bite. I might have even cleaned the bowl, but I'm not one to lick and tell. If I was going to cheat, I might as well go all the way, so I decided to polish it off with a manhatten of my own. I traded the bartender my bowl for the drink, then took it back to my horn and got the thing ready to play.

Twenty minutes later, we were on stage in front of a packed house. Doing the routine just as we'd practiced it earlier that day. Maxine sang like a gem, wearing a knee-length princess cocktail dress that was black hollow to hem, except for two gold cut outs. One stretched across the bustline, while the other started at the waist and continued downward. Black polka dots patterned the cutouts, which were also adorned with large white buttons. Her kitten heels matched her dress, as did the buttons in her ears. She was a sight to behold as she belted out *That Man*, then followed it with *All that Glitters*, *Pack the Louie*, and *Tongue Tied*.

The crowd was feeling the beat: the band was hoppin', and I was playing like ol' Satchmo had granted me the use of his freak lips for the night. At the break between sets, after the crowed clapped their approval, we all went outside to get a bit of fresh air—as fresh as one can expect in the desert. Much to my surprise, Maxine joined us, leaving her shadow to do whatever it was shadows did.

Maxine opened her purse and pulled out a bag of tea. She tossed it to one of the musicians and instructed him to light it up. The musician did as told, inhaled deeply, then passed it around. I opted out, but when it was

Maxine's turn, she took a long slow drag, holding the smoke in her delicate lungs before finally letting it escape the way it came in.

"Oh, that is some fancy Juju," she said, passing it to the man next to her.

As my bandmates paired off, engaged in their own conversations, I focused on Maxine. The tea had kicked in and it was showing. She slowly started moving to some unheard sound, her eyes gently closed, her hips swaying side to side, her dress gliding back and forth like a bell in a tower. She tilted her head slightly and let the sound take her on a journey; the waves washing over her arms, hands, and fingers. It was a journey I would have liked to go on, but that was probably the sauce talking.

She turned to me and raised her hands high in the air, inviting me to a dance. Who was I to refuse? I stepped in and she wrapped her arms around my neck; I rested my own two mani on her ample hips, navigating them like a sailor on the high seas. We swayed back and forth, just the two of us, turning in small circles, me following her lead.

"What's your name?" she asked.

"Rossi, but you can call me Max."

"Ummm, Max." she repeated. "That's a strong name. Are you a strong man, Max?"

"I guess that depends on how you mean it.

Her laugh was light and airy.

"You've got a beautiful voice," I said.

She smiled genially. "Aren't you kind?"

"It's not simply kindness. The audience loved it too."

"It helps to have a swinging band behind you," she said. "You're pretty good on that horn of yours. You play for a living?"

"I dabble is all."

"Ever think of going pro?"

"Once, when I met this little blonde dish in a tight sweater."

She laughed a second time, and the sea got a bit more turbulent. "Then what are you doing here?"

"Slumming," I said. "Just a break from my real gig."

"Oh? And what might that be?"

"Drinking hooch and playing the Bees."

"You're funny," she said. "And cute."

"Aren't you kind?" I said.

She slid a gentle hand across my cheek. "Don't you go anywhere," she ordered, then removed her arms from around my neck, turned and headed to the musician holding the tea stick. She snatched it from him, placed it in her mouth, and took another drag. The eyes rolled into the back of her head and she smiled deeply. I'm not sure her shadow would have approved.

After she returned the stick to where she found it, she came back to me and we resumed our positions. Back on the ocean.

"Where'd you get the tea?" I asked.

"From a friend," she said.

"Your friend got a name?"

"I'm sure he does."

"But you don't know it." I said.

She nodded.

"He a musician?"

She nodded again. "A sax player, just like you."

"I don't think your escorts would approve."

She gave me a humph. "What they don't know won't hurt me."

I smiled.

We swayed.

"I'm slumming too," she said. "Just doing this gig while I wait for my sister."

"She performs at the Rouge, doesn't she?"

Maxine nodded. She was awake, but you couldn't tell it by her eyes.

"She like it there?"

"Sure, why not?"

"Ever run into Margaret Lee Paige? Your sister, that is."

"Sure," she said, her eyes still at half-mast. "All the time. Shame what happened."

"Isn't it though?"

"That sax player killed her, you know."

"Do I?"

"Sure. He was two-timing that dancer."

"Meriday?" I asked.

"That the dancer's name?"

I told her it was. "You saying there was something going on between him and the singer?" I asked.

"Well, I couldn't say for sure, but you know how it is, a sideways glance, a little laugh. Like I said, I couldn't say for sure, but I wouldn't bet against it either."

"You think Meriday noticed it?"

"Honey child, Ray Charles could have noticed it."

"Your sister tell you this?"

Maxine nodded. "Some," she said. "Some I saw for myself. Except the catfight. I didn't see the catfight."

"Catfight?" I questioned.

Maxine smiled. "Oh, it was a doozy, according to Ann. Margaret was going on about how this sax player was boiling her cabbage. Then that dancer just stepped right up to Margaret and slapped her across the face, like nobody's business. 'Stay away from my man!' she says to her."

"That must have gone over well," I said.

"About as well as you can imagine."

"What did Margaret do?"

"What could she do? She slapped her right back! It went downhill from there. Feathers and rhinestones were flyin' everywhere. They were rolling on the floor, according to Ann, when the stagehands got there. The dancer even attacked one of the stagehands when he tried to separate them. Kicked the man right where a man ought not to have been kicked."

As Maxine's hips swayed, I felt the poor stagehand's pain. Clearly, Meriday knew more than she pretended to know. "What happened?" I asked.

Maxine shook her head. "Nothing. Everyone went back to work; there was another show to do." She paused and cracked her eyes open. "You talk too much and don't dance enough."

I made more of an effort to get on board. I brought my hands up to her sides; she lowered them back down to her hips with a smile. "I like them there better," she said.

"Did your sister say how Margaret was to work with?" I asked.

"Oh, she was all right, at the beginning anyway. But she got difficult to be around at the end. She missed rehearsals and when she did come, she was always cross about something."

"Why did she miss rehearsals?"

"I don't know. Something about being sick."

"Do you think she was?"

"Well, she sure looked it sometimes. And she was always mopin' around, like she hadn't gotten any sleep and she seemed to spend a lot of time in the ladies' room on her knees."

"She ever miss performances?"

She stopped swaying and her face grew serious. "Honey, you don't miss performances, no way, and she didn't miss a one."

"How where they? Her performances I mean."

"Oh child, that woman had the voice of an angel." And suddenly we were back on the sea.

"Anything else you can tell me?"

"Just that you're killing my buzz."

Just then the door burst open and a stagehand announced, "Five minutes," before sliding back inside.

The dance was over.

TWELVE

WE FINISHED THE second and final set, with the crowd even more into it than they were the first set. Whether the stars were aligned just right, the tea was extra special, or because Maxine was sitting in with us, we were hitting on all eights and it felt good—almost made me want to do it for a living . . . almost.

As I packed up my horn, Johnny Boy came over and slapped me on the back. "That was sure some bad playing you laid down tonight," he said.

"You weren't so bad yourself."

"You're a good fit. Glad I discovered you," he said with a grin and another slap on the back. "We might just keep you around."

Not if you make it big, I thought, but didn't say it. "Do you know if Garwood's here?" I asked.

"He's here," Johnny Boy confirmed with a nod of the head. "Over there talking to Jimmy and Maxine's butter and egg man."

I thanked him, closed my case, and headed over to Garwood to make my report. There wasn't much to make. I was proving to be about as useless as a ham sandwich at a Bar Mitzvah. Perhaps this detective gig wasn't a good fit for me after all. Perhaps I needed a new career; maybe I could take up selling shoes to a snake.

I stood, waiting my turn, as Maxine's shadow shook hands with Jimmy and Garwood in turn before collecting Maxine and heading out stage left. Jimmy was all smiles, happier than a puppy with two tails. Apparently, things had gone well. He looked over at me and nodded, before leaving me alone with Garwood.

"You got a minute?" I asked.

"Of course, Max. Please, take a seat."

I did as asked.

"Great set tonight. You all were in the groove."

I thanked him, but wasn't in the mood for small talk. My thoughts were on the Bees and a manhattan at the Sands, so I got right to the point.

"Moses is still in stir."

Garwood nodded. I wasn't telling him anything he didn't know.

"It doesn't look good for your man," I said, then told him everything I knew. I told him about my visit to the Rouge, about my conversations with Benny, Meriday, and Theo, about my visit to Margaret's apartment, and about O'Malley's witness. It was just enough to fill a thimble.

"You're going to keep at it, aren't you?" Garwood asked. "Keep digging?"

"There's not much more to dig," I told him. "Nothing left but hard ground."

I heard a sigh. I think it came from Garwood, but maybe not.

"Something troubling you?" Garwood asked.

It wasn't a question I wanted to be asked because it wasn't a question I wanted to answer. But I'm a sap, so I answered it anyway. "The thing is," I said, "when a man is sore at another bird for two-timing his gal pal, he doesn't usually take it out on the gal, he takes it out on the bird. So why is it Margaret Lee Paige lying on a slab in the morgue and not Grafton Freeman? And why is Grafton suddenly in the wind?"

"Two good questions," Garwood said. "Are they ones you intend to answer?"

"I'm afraid they may not be answerable by the likes of me, and even if they were, it might require stepping on toes."

"I see," Garwood said. He placed a hand on his drink and swirled it around, then did it again and took a slow sip. I'd have put down one myself had I had one to put down.

"What if I got you some help?" he asked.

"Not to be impertinent, Garwood, but what I need isn't help. It's a stiff drink, a set of Bees, and a long-legged Copa Girl."

That got me a gruff laugh, but it didn't last. He stared at his drink, swirled it again, then told it a tale. "They'll hang him, you know," he said solemnly. "And they won't even think twice about it. He's black, she's white. He was dead before they even cuffed him."

I thought about Moses sitting under glass, his face pressed through a meat grinder, an angry man with no prospects. I thought about O'Malley in his dingy gray suit and Stacy Adams and his raw knuckles. It didn't sit well, and I knew it in the pit of my stomach.

Garwood knew it too.

THIRTEEN

I LAID MY sax in the back seat, climbed into the front and pointed my Roadmaster toward the Sands. I wasn't kidding about the manhattan, the Bees, or the long-legged Copa Girl. I needed to clear my head and there was no better way to do that than at the tables, relieving some egg from his hard-earned cabbage. Why should I be the only sap in Las Vegas?

When the valet attendant came, I handed him my keys and a nugget that was hiding in my pocket. I took a step, then turned and tossed him another; I didn't want the first to get lonely. Once inside, I headed straight for the poker tables—the only honest game in the joint. It was Saturday night, and the place was bustling with all manner of people wasting their nickels and dimes on one-armed bandits. Bells whistled, lights blinked, and coins clanked into trays while Freddy Bell and the Bellboys played to a packed house in the Silver Queen. I snaked my way to the poker tables, looked for Texas hold 'em, and took a seat at the only open spot I could find, then I placed my lid, along with a couple dixies, on the felt in front of me.

The croupier was a nondescript man with short-cropped hair, a sharp nose, and a cleft in his chin that could have been cut with an axe. Clad in the usual white shirt, black vest, and matching bowtie, he eyed me casually, then snatched my offering before stuffing it into the box at his side. Then he pulled several of the little clay chips from the tray in front of him, counted them twice, and slid them over to me. Chips weren't actually worth anything, outside the casino that is; they simply took the place of cash, diverting people's attention from the amount of money they were blowing on the tables—a neat trick.

Accompanying me in my solitude was a dish in an emerald swing dress with a blue plaid cutout and a matching bow collar. She wore black gloves that stopped at her wrists and her blond hair was done up in some sort of Italian wave with a rounded-up horsetail in the rear, making her look younger than she was. I didn't mind. She was a fancy little dish, blessed with the kind of face that could make a preacher lay down his bible. Accompanying her, though not formally, were two fellows, one on either side. The first was in a fancy gray sack suit, the other a wheelchair. A jasper in a porkpie hat took the fifth spot. He was the nervous type, tapping on the table like he was waiting for a late bus.

Poker tables set low, unlike their blackjack counterparts, and came shaped like kidney beans, with the dealer positioned in a seat at the curve of the bean and the players on the outskirts. Thus, a goose in a wheelchair could fit in just fine. Everyone in Vegas had an equal chance of losing.

A cocktail waitress approached, and I ordered a manhattan and another to keep it company. The waitress smiled at me, so I handed her a single before she left; I didn't want my drink to get lost in the crowd. By the time she returned, the current hand finished, with the goose in the wheelchair winning the pot. My manhattans had arrived unscathed, so I gave the waitress another single, and she gave me another smile.

With the next hand underway, we all threw in our buy-in, also called an ante, which was simply the amount each player must toss into the pot to get the game started. With most games of chance, play is against the house. Not so with poker. In this game, each player is pitted against every other player with the house taking a percentage of the final pot, regardless of who wins. The role of a dealer is more of a mediator than anything, watching to ensure the play goes on without a hitch.

Poker is a game of nuances, trying to get your opponents to bet when they shouldn't bet, raise when they shouldn't raise, and fold when they shouldn't fold, all the while knowing when *you* should bet, raise or fold. The winner isn't always the bird with the best hand. More often than not, the winner is the one best at reading the table.

That was the reason I played poker; I enjoyed watching people—always have. The raise of an eyebrow or curl of the lip, the way a goose plays with his chips while waiting to bet, checks his cards, or even how he lays those cards down on the felt are all signs. Tells, they're called. Movements people make unconsciously that clue a joker in to the thoughts behind the cards, so long as that joker is paying attention. I pay attention.

This was a relatively low stakes table, so a single chip from each of us took care of the buy-in just fine. The dealer delt the hole cards face down so that only the holder of each pair could see them. Most dealers have a smooth style, gained through repetition, pulling cards from the deck and sliding them effortlessly in front of each player. One dealer I knew liked to spin his cards when he dealt them. He'd pull a card from his hand and, with a flick of the wrist, spin the card, landing it exactly in front of the intended player.

This dealer had none such panache. His movements were awkward, and he seemed wholly unsure of himself. He laid the cards down slowly, pausing briefly before dealing the next. He held the deck at the wrong angle, at times revealing the bottom card to anyone who chose to notice, forcing the pit boss to correct him fairly frequently. This was obviously a croupier who had not been croupiing very long.

I lifted the corners of my cards and had a peek—a three of clubs and five of spades. Hoping this wasn't an omen of things to come, I folded.

Each of my four compadres threw in another chip. The dealer discarded the top card on the deck, then dealt three additional cards face-up directly in front of him, taking more time than needed to arrange them. These three cards, known as the flop, were community cards, which meant everyone played off them to make their hands. The flop was a ten of spades, a queen of hearts, and a jack of diamonds. It was the makings of a straight, if one was so inclined.

The guy next to me was the nervous type, always checking and double checking his cards, as if they would magically change. Cards don't change. It was the sign of an inexperienced, unsure gambler, and while he may get lucky once or twice, before the night was through, he was destined to lose all he had and walk out a broken man, sour and disgusted.

The blonde, on the other hand, seemed to know what she was doing. She glanced at her cards but once and took her time with her bets. She looked at me with bright eyes, curled a ribbon of hair between her first two fingers, and flashed me a coy smile once I folded. I lifted my glass and returned the favor.

The inexperienced gambler made a bet much larger than he should have at this point in the hand. It was far too soon to know how strong a hand he had and betting so high he was announcing his ineptitude.

"You must have a peach of a hand," the woman said to him in a soft, Southern drawl. She pulled her fingers from her locks, grabbed a couple of chips, and raised the bet. He foolishly called. It wouldn't be the last mistake he made that evening. The porkpie hat folded, leaving only the bloke in the wheelchair, the dame, and our imminent loser to continue on, and lose he did, with the dame taking the pot when all was said and done.

"Better luck next time, honey," she said to the man, and flashed me another of those smiles she seemed to dish out like candy.

"Behaving yourself?" a voice from behind me asked. It was a soft voice, a familiar voice, and it floated on a hint of lavender.

"As much as any man can," I said.

"Well, that's comforting," she responded with just the right amount of snideness.

"Shouldn't you be dancing?" I asked.

"Shouldn't you be winning?" she countered.

"I thought I was the pistol around here," I said.

"Oh, you're still a pistol," she confirmed. "Don't worry." She placed a hand on my shoulder. "Wanna buy a gal a drink?"

"More than anything," I said.

I motioned for the pit boss and, when he came over, I asked him if I could leave my chips where they had grown comfortable while I entertained this young lady from the Copa Room. Virginia commented that it was more like corruption. Who was I to argue? When the pit boss assured me my chips would be here, untouched when I returned, I rose from my chair, placed my lid in position atop my head, offered the dancer my arm, and lead her to the bar.

I ordered Virgina a tom collins and myself a manhattan. "Packed house?" I asked.

"And how!" she said. "Packed house, new routine, and unhappy bosses."

"Oh?"

"Jack's madder'n a wet hen," she said, her Texas showing.

The Jack she referred to was Jack Entratter who was once the manager of the Copacabana club in New York City but had moved to Vegas to run the Copa Room at the Sands.

"Show not going well?" I asked.

The bartender appeared with our drinks. I handed him two bits just to be nice.

"Oh, the show's going fine," she said, taking her drink. "At least our part, anyway. It's the talent that Jack's sore at. He tried to get Lena Horne for next month, but she refused to come. Said she preferred to perform where she was welcome in the casino, not just on the stage. Harry Belafonte is trying to cancel his contract as well. So is Dorothy Dandridge."

I walked her over to a table with two vacant seats. Virgina nestled into one of the padded chairs, crossing one long, beautiful leg over the other. "How'd you come by all this?" I asked as I sat.

"You kidding me? Jack's been yelling at the top of his lungs all week. Cursing every colored entertainer in the book. He's so mad, he forbade any of us from even going to the Moulin Rouge."

"Well, ain't that something," I said. It wasn't much

to say, but I said it anyway. "What does he plan to do about all this?

"How should I know? Said something about talking to Jake."

That Jake was Jake Freeman, an "oil tycoon," and owner of the Sands. Truth was, he was a Texas gambler and while his name might have been on the deed, it was Meyer Lansky and Frank Costello who really owned the place. If Jack was going to talk to Jake, it meant Fingers would surely be involved. Frank "Fingers" Abbandandolo was my boss. He was also a capo out of New York, sent here by Lansky to keep an eye on their properties, specifically the Sands. Frank started his illicit career on the streets of New York as a young boy, picking the pockets of tourists. He was small and thin then, with nimble fingers. But he was a big boy now, a very big boy, and while the moniker no longer fit the man, once given, a moniker is never retracted.

I didn't particularly relish working for mobsters, but what was a boy from the north end to do? I couldn't beat them and I sure as heck didn't want to join them. This seemed like somewhat of a happy medium.

"It appears the Rouge is having a much greater effect than anticipated," I said.

"You don't know the half of it. I hear the head chef left to run the kitchens there, along with a fair number of maids and porters."

That explained my four-dollar club.

"The grass must be greener on the other side of the tracks," I said.

"Isn't it always?"

I couldn't argue with that. As we sipped our drinks, Virginia inquired about my night, and I told her. I explained how well everything went, how smoothly I played in particular, and how Jimmy scored with Maxine on the bill. "Looks like he might have a shot at something," I said.

"Something that would take him from Las Vegas?" she asked.

"Highly likely."

"That won't make Nancy happy."

I wanted to say, "She'll get over it," but thought better of it. We talked for a few minutes more before Virginia had to ready herself for the late show—her third of the night.

"I've got to scoot," she said. "I have to get made up. Olivia is ill, and I'm taking her part."

"Oh, and what part is that?"

"Queen of the Pacific Island," she said, with the appropriate fanfare.

I was confused. "But you don't look like someone from the Pacific Islands."

"You'd be surprised what a little make-up can do," she said as she stood. "What are your plans for the evening?"

"Drink a little, play a little, drink a little more," I said.

"You're incorrigible."

"I do my best. Don't suppose you're available for a nightcap?"

Virginia wrinkled her nose and shook her head ever so slowly. "I've already told you; my only date tonight is with my pillow."

"Perhaps another time," I said and downed the last of my manhattan. I stood and placed a hand on Virginia's lovely waist. I knew better than to kiss her at work. Dancers were tasked with mingling with the guests in between shows—spice up the tables a bit. It wouldn't do well if one of them showed to be unavailable. They needed to give the impression that every bird had an equal shot with them—even if it was all a grand illusion.

After Virginia left, I returned to the table I'd started with. All the players were still present, except for one. The porkpie hat had skedaddled for parts unknown, but another bird had taken his place, creating a full house with the dame, the goose in the wheelchair, the inexperienced player, and me.

I hit the table at just the perfect time and was able to jump right into the next hand. Resting my lid on the table, I threw in my ante and waited for the Bees to come to me. Two tens; I liked this pair much better. The flop produced another ten, along with a two of hearts and an eight of spades. My prospects had suddenly gotten brighter.

The guy to my right checked when the dealer came to him, meaning he wanted to stay in the game, but didn't want to raise the bet. It could be the sign of an unsure hand, or a player who understood the first round isn't the time to bet big. If you have a fish on the line, it's best to set the hook before reeling it in.

I checked as well.

The inexperienced gambler must have had a hand he was terribly proud of because he'd been fingering his chips the whole time, eager to bet. He threw two more chips into the pot, only these were five-dollar chips.

The dame whistled loudly. "What're you holding, honey?" she asked with a smile, twirling another ribbon of hair between her fingers. "That flop must have been kind to you."

He gave her a confident grin. "I guess you'll have to bet to find out," he said.

"Oh, I don't have to bet, Sugar," she said. "I can fold and still find out what you're holding when the hand is through."

That shook his confidence a bit.

The bet came to the goose in the chair, he called, meaning he threw in two five-dollar chips as well. The dame stopped the twirl. She picked up her last two chips and brought them close to her ruby red lips. Then she eyed the inexperienced gambler, and looked to the goose in the chair, before finally turning her attention to me.

She winked.

"Maybe I'm just a sucker," she said, then added the chips to the pot.

The guy next to me called. I did too.

The dealer burned another card, then dealt the turn: a jack of diamonds. The fellow next to me checked again, and when the bet came to me, I threw in two more nickels, just to make it interesting. The most the inexperienced guy had was three of a kind and since I had three of the four tens in the deck, the highest he could have would be three eights. The jack wouldn't have helped him any more than it helped me, so it seemed like a safe bet. Of course, he could have had a gutshot—four cards into a straight—and the jack could have finished that straight for him, but nobody in his right mind would have bet on an inside straight that early in the game.

The inexperienced gambler matched my bet and raised it two more, dwindling the stack in front of him significantly.

The dame had returned to twirling her hair. "Well now, Darlin'," she said. "What've you got in that hand of yours?"

"Enough to double my money," he said.

She bit her lower lip slightly, then said, "Honey, the quickest way to double your money is to fold it over and place it back in your pocket."

I laughed, so did the bird next to me. The gambler did not.

The wheelchair folded.

"That's a lot of green," the dame said. She slid a hand down beside her and brough it up under her dress, then pulled it upward, lifting the hem as she slid it along her stocking, up her thigh, past the clips and straps of her garter belt, until she found a black, lace garter. Folded in the garter was a fine bit of cabbage. She removed it, slipped out a couple bills, and returned the rest whence it came, before slowly pulling down her hem. It was a show meant for all the guys to watch—and watch we did.

She placed the bills on the table in front of her. The dealer took them eagerly, exchanged them into chips, and pushed those chips back to her. As she removed the top four from the stack, she had all the eyes on the table, still watching her with eager anticipation. She looked to each one of us in turn, but this time, when she glanced toward the wheelchair, I noticed something I hadn't before.

It was a meager movement of the hand, a finger raised ever so slightly, followed by an almost imperceivable nod of the head. "Oh, what the heck," she said and tossed the four chips into the pot.

The man next to me folded. I threw in two more chips.

The dealer burned the last card and dealt the river. Having the pit boss hover over his shoulder did little to settle his nerves, and it showed. The river was another eight. The suit didn't matter. I was a river rat with a full house.

With two players having folded, there were only three of us left. I tossed two more chips into the pot, then waited for the inexperienced gambler to make his move. He was too far into it all to pull out now. He either had what he thought was a good hand or was bluffing poorly. Either way, he had to go on, see it through.

He fidgeted with his chips, then checked his cards one more time, just to make sure they hadn't changed. They hadn't. His eyes darted from the pot to his cards, then to his chips.

"Sir," the dealer said. "It's your bet."

"What're you gonna do, sugar?" the dame asked.

He picked up two chips, studied them for a moment, then threw them into the pot. Then, much to my surprise, he picked up two more and threw them in as well. It must have surprised the dame too, because for just a moment, she lost her smile, and stopped twirling her hair, but quickly regained her composure. She, too, was in a bit of a pickle, having placed enough in the pot that it would be hard to walk away.

Then she did it again. Glanced ever so quickly at the goose in the chair. This time, he raised a different finger on a different hand.

"That's quite a pot," she said, "enough to make a girl swoon. But I'm afraid you've all raised the stakes just a bit too high for little 'ol me. I'm going to have to bow out of this one." She placed her cards down on the table and said, "I'll leave you to it then."

I turned to the inexperienced gambler and tossed two chips into the pot, then tossed two more. "You plan on seeing it through?" I asked.

He tried to give me steel eyes, but it didn't take.

"If you've got those two eights, then call or raise," I said.

He fingered his chips.

The dealer chimed in, "Sir?"

He took two chips and slowly added them to the pot. Then he returned his hand to his now much diminished stack.

"Sir?" the dealer asked. "Have you finished your bet?"

"Oh, just do it," the dame said. "You came here to gamble, didn't you? Then gamble."

Her words had the same effect on him alcohol has on a sailor. He girded up his loins and threw two more chips onto the pile. Normally, I would have called. I had a good hand and was willing to wager it was better than his, but something was going on here that I couldn't quite put my finger on and I needed this rube to stay at the table long enough for me to figure it out. So, I pushed my cards into the pot and folded.

There was no one at the table more surprised than him. He laughed and turned over his cards: a six and a seven. The fool was indeed trying for a straight. "Ha!" he said. "I bluffed both of you."

I eyed him sternly, practicing the look my father would have given me. "Let me give you a little hint," I said. "A little humility goes a long way."

The dealer collected the chips, took the house's cut, and slid the rest of the pile over to the winner. Then he took to shuffling the deck. When done properly, the shuffling of a deck is a thing of beauty. There was no beauty in this man's shuffling.

I finished the rest of my drink while I waited for the next deal, hoping a cocktail waitress wasn't too far away. I caught her out of the corner of my eye and was about to order another pair of manhattans when I was suddenly overcome by a very large shadow.

FOURTEEN

"THERE YOU ARE, Rossi," the voice behind me said. It came from my boss, Frank "Fingers" Abbandandolo, as did the shadow he cast. "I figured I'd find you here," he said. "Haven't seen you in a while."

"Really?" I asked. "I was here just yesterday."

"Come. Take a walk with me."

"I kind of have something going here," I protested.

"It'll wait."

I stood, reluctantly, and put my lid in place, then tossed the dealer a chip and the dame a smile, before turning and following Fingers. He was chewing on another one of his stogies, at least what was left of it. He'd mushed the end into a wet mess that he bit down on hard as he sucked the tobacco into his lungs.

"Not your normal dress," he said as we made our way to the stairs that led up to the mezzanine level.

"I had a gig tonight, at the Bootlegger," I explained. "Came right here from there."

He started up the stairs, then stopped and turned to me. "Gig?" he asked.

"Oh, didn't I tell you? I fool around a bit on the saxophone. Been playing with a local band."

"You any good?"

"I get by."

Fingers gave me a humph and started back up the stairs. When we got to the top, he paused, sucked air into his pleading lungs, then continued on toward the executive offices. Every office was clearly emblazoned with the name and position of the person who occupied the thing—the important people who ran the place. The size of both the office and the letters that made up the name on the plaque revealed the level of importance. Jake had the largest office, followed by Fingers, though that arrangement was just for show. Everyone knew Fingers ran the place—under the direction of Meyer Lansky, of course. I'd been in Fingers' office on occasion. It wasn't a place I ever felt comfortable. Choices often accompanied it—ones I didn't enjoy making.

I was about to get the door for him when Fingers suddenly switched directions and headed into an office just to the left of his own. I followed. He flicked on a light, revealing an office, complete with the usual accouterments: desk, chair, phone, matching pen and pencil set. Behind the desk, a bank of gray file cabinets stood at attention, waiting for orders. To the right was a wet bar, complete with shiny new bottles of Old Forester and sweet vermouth, accompanied by another, much smaller bottle of bitters—a manhattan just waiting to come alive. There were other bottles and some decanters as well, but I didn't pay them any mind.

The whole place had that new office smell.

"What's this?" I asked.

"An office," he answered, then walked over to the wet bar, popped the top off one of the decanters, and poured himself a couple of fingers. "You catch the name on the door before you walked in?"

It embarrassed me to admit I hadn't, but I didn't let it stop me from looking. It said:

Max Rossi

House Detective

The letters were rather small in comparison, but I didn't mind. "Do I need an office?" I asked.

"I guess that depends on you," Fingers said, obscurely.

"I'm afraid I don't follow."

"Where've you been all day?"

"I told you. I had a gig."

"You had a gig tonight, not today," he said and took a slow, deliberate sip. "Why don't you try out your new chair," he said.

I wasn't sure where this was going, but thought it best to play along, at least for the time being, so I went over and took a seat behind the desk. Fingers folded himself into one of the two chairs in front of that same desk.

"There, how does that feel?"

"It feels like a chair behind a desk. What's it supposed to feel like?"

Fingers ignored me. He took another puff of his cigar before pulling over the Sands logoed ashtray and resting it inside. "Leona will take messages when you're not here, but you shouldn't consider her your secretary."

I nodded.

"Oh look, there's one now."

I looked down at a folded piece of paper on my desk. I opened it up to three words written in the most beautiful penmanship I had ever seen: Call your mother.

"Do you like it here, Rossi?" Fingers asked. "Everyone treating you well?"

"I like it just fine," I said.

"You don't want to be anywhere else?"

"Why would I want to be anywhere else?"

Fingers looked at me the way mobsters do, with cold, dead eyes. "Why indeed," he said, then took another sip.

I tried changing the subject. "I hear Belafonte is trying to get out of his contract."

"You know what's good?" Fingers asked, ignoring my question. "Bagels are good. I miss a good New York bagel. You can't get one here. They try, but they just can't get it right. They say it's the water. I don't know. I guess it could be. When I was a kid, my folks would take me to Katz's and I'd get an onion bagel with butter. But when I got older, I preferred Eisenberg's over on Fifth—cream cheese with that Nova Scotia Lox and capers. I know, it ain't Italian, but damn it was good. I miss that."

I wasn't sure what was bringing on this trip down memory lane, but who was I to stop it? "We went to Jack and Marion's in Brookline," I said.

Fingers nodded. "It's good to know where you're from, Rossi. Where your roots are. Which side you're on." He paused, then asked: "Which side are you on?"

"What exactly do you mean?"

"You the Sands' man, Rossi?"

"I told you when I took the job that I didn't want to be tied to the Sands. You agreed."

"I suppose I did. But it's one thing not to be tied to the Sands, quite another to be working for the competition."

"What are you talking about?"

"You spent the day at the Rouge, chasing down ditsoon. Maybe it's time for you to remember which side your bread is buttered on, Rossi."

Fingers had chosen his words carefully. Mulignan wasn't a nice term, ditsoon was even worse. That was his intention.

"I was asking questions for a friend," I said. "A goose gets popped for a murder he may not have committed. It just didn't sit well with some people is all. I wasn't officially working for anyone, just promised I'd ask a few questions, nothing more."

"I see," Fingers said. "Your questions weren't addressed to any G-men were they?

"G-men? What are you talking about? Why would I be talking to G-men?"

"Why indeed." Fingers lifted his stogie from the ashtray and examined it. "You get your questions asked?"

I nodded, but he wasn't looking at me.

"Good," Fingers said. "Now you can get back to work . . . at the Sands. Unless you don't like this office. Unless you want a different office."

"I like it just fine," I said.

"Good." Fingers stood. "Pour yourself a drink. Make yourself at home. Then go downstairs. There's a whale in pit three, playing baccarat. Oriental. Just came in. Keep an eye on her."

I nodded.

He emptied his glass, set it on the desk, and headed for the door. He stopped just as he got there and turned to me. "The only way Belafonte gets out of his contract is in a box," he said, and with that he left.

I sat there behind the desk, staring at the door. Fingers had just warned me to stay on my own side of the street and I'd received the message loud and clear. I didn't have to guess where Fingers got his information; that was clear as well. So too was the fact that this little warning had more to do with the Rouge and its clientele than with my working a side gig. I'd had a bad feeling about this whole thing from the moment Garwood asked me to look into it, and that feeling had just gotten worse. I was, however, left to wonder just what it was about the Rouge that made Fingers feel the need to keep me away.

FIFTEEN

I DID JUST what Fingers told me to do, went to the wet bar and poured myself a drink. I didn't bother to mix a whole manhattan, just dribbled some rye into a clean glass; that was good enough for a two-bit house detective. I took the glass, and the rye in it, back to the desk—my desk—and just sat there, staring at the empty walls, trying to erase the thought of Casper Moses Jones rocking back and forth in the can, after having had the tar beat out of him for something he may not even have done. I thought of Margaret Lee Paige lying dead on a slab in the morgue, still keeping the secrets in death she had kept in life, and of Meriday—a woman scorned—and the fight the two had in the dressing room, and I couldn't help but wonder who was more likely to have done the dirty deed, man or woman.

Of course, the answer to that question involved a piece of the puzzle to which I was not privy: just how did Miss Paige meet her maker? Was she shot, stabbed, or something more sinister? Stabbing is an angry crime, my father used to say. It's personal. Stabbing is what one did when vengeance demanded the death to be at the hands of the one offended. The only thing more personal is strangulation. But strangulation was usually a crime of passion. Who hadn't heard, "I'll kill you with my bare hands," at some time in their life, except, well, maybe decent people, but who was I to know what decent people hear or don't hear?

Most people think dames are opposed to using such things as a knife, but it isn't true. They can often be far more violent than their male counterparts. Working with my father, it was not at all uncommon to find a stiff—often a male—stabbed or beaten to death with whatever was handy at the hands of some depreciated dame. I think it's because women are more passionate when it comes to knocking someone off. It may take them longer to get there, but when they do . . . watch out!

Most people mistakenly believe dames prefer poison, and while they do use it, it's not as prevalent as one might think.

Of course, shooting someone is much easier. Pull the trigger and a button does all the work. There's a distance to it, something that somehow makes the thing less personal—if that's even possible—and just like gooses, dames use gats.

I needed to see the coroner's report, but the chances of O'Malley showing me that little gem was about as likely as my mother not trying to set me up with a good Italian girl from the neighborhood.

If Casper Moses Jones did kill Margaret Lee Paige, the question was why. Just because she cut him out of a record deal? That didn't seem likely. He'd cut records before—granted with other musicians—but this didn't seem like his big break. Gigs come and go, everyone in the life knows that. Hustling for gigs is just part of the game. Love, on the other hand, is a much more powerful emotion—one that all too often leads to the ol' bone yard. A breakup could prime the pump, but if Margaret was sharing men, Moses likely knew about it, and even if he didn't, why wouldn't he go after the goose, not the dame?

Meriday, now that was a different story. As I, myself, knew all too well, it is true what they say: *Hell hath no fury like a woman scorned.*

But there I was, thinking in circles again. Each and every one of these thoughts had already crossed my feeble brain more than once along the way, and all of them with no answers. Who was I to expect answers anyway? This wasn't my case. I wasn't involved. I was the Sands' man. I was just supposed to ask questions for a friend. All those questions had gotten me was kicked out of a casino, and my own livelihood, such as it was, placed in jeopardy.

Fingers' empty glass, there on *my* desk, looked back at me. "*Are* you the Sands' man?" it asked.

I swirled the rye in my own vessel, eyeing the rusty liquid as it caressed the bottom of the glass, then slammed it down my throat. It should have stung, but it didn't. I was already behind the eight ball, what more harm could the rye do? I stood, slipped the note into the pocket of my trousers, and crossed over to the bar. I rested the glass on the tray, then left the office the way I'd found it.

Closing the door behind me, I turned and took one last look at the words written there.

Max Rossi

House Detective

I *was* the Sands' man, and it was about time I started acting like it.

I was about to head down to the casino floor and pit three when I decided to take a detour onto the catwalk. The mirrored glass above the table games not only helped the pit bosses keep an eye on everything going on in the pit, it also concealed a secret, a system of pathways, via suspended platforms, that allowed the boys in surveillance to keep a weather eye on all the games being played in those pits. If players did look up—which most of them did not—all they'd see was a reflection of themselves. What they never saw were the men looking down on them from above, making sure no monkey business was afoot.

You could see everything from up there, and that's just what I intended to do.

A knock on the door resulted in a panel being slid open, and a set of eyes giving me the once over.

"What's the take, Charlie?" I asked.

The panel slid closed, and the door opened. I stepped through and was met by a diminutive man in Coke-bottle glasses. How he saw anything through those things, I'll never know.

"You here about pit three?" he asked.

I tapped my nose. Whales caught everybody's attention. It was the moniker given by the casino to a gambler who came to play, and just to prove it, brought along a whole patch of cabbage with him, or in this case, her. It was good to catch a big fish, better to catch a whale.

Charlie grinned, then turned and headed down a path to the pit in question. I followed, trying my best to get my sea legs as the gangway rocked back and forth with each step. This journey on the sea, I had to admit, was not as pleasurable as was my previous one. The movement was so severe I had to take hold of the handrail for fear of falling. Charlie walked quickly, sans handrail, seemingly unphased by the movement. He arrived first and waited for me to catch up.

When I finally got there, he pointed to the baccarat table in the pit below. "There," he said. "In the red dress."

I looked down at the pit and saw her immediately, a dark-haired Oriental woman in a red, silk, floral-patterned dress, that hugged her body like a doting lover. Her hair was done up in a bun and held in place by a pair of chopsticks that matched the color of her dress. Long, dangling baubles hung from each ear and both her wrists were clad in loose fitting, gold bracelets, that tinkled when she moved her hands.

I wasn't a fan of baccarat. It was a confusing game, and I didn't trust it. Players could bet with or against the house and they could even change which side they bet on. They were also allowed to keep track of the hands dealt. When a casino allows the player to have that much information, it's a rouse meant to give a false sense of fairness. Trust me, faithful reader, there are no games in any casino in which the house doesn't hold the advantage.

In baccarat, nine is king and whichever hand—house or player—gets closest to nine wins. Face cards, that is, any card with a face on it—kings, queens, jacks—coveted in all other games, have no value in baccarat. None. Nada. That in and of itself is a crime, and it gets worse from there. Tens suffer the same fate as face cards, and aces are only worth one. Each hand—player and house (called banker)—get two cards, dealt face up. Whichever hand is closer to nine wins. It's that simple. All bets are made before the cards are turned and bets cannot be raised.

Of course, it's not as simple as that—but what in Vegas is? If the player is dealt cards that total six or more, the player must stand. If the player is dealt cards that total five or less, the player gets one more card and then must stand. If the player stands on any total, the bank will take another card, if their cards total five or less.

If the cards in any hand add up to more than nine, they must all be added together and the one dropped. So, if the cards add up to thirteen, the one is dropped and the total now becomes three. It's dangerous to go above nine—unless, of course, you have something high, like eighteen. Ties pay eight to one, a winning bet with the player results in even money, but anyone who wins by betting with the bank gets only ninety-five percent of the total bet, with the house keeping five percent. If that doesn't clue a Joe into where the odds lie, nothing will.

That was yet another reason I didn't like the game. It was too hard to make any dough, and I don't particularly like to work for my money.

"What's her name?" I asked.

"Madame Wu," he said.

"Be serious!"

"I am being serious. She came in late this afternoon and deposited five large in the cage. Signed her name as Madame Wu. They comped her room, gave her a meal, and she's been at the table ever sense."

Sitting next to Madame Wu was the largest Texan I'd ever seen. By the size of him, he could have been Fingers' own brother—stogie and all. Maybe a second cousin twice removed? The only thing bigger than the man was the size of his lid. It could have easily provided shelter in a storm for a family of six—maybe seven. I didn't know much about Western attire, but that was what I assumed to be a ten-gallon hat, with an extra ten thrown in for good measure.

"The big guy in blue. Texas?" I asked.

Charlie nodded. "One of Jake's friends. Samuel J. Latisse."

"Who's the dame on his arm?" I asked.

"That would be his new wife," Charlie said.

I looked at Charlie incredulously. "A bit young, ain't she?"

"If you had this bird's bank, you could get the young ones too."

Not that I'd want them, I thought. "He staying with us?"

"He's got the Man O' War suite. Just came in a couple days ago. Celebrating his honeymoon."

"Doesn't seem to be doing much celebrating."

That got me a chuckle.

"He's on the table a lot," Charlie admitted. "Likes to play baccarat."

"Really?" I questioned. "I thought all Texans played poker."

"Not this one. He hasn't even been to a poker table. Comes in, gets a drink, and goes straight to baccarat. The wife usually comes in a bit later."

"She stay with him while he plays?"

Charlie shook his head. "Usually she asks for money, then disappears. Comes back with new clothes. Hangs out at the pool quite a bit. He plays, breaks for dinner, then goes back to the table."

"Winning?" I asked.

"He is today. Up about twenty grand."

I whistled.

"Course he lost thirty yesterday."

"Still ten in the hole then."

"More or less," Charlie said.

"What about the other jokers at the table?"

"They sat down shortly after she did," Charlie said. "They all seem agreeable enough, but there's nothing to indicate they're together. I've been keeping an eye on

Madame Wu. She's the friendly type, talking to all the players at the table and tipping heavily."

"That a problem?" I asked.

"Can be," Charlie said. "Cheaters often tip heavily. It's a common misdirect. They know a constant flow of money will keep the dealer distracted. Chatting up the other players does the same thing."

"How are her bets?"

"All over the place at first. Played the bank for a while, then the player, then went back to the bank. Nothing steady or methodical. Nothing that would warrant attention. Typical baccarat player, trying to stay one step ahead of the cards."

"Winning?"

"Not at first, but her luck seems to have changed recently."

I looked down at the table and watched the players play, making their bets with each hand. It was strange watching from above, like a bird in the sky peering down over the top of heads. With only four cards dealt, most of the time, baccarat is a fast game, with money won or lost in an instant—another reason not to trust the thing.

Though Charlie was concerned with cheating, it was his job after all, I knew there wasn't any real way to cheat at baccarat; everything was already out in the open and nobody ever touched the cards but the dealer. Of course, that doesn't mean it's impossible, it's just not something that can easily be accomplished without it being an inside job, and it usually doesn't end well for dealers who cheat.

One of Charlie's employees called after him. Charlie excused himself, then went to join the younger man on an adjacent walkway. When he got there, the employee pointed down at the table below. Charlie peered down at the game, bending over the railing and adjusting his glasses a bit to get a better look. After a moment, he straightened himself and shook his head. Then he came back to me.

"What was all that about?" I asked.

"Gypsies are in town," he said. The look on my face must have clued him into my confusion, as he added, "They'll rob us blind if we don't catch them."

"Really?" I asked. "I knew several gypsies back east. They didn't seem like the robbing kind."

"Oh, I'm sure most of them are upstanding citizens, but some particular families are more inclined to the criminal lifestyle. You know how that is."

I knew. Better than most.

"Got a call from my friend at the El Rancho, told us to be on the lookout. Said they hit his casino the other night."

"They catch them?"

Charlie shook his head, just like he had with his employee. "No, this group is a sneaky bunch. Slipped in and out before anyone was the wiser."

"He tell you what to look out for?"

"Tall, thin redhead," he said.

"Dame?"

He nodded. "It's the women who commit the crimes in that family. Men send their wives and girlfriends out into the world to make a buck, while they sit at home, fat and happy."

"Nice work if you can get it," I said.

I thanked Charlie and turned to leave, but stopped when another thought came to me. "You see a goose in a wheelchair playing poker?"

Charlie nodded. "Yeah, he was in here earlier."

"You see a bird in an emerald swing dress at the same table? Black gloves, hair done up in a horsetail."

Charlie thought for a moment. "Now that you mention it, I did see her. Why do you ask?"

"I don't know, something about them just didn't sit right with me."

"You think they were together?" Charlie asked. "They left separately."

"Maybe it's nothing," I said, but my big toe didn't agree.

"Well, if either of them come back, I'll keep an eye on 'em."

I nodded, left surveillance, and headed down to the casino floor. It was time to get a better look at our whale.

SIXTEEN

WHEN I ARRIVED at the baccarat table, Mr. Latisse was even more cowboy than his hat led on. A right shiny peacock sitting atop a sunflower decorated each of the lapels on his light blue suit jacket. Rhinestones trimmed his collar and his sleeves, though I couldn't make out the pattern. His dress shirt was white, and he sported one of those black, mid-length Apache scarf ties worn by the likes of Chet Atkins. It was a bit much for a boy from Beantown, but I didn't mind.

The dolly on his arm was no less adorned. She was trimmed in a black cocktail dress, emblazoned stem to stern with yellow roses—just like the song—a black sash tied around her middle. Her hair cascaded downward from underneath a black, flat-brimmed bolero hat; its brim covered in dangling baubles that looked like something a cat might enjoy. Jade and silver decorated each wrist. She was young, thin, and blonde . . . very blonde and very young, much more so than her new amorato.

It was clear what he saw in her. The question was, what did she see in a man more than twice her age? Love of the man, or love of the man's money? I had a pretty good idea, but then again, I was a cynic, an infidel—something the priests were prone to remind me—a wet blanket through and through. Or perhaps I was just jealous.

There were only four people at the table: the Texan, an ordinary-looking gent, Madame Wu, and the bloke in the porkpie hat I'd seen previously at the poker table. I guess he was hoping his luck would run better here than it had there.

I took a seat at the table, but didn't count in. That unnerved the dealer a bit. They don't particularly like it when people come to watch, instead of play. Pit bosses like it even less.

Madame Wu eyed me cautiously. I returned the favor.

"Latty, I need another couple hundred," Latisse's young wife said to him in a southern accent that seemed less than authentic.

"I just gave you three hundred this morning," Latisse responded in an accent much more fitting of the South.

"Oh, honey, I'm wearing that money," she said.

"Then what do you need more for?"

"Well, sugar, I have to wear something to bed when I take off these clothes. Don't I?" she said, snuggling up to him.

The man's face turned redder than Madame Wu's dress. He handed her several black chips. She accepted the offer, removed two more from atop the stack in front of him, kissed him on the cheek, and skedaddled.

I watched as she made her way out of the pit area, past the slot machines, then disappeared into the crowd.

A male voice brought me back.

"Sir, if you are not going to play, could you please free up the table so others may have a chance to try their luck?"

I turned to face a pit boss standing behind the dealer. He eyed me intently, arms crossed, waiting for a response. He had my attention. He had the table's as well. I didn't know this pit boss, and he didn't know me. There were chips in my pocket and I would have thrown them down on the felt, but baccarat is a rich man's game, with single bets often higher than the average man's yearly salary. Well, higher than mine anyway, and much more than I could afford to lose. So, since I wasn't playing with the house's money, I chose the better part of valor, excused myself, and left the table. I didn't ask "Latty" for chips before I left. I didn't expect he'd give them to me anyway. I didn't have the right parts.

Instead of sticking with Latisse, I decided to give finding his dolly a go. I doubted she was still in the casino, but one never knows, does one? I traced her steps as far as I had seen them and had a look around. Nothing. No dolly in a black dress emblazoned with yellow roses. The casino wasn't as full this time of the night and few stores were open, so it was most likely that she had gone back to the suite.

Luckily, I was only steps away from the Garden Room, so I decided to stop in and have a bite . . . and a manhattan . . . not necessarily in that order. I took a seat, ordered food and drink, and was halfway through my curry of lobster I'Idienne when the smell of lavender filled the air.

SEVENTEEN

VIRGINIA SLIPPED EASILY into the booth next to me, clad a different dress than she wore when I saw her earlier that evening—or was it morning? Who can keep track of such things? This dress, I assumed, was the one she had worn to work. It was a plain, cranberry swing dress with cap sleeves. A matching ribbon kept her hair in a tight ponytail behind her head.

"Don't you ever leave this place?" she asked with tired eyes.

"I could ask you the same question."

She gave me a weak smile.

"You look sapped," I said.

She took hold of my manhattan and helped herself to a sip. "You don't know the half of it," she said.

"I thought you were headed home after the last show."

"I was, but I got side-tracked," taking her time with my drink.

"You decide to take me up on my offer of a nightcap?"

Her smile brightened a bit. "In your dreams, lover boy."

"Then you weren't looking for me?"

"Oh, I was looking for you, but not for what that wicked mind of yours conjures."

I was intrigued. "If not for that, then what?"

"There's a woman here to see you."

"Me?" I asked.

"You," she repeated.

"Are you hiding her in your purse?"

"Funny," she said. "If you want to see her, you'll need to come with me."

"Who is this woman?"

"Someone you know."

I frowned. "It's not Nancy, is it?"

Virginia slapped my arm. "Be nice," she said. "No, it's not Nancy. Her name is Theodosia and . . ."

"No thank you," I said, cutting her off with raised palms. "I'm done with the Moulin Rouge and all her players. I'm the Sands' man. Something that's been made abundantly clear to me this very evening."

"Don't be like that," Virginia said. "She looks desperate, and she's been crying."

"I don't work for the Rouge," I reiterated.

There was an awkward pause.

"How did she know to come to you?" I asked.

"She didn't come to me directly," Virginia said. "She showed at the back door of the stage and asked if anyone knew a Max Rossi. Cat heard the conversation and came to me. So, I went to see what she wanted. When I asked her what this concerned, she said she'd already spoken with you today and that you'd know what it was about."

"What did you tell her?"

"I told her I wasn't sure if you were still here, but I'd check."

"Well, tell her you checked, and I wasn't here."

That got me a look. "What's this about, Max?"

"The sax player that got pinched the other night," I said. "Garwood asked me to look into the case a bit, thinks the bird wasn't given a fair shake. I asked a few questions, but it didn't go well."

"Is he wrong? Garwood, I mean?"

"Probably not, but what business is it of mine?"

Virginia placed a soft hand on my arm. "Go see what she wants, Max. What harm could it do?"

"It could cost me my job," I said. "Fingers told me to stay out of it in no uncertain terms, and that is exactly what I plan to do."

That got me another look. Damn those brown eyes.

I called the waitress over and signed the tab. She gave me a sizable grin when I pulled out one of the chips hiding in the pocket of my trousers and laid it on her tray. I downed the last of my manhattan and followed Virginia to the showroom, taking in the scenery as I went.

Once we reached the Copa Room, we made our way onto the stage and out the door in the back—the one used by the dancers, singers, musicians, stagehands, and the like. Theodosia was standing there, hugging her body against the night air. A cigarette in one hand. When she saw me, she took one last puff, then dropped it to the ground, crushing it out with the tip of her shoe.

"He's gone," she said, as she came up to me.

"Who's gone?" I asked.

"Grafton. He's gone, and I can't find him anywhere. He hasn't shown for work and he isn't at his place. It's not like him. I'm worried, Mr. Rossi."

"Maybe he's off tying one on," I said.

"He's not like that," she assured me.

"You sure?" I asked.

"What kind of remark is that?"

"The kind most appropriate for a man accustomed to parties after hours at a certain blonde's apartment."

Virginia slapped my arm. "Be nice," she admonished.

Theo kept silent.

"Did you know?" I asked. "Did you know he attended after hour parties at Margaret Lee Paige's apartment, playing sax and smoking juju?"

The look on her face told me all I needed to know. Meriday wasn't the only one choosing to be blind.

"Have you called the police?" I asked.

She nodded, helplessly. "They told me there wasn't anything they could do. That he'd show, eventually. You've got to help me, Mr. Rossi."

"What is it that you think I can do?"

She clutched herself even tighter.

I took a deep breath and started over. "When was the last time you saw him?" I asked.

Theo was shaking, but it wasn't from the cold. "I haven't seen him since the night they took Moses away," she said as she fiddled with the bracelet around her wrist. "He left the show very upset, said 'this isn't right' and left. I tried to get him to come home with me, but he wouldn't."

"What did he mean by that?"

Theodosia looked puzzled. "By what?"

"This isn't right.' What did he mean by that?"

"I don't know. He was upset is all. Just kept shaking his head, mad as all get out. I tried to get him to come home with me, but he wouldn't."

"Yes, you said that. Do you know where he went after the show?"

Theo shook her head. "Home, I guess."

"And where is home?"

"The Harrison Boarding House."

"Did he contact you after that?"

"No."

"And that didn't bother you?"

Theo gave me wide eyes. "Why should it?" she asked. "Men need time when they're angry. You know that, Mr. Rossi. They need distance. It's best to give them that distance."

I didn't want to say it, but I was beginning to think Theo had a legitimate reason for concern. "Why did you ask me if Meriday had told me Grafton killed Miss Paige?"

"Did I?" she asked.

"You did," I confirmed.

She hesitated.

I folded my arms and waited.

"Meriday hates Grafton," she finally said. "Blames him for all Moses' problems."

"Yet it was Moses who was playing backseat bingo with Miss Paige?"

"Max!" Virginia exclaimed.

"Oh, it was more than just bingo, Mr. Rossi," Theo said. "I assure you."

"And Grafton?" I asked.

Theo's face hardened. "What about Grafton?"

"Did he play bingo too?"

I don't know which happened first, Virginia yelling at me or Theodosia slapping me across the face, but I deserved them both. Still, it was a question that needed asking, so I asked it—for all the good it did me. Did Theo slap me because my question offended her, or had I hit the nail on the head? After all, Grafton had disappeared the very night Moses got pinched.

I gave Theodosia a moment to collect herself before continuing. "Why do you think Moses killed Miss Paige?" I asked.

She looked confused.

"When I asked you if Grafton killed Miss Paige, you told me that Moses did. Why did you say that?"

"Moses has a temper. A very bad temper."

"That why he took a swipe at Grafton?" I asked.

She nodded.

"Who else did he take a swipe at?"

Theo didn't answer.

"Meriday?"

Theo hugged herself tightly and kept her eyes on the ground in front of her. Virginia once told me a girl knew how to cover imperfections. I wondered if Meriday knew those tricks as well.

"Why did Benny almost fire Moses?" I asked. "It wasn't just for the fight, was it?"

Theo looked up at me, then shook her head.

"What was it, Miss Paige?"

"Moses was . . ." she hesitated. "Mosses was on the pipe."

"Opium?" I asked, more than a bit surprised. "I thought jazz musicians only smoked tea. You know this for a fact?"

She nodded. "Meriday told me. It affected his playing and Benny noticed."

"I'm sure he did," I said.

"He told Moses to get off the pipe or find another job."

"So why didn't Grafton take advantage of it?" I asked. "I mean who, when relegated to second fiddle, wouldn't want to be top dog? If Moses was having so many problems, why wouldn't Grafton step up to the plate and claim the prize?"

"Because, Mr. Rossi," Theo said, "Grafton and Moses were friends.

EIGHTTEEN

I COULDN'T HAVE been more surprised had I discovered my mother's gravy came from a jar. Grafton and Moses weren't rivals, like Benny had implied. They were friends. Of course, the rivalry could have been amicable, but it hadn't come off that way. *Why was that?* I wondered.

"If Moses and Grafton were friends, why did Moses take a poke at him?"

"Because Grafton was trying to straighten him out. He told Moses he needed to get off the pipe and to stay away from Margaret. That he wasn't doin' Meriday right. But Moses was mad. Spittin' mad. He accused Grafton of movin' in on Margaret, told him she was his girl and that he had no right to take the gig away from him.

"Margaret Paige may have named Grafton to take Moses' place, but he refused to play for her, and he told Moses as much. But Moses didn't believe him, called him a snake in the grass. That's when he took the swing."

"You saw this?"

She shook her head. "Grafton told me about it, but all the other musicians saw it. They raised quite a ruckus."

"Have you spoken to the police about all of this?" I asked. "After Moses got pinched?"

"Me?" she questioned. "I haven't told the police a nickel's worth a nothin'. They never asked."

"The police never spoke to you about Moses?"

She shook her head. "None of us have. They didn't ask a one of us anything. They just hooked him up, left, and never came back."

Why didn't that surprise me? O'Malley was an idiot. He'd gotten his man, and that's all he cared about. Never mind whether that man was or wasn't guilty. None of that mattered. Moses was the most likely suspect, so he was guilty and that was all O'Malley needed. I was beginning to understand Garwood's concern. But notwithstanding that concern, I was still the Sands' man and while my big toe was telling me otherwise, I wanted nothing more to do with this predicament.

"You need to go to the police," I said. "Speak with a man named McQueeney, Connor McQueeney. Tell him about all this. He's a lieutenant. You can't miss him. He puts mountains to shame."

Theo looked sullen. "I've already gone to the police." She looked at me with pleading eyes. "Don't you understand, Mr. Rossi? They don't want nothin' to do with the likes of me. They don't care a lick about what I have to say. Grafton is missing and they have no intention of finding him." Tears rolled down her cheeks. "I've got nowhere else to turn, Mr. Rossi. You're my only hope."

Virginia went to Theo and hugged her. Then she took hold of my hand, squeezed it, and flashed me those big brown eyes of hers. Damn brown eyes.

As I rubbed the back of my neck, someone said: "Let me see what I can do." Maybe it was me.

Theo rushed over to me and wrapped her arms around my neck. "Oh, thank you, Mr. Rossi! Thank you!"

She probably would have kissed me, but I didn't give her the chance. Instead, I took hold of her wrists and pulled her arms from around my neck. "I'm not making any promises here," I stated firmly. "I can't guarantee it'll do any good."

"I understand," she said, but I didn't believe her.

As I looked into her eyes, my thoughts went quickly to Maxine and the reefer she said came from a sax player. At first I had Moses doped for that player, but if Moses was on the pipe, he probably wasn't dealing marijuana at the same time. Dealers aren't typically users—of course there are exceptions, but I didn't think this was one of them. Then something came to me.

"Did Grafton peddle?" I asked.

"Peddle?"

"You know," I said. "Was he free with the juju? Was he a bellhop?"

I expected her to get angry again, but that didn't happen. She just looked down at the ground and rubbed her hands against her arms.

I waited.

"Yes," she finally said. "I saw him sell marijuana sometimes." She looked directly at me, then said forcefully: "But that is all. My Grafton didn't sell opium, and he did not use it."

Maybe it was the way Theodosia answered me, or maybe it was the look I received from Virginia, but I decided to let that stand. This little meeting had put a damper on the night, and I didn't hold much hope for it getting any better. After she left, I took Virginia to her

Thunderbird, patted her on the bottom, and kissed her goodnight. It was a long kiss, a nice kiss, the kind of kiss that makes a fellow want more, but I didn't ask. Virginia was tired, and I knew better than to press what little luck I had left.

I went back to the casino, expecting my whale to have already fluked, but that wasn't the case. She was still at the same table, with the same Texan in the same suit. The only thing that had changed was the stack of black chips in front of both the Texan and Madame Wu. That caught my attention. I needed more information, and I knew just who to ask.

Luckily, Charlie was still in surveillance. He let me in the magic door, and I followed him to our previous spot on the catwalk, holding onto the rails as I went.

I leaned slightly over the handrail and looked down at the table. "Madame Wu's in the chips."

Charlie agreed.

"She a friend of the Texan?"

"Not as far as I know."

I knew the basics of the game, but not much more, so I didn't know what to look for as far as cheating went. That was Charlie's field, and he was good at it, very good at it. Much better than I. But as I looked down at this little scene playing out in front of me, it just didn't feel right. Something was amiss, but I couldn't put my finger on it.

Madame Wu was winning and winning big. Sure, losses came, but not very often. She was doing so well that the Texan started following her play, putting money on either the player or the bank when she did.

I watched for quite some time as Charlie went about his duties, and the more I watched, the more something seemed to stand out. I called Charlie over.

"She able to switch her bets like that?" I asked.

"What do you mean?"

"She places a bet on the table before the cards are dealt, but then she often switches her bet from the player to the bank, or vice versa, before the dealer turns over the cards. Is she able to do that?"

"Depends on the pit boss," Charlie said. "Technically, they're not supposed to, but some pit bosses are fine with it as a courtesy, so long as the cards haven't been exposed. Some player gets a late hunch and wants to change his bet; a lot of pit bosses will look the other way."

"Yeah, except when she changes her bet, she wins most of the time."

That caught Charlie's attention. "Is that so?" he asked. "You think she's cheating?"

"I don't see how she could be. She never touches the cards. But something there seems off to me. I'm gonna head down and have a closer look."

I was about to leave when something caught my eye—a croupier with a cleft chin. "You know that dealer?" I asked.

Charlie leaned over the rail and looked down at the table. "He's new. Hasn't been on the tables very long."

"He was just on the poker table earlier."

"That's no surprise," Charlie said. "Dealers rotate games every so often. Pit bosses like to try them, especially the new ones, on different games to see where their strengths lie. It's not uncommon at all to see them dealing poker, then baccarat, then blackjack, or even roulette."

It was a sensible explanation, so why was my big toe not buying it?

NINETEEN

WHEN I WAS at the table before, I didn't bet. That made the pit boss most uncongenial, so I decided it would be best if I laid some scratch down this time. A couple of Cs were burning a hole in my pocket, so I threw them on the table just to cool them off. The dealer snatched them up quickly and returned to me two black chips. A meager pittance.

I pushed them back to the dealer. "How about we try the green ones?" I said.

"Sir," the dealer stated, "this is baccarat. There are minimum bets that don't involve the green chips."

"And yet, there they sit in your tray," I said.

"But, sir, if . . ."

"Aw, give him the chips," the Texan said in a smooth Texas drawl. "It ain't gonna hurt nothin'. He'll just lose a little slower's all."

The dealer looked to the pit boss. The pit boss glanced over at me. I flashed him my best forty-watter. He nodded, and the dealer exchanged the chips.

Madame Wu gave me the once over. "Big spender, huh?"

"I have my moments," I retorted.

"You decided to play this time. Thought maybe we'd scared you off."

"Not a chance," I said.

The dealer was nearing the back end of the deck, so he stopped the game to shuffle. He was no better at it here than he was at the poker table. And as the dealer prepared the deck, I turned my attention to Madame Wu. Black mascara encircled her almond eyes, ending in a line that trailed off to the side of her porcelain face. Dark eyebrows and bright red lips finished off the look. She sat pristinely in the chair. Her back board straight, her movements slow and delicate. A strand of black hair rested near her ear.

Madame Wu looked the part all right, but somehow, something just didn't seem to fit.

"That's a beautiful dress you have on, Miss . . ." I let the end drop, hoping she would supply her name.

"Thank you," she said, leaving me hanging.

"Tokyo?" I asked.

"Hong Kong," she replied.

There are many Oriental accents in the world, and I am familiar with none of them—except those I've heard in the movies. Where Madam Wu's accent originated was as much a mystery to me as the woman herself.

I was about to ask her another question when the porkpie hat spoke up.

"First time in Vegas?" he asked.

"Not exactly," I said.

"You sound like you hail from back East somewhere,

possibly Massachusetts."

I complimented his ear for accents, adding that I hailed from Boston.

"You a Red Socks fan?"

"Of course," I said. "Who isn't?"

"I'm a Red's fan myself." He extended his hand. "Name's Coca, Jonathan Coca."

I shook his hand. He was fishing for my name, but, like Madame Wu, I wasn't biting.

"What is it that you do, Mr. Coca?" I asked.

"Oh, call me John. Everybody does. I'm a wall coverings designer."

"Is that so?"

"Sure is. I know all there is to know about wall coverings. Been doing it for twenty years. Take that one over there on the wall. It's a toile, which is like a fine batiste with a cloth weave. It's probably got some silk in it too, I would imagine, seeing as how casinos seem to spare no expenses—especially this casino. I'll bet you dollars to donuts that paper came from Dupenny's or Bradbury & Bradbury."

It was much more than I needed, or wanted, to know. Luckily, the dealer saved me from further delirium. He had finished shuffling and was now ready to deal. It was time for bets. I placed a green chip on the felt in the area marked for the player. The porkpie did the same only with a black chip. The Texan chose the bank, as did the fourth man at the table, each throwing down a single black chip. Madame Wu placed her black chip with the player.

"No more bets," the dealer said.

He dealt one player's card face down, then delt a face down one for the bank, repeating the order one more time. I watched as he picked up the banker's hand and did a quick shuffle, taking the bottom card and placing it swiftly over the top of the other card. He was about to turn over the cards when Madame Wu spoke.

"I'd like to change my bet," she said.

The dealer turned to the pit boss with questioning eyes.

The pit boss nodded. "You know the rules," he said.

Madame Wu smiled and moved her chip to the bank, placing it in the spot indicating a pair—meaning she was betting that the banker was holding two of the same type of cards.

"I just have a feeling," she said, more to the Texan than anyone.

"I think I'll up my bet," the Texan said.

The pit boss nodded his approval.

The Texan tossed a second chip onto the table to accompany his first, then he moved his chips to the same spot as Madame Wu, betting on the pair.

The dealer turned the player's cards over. A jack and a ten—suits didn't matter. That meant the player had nothing. He turned the bank's cards over: two queens—a pair.

Pairs paid eleven-to-one. What were the odds?

"Hot damn!" The Texan exclaimed. "A banker's pair! You're one lucky lady. I think you're my good luck charm."

Because both hands added up to zero, each got another card. The first card went to the player. It was a three. An eight went to the bank. The Texan hooted again as the dealer collected chips, adding up to one hundred and ninety dollars, then added another twenty-two black chips and scooted them all across the table to him. He did the same with Madame Wu; only her total was eleven hundred and ninety-five dollars, since she had only bet one black chip. I lost, as did my lidded companion, with the fourth man getting a ninety-five-dollar return.

I watched the table for the next few deals. Each time placing my green chip in the player's spot. With every deal, the two gooses at the table bet opposite of each other, while the Texan bet whatever Madame Wu bet. Also, with every bet, the dealer dealt the cards the same way he had originally, shuffling the two cards each time before he turned them over. Sometimes Madame Wu stayed with her bet and sometimes she switched it before the cards were exposed. Sometimes she lost, but mostly she won.

After several more hands, the dealer went through enough cards to reshuffle. As we all sat there waiting, the bird next to me began flapping his gums anew. I didn't much pay attention to what he was saying. My eyes were on Madame Wu as she twirled a strand of hair between her fingers.

She exchanged an ever so slight look with the male at the end of the table, then turned to the Texan. "I believe I shall call it a night," she said before the dealer could finish shuffling.

"What? So soon?" the Texan questioned.

"It is well past a respectable hour for a lady to be out," she said.

"Hogwash," the Texan countered. "We're just getting started. You can't leave on a streak like this."

"Tomorrow is another day," she said and motioned for the pit boss, who, in turn, motioned for an attendant to help collect her chips. He'd take them to the cage where they'd be placed in her account. Before she left, she removed a black chip from the stack and laid it on the felt for the dealer with a smile.

"Aw, hell," the Texan said. "I guess I best call it a

night as well." He followed Madame Wu's lead and tossed the dealer a black chip of his own. Then he collected his chips all by himself and made his exit.

I smelled a rat, but I couldn't see just how that rat was getting the cheese.

TWENTY

IT HAD BEEN a long day, and I was eager to hit the sack, so I jumped into my Roadmaster and pointed it toward home. Somehow, I managed to get the thing safely into my make-shift garage with my eyes still open, just don't ask me how. I should have just taken a room at the Sands, but I needed to make a call and it wasn't one I could make from there.

Boston was three hours ahead of Las Vegas and my father was an early riser, which meant my mother was as well. I picked up the blower, bringing the receiver to my ear. When the operator answered, I gave her the number.

"Madison six three five eleven," I said.

"One moment, please."

The next voice that came on the phone was my mother's, repeating the same thing she said every time I called. "Oh Massimo. It's so good to hear from you. When are you coming home?"

"Hi Ma," I said, ignoring the question. "How did you know it was me?"

"What? I'm supposed to know other people who live in that town of yours?" she asked. "The operator tells me I have a call from Las Vegas, I know it's my son who finally found a bit of time to remember his only mother."

"Ma, I called you only two days ago."

She let that pass. "Guess who I ran into at Antonio's"

"I don't know, Ma. Antonio?"

"Silvia Bellafiore. She told me her daughter Angela is back home from college."

"That's nice, Ma."

"She's a beautiful girl, Max."

"I'm sure she is, Ma."

"She would make beautiful babies."

"I'm sure she would, Ma. Is Dad home?

She ignored me. "Didn't you go to school with her?" she asked.

"I went with her brother Frankie," I said. "Angela is his kid sister. Is Dad home?"

"I told Silvia you were in Las Vegas on vacation, but would be coming home soon. She seemed very interested."

"I'm not on vacation," I said, trying to conceal my frustration. "Look, Ma, is Dad home? I really need to speak with him."

"She's a beautiful girl, Max."

"Dad, Ma."

I waited while she yelled for my father to come to the phone, burying the handset in her breast as she always did when she called for him. My father had left me a message to call him, and I was eager to know why. There were no frivolities with my father. He answered the phone and got right down to business.

"What the hell are you doing out there, Max?"

"You're going to have to be a bit more specific," I said.

"Out of the blue, I get a call from Abbandandolo telling me I need to keep my son in check before something bad happens. What have you gotten yourself into now?"

Why did I suddenly feel as if I were in high school all over again, called into the principal's office? "I did a favor for a friend," I said. "One that ruffled a few feathers."

"Sounds like more than a few. What kind of favor?"

I told my father about Garwood Van, about Marget Lee Paige, and about Casper Moses Jones. I told him about my trip to the Moulin Rouge and my interviews with Meriday and Theodosia. "Moses is colored," I said, "but Margaret Lee Paige, the woman he is supposed to have killed, is not."

"I see."

And with those two words, my father said more than could have been written in an entire Encyclopedia Britanica. A colored man had been accused of killing a white woman and Boston Rossi's pride and joy, his son, his only namesake, decided to poke his beak right in the middle of it. I knew what he was thinking. I was thinking the same thing: this could only end poorly.

"I just did a favor for a friend," I assured him. "Nothing too involved. A few quick questions. In and out. I'm not interested in being any more involved than I have to be."

"Did you get your questions answered?"

"Mostly," I said.

I hesitated.

"There something else?"

"One of the possible players has vanished," I said.

"Oh?"

"Grafton Freeman; plays second horn to Moses. When the singer canned Moses, she turned to Grafton to be his replacement. It caused quite a stir and ended up in fisticuffs between Moses and Grafton."

"So, what's so strange about that?"

"Nothing," I said. "Except there could be a complication. Moses was fooling around with the singer and Grafton was likely the backdoor man."

"I see. How long has this Grafton character been missing?"

"Ever since Moses was pinched."

"You like Grafton for this then?"

"I can't quite get there," I admitted. "Problem is, I can't quite get there with Moses either. Sure, I understand a love triangle can easily lead to murder, but why would either of them kill the dame and not the rival?"

"Maybe she was playing one against the other."

"But what about the girlfriends? Where do they fit in all of this?"

"It's a good question and maybe if you were a cop you should answer it, but you're not, Max. At best you're a private dick who, apparently, is on shaky ground."

Ain't that the truth? I told my father about my new office and how it was presented to me. "It was definitely a message," I said. "One received loud and clear. What I don't get is why they want me to stay away from the Rouge."

"Isn't that obvious?" he asked.

Maybe it was to him.

He sighed, then continued. "I did a little digging. Looks like that place has been very successful since it opened its doors."

"That's a bit of an understatement."

"No one's claimed the place," he said.

I thought of Sal's trip to the Rouge and how he was escorted out by the Brown Bomber and his wrestling pal. And then it hit me. "They don't want the casino to succeed," I said.

"Not when they don't have their mitts in it."

But it was more than just that. I thought of Belafonte and his desire to get out of his contract. Sure, they might not care about the coloreds going into the place, but when the talent doesn't want to perform in their casinos any longer, not when they can perform and stay in the Rouge, well, that's a zucchini of a different color, isn't it? Leave it to my father to figure it out.

"You need to wash your hands of all this, Max. Keep your nose clean."

I knew my father. His warning was a departing statement, but before he could hang up, I threw out another fastball.

"You know anything about a boxer named Booker Percy?"

"I've heard of him," my father said. "Watched him in the ring once. He had a helluva right. He probably would've gotten a shot at the big time, if he hadn't made a mess of things."

"Oh?" I asked, curiously. "What'd he do?"

"Put his hands on a made man, tried to strangle him."

"And he's still around?"

"You tell me."

"He's around," I said. "Here in Vegas, but I don't get why."

"Money," my father said, matter-of-factly. "They decided they could make more money from him throwing fights. He was worth more alive than dead. It's that simple."

"Yeah, but you can only throw fights for so long," I said.

"They must be using him for muscle or something else. Why don't you ask your buddy Manella?"

"Why would I ask him?"

"Who is it you think Percy choked?"

"Manella?" I repeated incredulously.

"Why do you think he always has those two goons with him? You're on dangerous ground, Max. Don't stay on it very long." And with that, he hung up.

I put down the receiver and closed my gaping pie hole. Percy, at some point, had tried to choke out Manella—a made man. Which means now Manella owned him.

I thought about what my father said, me being on dangerous ground. Who was I to argue? After all, I knew he was right. The smartest thing to do was what he said and keep my nose out of it. That would make Fingers happy and me happy as well. But then I thought of Theodosia and the bluebottles who were unwilling to help. I thought of Moses sitting in a cell after having received a beatdown, and Virginia's damn brown eyes.

I took a shower, changed into my nightclothes and climbed into bed. A good night's sleep would do me good. After all, I had a busy day ahead of me. I needed to find Grafton Freeman, and I knew just where to look.

TWENTY-ONE

I WOKE EARLY, washed my face, brushed my teeth, and made myself nice. I decided to dress casually, figuring I might get further if I didn't go in looking like a G-Man or an inspector of some type. I chose trousers and a camp collar shirt with a straight hem that I left untucked, argyle socks and my same shoes from last night.

Before I headed down to my favorite diner, I had a bone to pick, so I jerked up the receiver and asked to be connected to Garwood Van's Music Land. A clerk answered and told me Garwood was busy, but he'd be happy to tell him I called.

"Tell him it's Max, please, and that I need to speak with him."

It took less than five minutes for Garwood to come to the phone. "Max, how great to hear from you," he said. "Everything all right?"

"Whiskey and soda," I said. "Except for one thing. A small fact you left out about Moses' addiction to opium."

The phone went silent.

"Still there?" I asked.

"I'm still here," Garwood said.

"Why didn't you tell me he was an addict?"

"I was hoping that wouldn't play into things."

I thought of Moses sitting in jail, rocking back and forth, picking his fingernails. He'd barely looked at me when he spoke. I had thought it was on account of the beating he took. Now I knew otherwise.

"How could it not?" I asked. "He isn't just a black man who may have committed murder, he's a black man who is also an addict."

"Would you have taken the case if I told you?"

"There's no case to take here, Garwood. You wanted me to ask a few questions, and I did that. Now I find out Moses was kicking the gong around. What else are you hiding?"

"Now look here, Max . . ."

"Don't give me the song and dance," I said, cutting him off. "You've got me wondering how much of what anyone tells me is the truth. Carter tells me Moses and Grafton were rivals, but Grafton's gal pal tells me they were friends. While Moses' girl is ready to hang the lot of them."

"Benny didn't lie to you," Garwood said. "Moses and Grafton are rivals as far as the horn is concerned. Benny is not one to delve into a man's personal affairs unless it affects his playing."

"Like the opium?" I asked.

"Yes," Garwood admitted, hesitantly. "Like the opium."

"What else do you know that I should know?"

"You still on the case then?"

"For now," I said. "Tell me about the fight."

"Far as I know, Moses was to play on Margaret's album until one day she told Benny that Moses was out and Grafton was in."

"Yeah, that's nothing new," I said. "But why did she choose Grafton?"

"Who knows," Garwood admitted. "Most likely because she knew Grafton, knew his playing. It's better to pick a player you know and have played with than a session boy. Not that there's anything wrong with a session boy, it's just easier with a horn, you know. Get it?"

"I get it," I said. "You don't think there was a little on the side there? A little hanky panky?"

"With Grafton?" he asked. "I wouldn't know that."

I wasn't sure I believed that, but I let it go for the time being. After my phone call with Garwood, I donned my grandfather's lid, locked the front door, then climbed into the Roadmaster and headed to my favorite little diner for a bite to eat and a cup of Joe. Once settled into a booth, I chose something my waitress called Adam and Eve on a raft with a side of axle grease. The food was delightful and the coffee strong enough to wipe off paint with. Best of all, I wasn't disturbed for the entire meal. I was feeling good, so I ordered a side of fisheyes to complete the meal. I have a weakness for tapioca pudding, don't ask me where that came from.

When I was through, I headed to the Sands to check on our whale. She wasn't there, but the Texan was. Fat and happy, sitting at baccarat nursing a pile of black chips. His dolly was nowhere to be found. I went to the front desk, picked up the blower, and called surveillance. Charlie answered on the third ring.

"Any of our friends show today?" I asked.

"Not a one," he said.

"And our Texan's dolly?"

"Out by the pool, soaking up the sun."

I told Charlie I'd check back later and hung up. Then I headed outside to the pool to see what I could see. It was quite the sight. The Texan's wife was clad in a lemon-yellow princess bathing suit, with a sweetheart neckline that clung to her ample bosom like a kitten on a limb. White vertical stripes cascaded downward, ending at a pencil skirt-style bottom. The suit hugged her just where a suit oughtta hug a woman, without showing lumps or bumps that weren't meant to be shown. She was sitting on the edge of the pool, her feet dangling in the water, drinking something with an umbrella in it, while watching a floating craps game.

I thought of the Texan sitting at the baccarat table and wondered why he wasn't sitting at the pool, enjoying the same sight I was. It was amazing what money could buy. I stood there much longer than I should have, but finally left before I was arrested for leering. The sun was more than halfway through its daily journey and I had work to do.

I jumped in my Roadmaster, turned right on Hiway 91, and headed over to Bonanza. Then I turned right on F Street, and just as I did, the world changed around me.

Las Vegas, Nevada is no Boston, Massachusetts. It's a small western town, barely fifty years old, in the middle of a very large desert. There are great expanses of dirt and cactus, unwilling to succumb to human occupation, dotted with resort casinos, each eager and able to separate a man from his hard-earned scratch.

Unlike my bean town, there are no streets lined with four- and five-story apartment buildings, pressed so close together a jack of spades couldn't find purchase between them. Cars don't line the curb on Court Street outside The Golden Teapot at Scollay Square, and there are no parades and festivals honoring the Saints as in the North End. You can't get a decent fish sandwich anywhere in Las Vegas and a good bowl of chowder is simply out of the question.

Yet even with that, this little town has a certain charm about it—at least it has for me. Which is why I stayed here after Tony Cremonesi's bachelor party. Casinos will take your money unless you know the game and don't try to buck the odds. And while the resorts draw the crowds, outside the casinos rests a thriving community—small cottages on manicured lawns, a main street that brings you into its bosom and hugs you like an Italian mother at first communion. Honest people looking to make an honest buck . . . well, most of them anyway.

Admittedly, I hadn't explored all Las Vegas had to offer and hadn't ever made it to the area just west of Fremont Street, known appropriately as the Westside. The closest I had come was the Moulin Rouge only one evening past. But F Street was not the main street that was Bonanza, and just as I turned off Bonanza and onto F Street, I entered into a place I had not expected to find—a crumbling, shabby, dusty town. F Street itself was hardly a road at all, nothing more than a patch of dirt, barely distinguishable from every other patch of dirt in the barren void. There were no gutters, no traffic signs, not even a single streetlight. Instead of sidewalks, trails snaked their way down make-shift blocks, molded by dirt-stained shoes treading the same paths again and again.

The whole area was known as the Dust Bowl or Dustville and it was easy to see why. Dusty children played on dusty streets with dusty balls they kicked at one another, stirring up brown clouds of desert dust with every strike. Old men perched in old chairs with blank faces on what passed for porches under failing roofs, waiting to die. Mothers emerged from houses with broken doors resting slanted on equally broken hinges, wiping sweat with soil-stained cloths from foreheads burnt with age, yelling castigations at no one in particular.

None of the basics of suburbia were wasted on these ramshackle dwellings. There were no lawns, no greenery of any kind, no ornamentation distinguishing one shack from the next. It was a town that should have been abandoned, lost to time, long ago. But there it stood, refusing to be forgotten.

I continued down F Street to the corner of Adams, named after President John Quincy, as were all the east/west streets in this area of town—though I wasn't certain he, or any of our other founding fathers, would be pleased with the veneration. That was, of course, until he caught a view of the Harrison Boarding House.

Unlike the rest of its counterparts on F Street, the Harrison Boarding House, with its shapely lawn and covered porch, could've easily fit into any neighborhood in any other part of Las Vegas. Curtains covered actual glass on actual windows. A thin brick chimney stuck out from the left side of the house, casting an equally thin shadow on an asphalt roof. The house was shiny and clean, a beacon of respect in a declining, decrepit neighborhood.

I parked my Roadmaster at a place that looked like it could have been a curb, if one was so inclined, and got out. I had barely made it three paces up the walk when I was greeted by a bruiser with rolled-up sleeves, a flat nose, brown slacks, and a gray pork pie hat. He emerged from a perfectly functioning front door, and seemed none too happy to see me, or perhaps he simply had a bug in his britches.

"You lost, mister?" he threatened more than asked.

I assured him I wasn't, then inquired as to the whereabouts of one Grafton Freeman.

"He ain't here," a woman said. She emerged from the same door as had the bruiser, only she did it with style and grace in a flower pattern new look dress, a high belt fitted tightly around her waist, her black hair done up in a modified pin curl, accenting her dark complexion. She smiled at me with perfect teeth. "And if'n he was," she continued, with a touch of the south, "he wouldn't want to speak to the likes of you."

"You don't even know me," I protested.

"Youse white, ain't ya?"

She had me there. The bruiser took a step closer. His intentions were clear, and he had enough meat to back them up. I was a stranger in a strange land—persona non grata. "Well," I said, "if he does come back here, can you tell him I'd like to speak with him?"

The woman I assumed to be Mrs. Harrison swung out a hip and shot me a look that made me feel about as welcome as bacon in a bowl of chowder. "And just who are you?"

"Name's Rossi, ma'am. Max Rossi. I heard Grafton play at the Rouge last night and I'd like to speak with him."

"What about?" she asked with raised eyebrow. "You an inspector? I run a clean house. I have toilet facilities, a bathtub, and even a shower."

"It's a private matter," I said. "I'm not here about your boarding house."

She let out a humph. "You don't look like a copper."

"That's because I'm not."

"What then? You some kind of detective?" she asked, emphasizing the "de."

"Not a very good one, I assure you."

"Well, ain't that something?" She thought for a moment, gave me the once over, gave it to me again, then continued. "What makes you think this Grafton of yours is staying here?"

"I have it on good authority from Benny Carter," I said, throwing the name out like a slider into home.

She cocked her head and raised an eyebrow. "You speak to Benny?"

"Yesterday," I assured her. "Told me Grafton was renting a room here. Perhaps he was mistaken."

I could tell she was trying to decide if I was a man who could be trusted. I could have saved her the time, but decided it best to keep my trap shut. After a moment, she relented. "Take yourself on over to the Town Tavern," she said dismissively. "You might find him there."

"The Town Tavern?"

"It's over on Jackson," she said, shooting a finger in what I assumed was the direction of the street in question. "Just go on up E Street. You can't miss it."

I tipped my hat, then tipped it again at the bruiser who did not return the favor. Instead, he watched intently as I climbed back into my Roadmaster. In my rearview mirror, I could see him come all the way out into the street, just to make sure I was gone.

TWENTY-TWO

TOWN TAVERN WAS an unassuming little building nestled on the corner of Jackson and E Street. The sign on the roof was almost larger than the building itself. Made to look like a top hat and cane, it was a bit too dapper to blend into its dusty surroundings—or perhaps that was the point. Several cars were parked outside the place accompanied by several able-bodied men resting their backsides against hoods, heels perched atop bumpers. Birds with little else to do but stand there and lie to each other.

I parked on the adjacent corner, then headed for the door, cognizant of the eyes upon me. The place wasn't any larger on the inside than it looked on the outside. A plain-looking jukebox rested atop a checkerboard floor against one wall to the left of the entrance door. On the opposite side of that same door was a cigarette machine under a fine painting of a stagecoach by C. M. Russell that was ferrying passengers to parts unknown—likely away from the Westside. It was a tavern struggling to find its identity.

A padded bar with padded chairs and stools—none of which matched—stretched itself along the adjacent wall. A large refrigeration unit took up much of the space behind the bar, but there was still enough room for a man to tend. A modest stage hugged the back corner of the place, with tables and assorted chairs occupying the floor in front. A big arts and crafts sign advertising Johnny Talbot and De Thangs in sparkling letters was pinned to the curtains at the back of the stage—though neither Johnny nor the De Thangs were currently present.

A group of elderly men busied themselves playing cards at one table, while a young couple in front of the jukebox moved to The Turbans' *When You Dance*. They eyed me cautiously as I made my way to the bar. A lone man sat on one stool, clad in a navy jacket with matching pants and no lid. His jacket opened to reveal a white-collared shirt—not a dress shirt—which he wore with no tie. What was the world coming to? He leaned over a pint glass, hugging it like a long, lost lover.

I tipped my own lid at the man as I approached. He nodded, then gave me his back. A weary bartender drew near, scrutinizing me with seasoned eyes. The few hairs that remained on his brown head had migrated down his face to his upper lip, jowls, and chin, giving him the warm comfort of an Uncle Remus. I wondered if that was intentional.

"Don't ask if I'm lost," I said.

"Can I help you with something?" he asked intently.

"I could use a manhattan."

The man in the chair turned and gave me a disdainful eye. They apparently didn't get many requests for manhattans in this establishment.

"I ain't got no rye," the bartender stated.

"Have you bourbon?" I asked.

"I gots some Old Forester."

"That'll do."

The old man shook his head and let out his breath. "I ain't made one of these in some time," he said. "I can't guarantee I'll get it right."

"Just do your best," I said. "I'm sure it'll be fine."

As the bartender concentrated on my drink, the man at the bar turned to face me. "You're a long way from home, ain't ya?" he asked in speech less slurred than I expected.

"Oh, I don't know," I said. "We're all part of the same city, aren't we?"

He snickered. "Sure mister," he said. "Whites and coloreds, one big, happy family."

I smiled cautiously.

His eyes tightened. "What you doin' in the colored part of town, Ginzo? You tryin' to put the pinch on the tavern? Cause it ain't gonna take."

"Army or Navy?" I asked.

"'Scuse me?"

"I haven't heard that term in some time," I said. "Figured you for a GI. You must've served in the pacific. I had an uncle who served there too, picked up the word from the Aussies." It was a lie, of course, but he didn't know that. "Can I buy you a drink?"

He softened a bit. "Sure," he said. "I guess your money's as good as anyone's."

"It's the requisite green."

The bartender returned with my drink and pushed the glass over to me. "It's as close as it's gonna get," he said.

Thankfully, he'd chosen the proper glass. I was a bit concerned he'd go for a highball or, heaven forbid, a pint glass. But he didn't. He chose the rocks glass, the only glass, in my humble opinion, in which a manhattan should ever be served. Not only was the glass correct, the liquid inside had the proper hue as well. However, the missing garnish made me a tad skeptical. Not that I needed a garnish. I was a big boy after all.

It seemed the old man was as anxious as I to know how he'd done, because he stood waiting, eyes focused on me, as I picked up the offering and brought it to my lips. Before they had a chance to even touch the rim, the spice and vanilla from the bourbon combined with the orange from the bitters to make a right proper bouquet. We were definitely on the right track. The old man's eyes widened as he waited for me to make the initial taste. Much to my surprise, he'd nailed the mixture.

"That's quite good," I assured him.

He smiled and nodded his satisfaction.

"Could you bring my friend here another of whatever he's having, on me?"

"I ain't your friend," the man barked.

"Fair enough," I said, then turned back to the bartender. "Could you please bring my associate another of whatever he's having?"

"You talk awful fancy for a Ginzo," the man said, as the bartender filled his glass.

I thought we had passed that. Apparently, we had not. "It's how all the cool mobsters speak," I assured him.

"Then you are here to put the pinch on the Tavern. I knew it!" He said, slamming his now empty glass on the bar.

I turned and looked at the man with hard eyes, just as my father had taught me. "You knew nothing of the kind," I said, firmly. "First of all, if I were going to put the pinch on anyone, I wouldn't have come alone. I'd have come in heavy and brought muscle with me to emphasize the point. Second, I wouldn't have ordered a drink. I'd be all business. Get in and get out. The longer you stay, the more dangerous the situation becomes." I took a quick drink, set the glass on the bar with intent, then stepped closer to the man. "Third of all, the moment you called me Ginzo, I would have slapped you down, or had one of my men do it for me." I looked hard into the man's eyes, looking to judge his reaction. Fear or defiance, which would it be? "But I didn't do any of that did I? All I did was come in here and order a drink."

"Simmer down, son," the bartender said. "He didn't mean nothin' by it. Did you, Marcus?"

"You still didn't say why you're here," Marcus said.

"I'm looking for a friend," I said, returning to my drink.

"Really? And what's the sheboon's name?" Marcus asked.

"What makes you think it's a she?" I countered.

"All right, I'll bite. What's *his* name?"

"Freeman," I said. "Grafton Freeman."

The name sucked the sound from the room.

TWENTY-THREE

"NEVER HEARD OF him," the bartender said quickly, but his face betrayed his denial.

"Really?" I questioned, feigning surprise. "Mrs. Harrison seemed to think he'd be here."

"You speak to Mrs. Harrison?" Marcus asked.

"I did," I confirmed. "She's the one who sent me here."

"Well, I ain't never heard of him." the bartender repeated, then took to the bar with a wet cloth, moving it in tight circles.

"How about you, Marcus?"

Marcus focused on his newly filled glass, then shot a quick glance at the bartender. The old man shook his head ever so slightly. Barely enough to be noticed, but I noticed, and so did Marcus. He went all mum and gave me his back once again.

"That'll be two bits for the drinks," the bartender said.

I reached into my pocket, pulled out two bits, and laid them on the bar. Then I took out a clean, fresh dollar bill and laid in on the bar next to them. "Don't you want to know what I want him for?" I asked.

"Ain't no business of mine," the old man said. "I don't know him. No way, no how, so why should I care what dealings he got with you? You're barking up the wrong tree, mister."

He collected the two bits from the bar and went for the buck, but I snatched it before he could get a good hold. "Mind if I ask around?" I asked, holding the bill between two fingers.

"It's a free country," the old man said, eyeing the bill. I passed it to him and he slid it into the front pocket of his trousers, then he placed the two bits into the register, turned and busied himself with polishing glasses that looked clean enough from where I stood. He cast a reflection in the mirror behind the bar. In it I could see him eyeing the telephone.

Having overstayed my welcome at the bar, I decided to mingle a bit while I waited for whomever the old man was eager to contact and made my way over to the men playing cards—a place I might feel more at home. Five men were squeezed around a table barely large enough for three. Sleeves were rolled up and lids pressed back. Glasses, mostly emptied, and smokes in trays fought over what little space wasn't occupied by cards. A plume of dingy white smoke lingered in the air above the men, who seemed barely to notice my presence.

Whatever game they were engaged in resembled nothing for which I had ever seen the Bees used. One man, playing the dealer, dealt out five cards, face down, to each of the other contestants—one at a time. Each man laid down a dime, then snatched up their cards. But before any move could be made, one knocked on the table and yelled out "tonk!" causing all the others to throw their cards down in disgust. The man who yelled tonk smiled proudly, then collected the coins laid out in front of him.

"That's one more for me," he said.

"One more'n you deserve," said another older man, a bent cigarette dangling from the corner of his mouth. He collected the cards and began shuffling.

"Ahh, what you say," the first man said. I guessed he was younger than the man shuffling the cards, though nothing I could put my finger on led me to that conclusion. He had a tuft of white gripping his chin and a way of smiling without involving his mouth. A likable enough chap.

"Can anyone play this game?" I asked.

"Anyone with scratch," the older man said, without expression.

I pulled up a chair and squeezed myself into the ring of men, ending up next to one who sported a steady, painful expression, like he was trying to ease himself onto a chair of cactus. His shirt, which had once been light blue, was frayed at the collar and he chose to keep his newsboy lid firmly planted in place atop his head; I rested my own lid on the back of the chair.

"You ever played tonk before?" the older man asked.

"I'm afraid not," I admitted. "Is that a prerequisite?"

He eyed me with raised brow. "No, but it don't hurt none to know how to play."

"I'm sure I can pick it up," I said. "With a little help."

"You ever play rummy?" the smiling man asked.

"A time or two," I said.

"This here tonk is much the same. You make books or runs and if you collect more'n a hundred points without laying down, you're out. If'n you get dealt fifty right off the top, you win that hand straight up, but you gotta yell 'tonk' or it don't count."

"And hit the table," I added.

"It don't hurt none to knock on the table," the older man said, "but it ain't necessary." Having finished, he held the deck at the ready. "You got it?" he asked.

"We'll see," I said.

He delt out the cards, five to each of us, and after we all threw in our antes, and no one yelled "tonk," he placed the remaining cards in the center of the table, before turning the top card over and laying it down next to the pile.

"You a hipster?" the man next to me asked.

I shook my head. "I fool around with the sax now and again, but we're not serious."

"A jazz man, huh?" He leaned closer to me and asked: "You layin' down the hustle?"

I leaned in as well and shook my head a second time. "Not my cup of chowder," I assured him.

He gave me a humph and returned to his cards. The man to the left of the dealer picked a card from the pile, then laid it down on top of the overturned card. The next two men did the same. When it was my turn, I picked up a three of clubs from the discard pile and laid it down in front of me with the four and five of clubs I had in my hand. I looked to the dealer; he nodded his approval.

The man next to me picked a card, then laid down both a run and a book, the satisfaction painted on his face. The game continued in succession, with guys laying down cards or slamming down useless cards onto the discard pile. When the table filled up, one of the smiling men yelled out "drop!"

"Oh, man," the player next to me exclaimed, "Why is you always yellen' 'drop' when I gots me a hand fulla cards?"

The smiling man laughed, as much as his face would allow him. Each player added up their cards. I sat there looking foolish until the man next to me offered his assistance. "Each of the court cards is worth ten points," he said. "Aces are one and all other cards are face value." He looked over my hand. "You've got thirty-nine points."

"Is that good?" I asked.

"Naw," he said. "You're gonna' lose. But I am too, so don't fret it."

He was right, we both lost to the smiling man who called "drop." We played several more hands, and I lost every one of them, trying my best to learn as I went, and doing a right poor job of it. The men were quiet at first, but after a while, they seemed to warm up to me—at least they stopped sneering. I'm sure my coins in their pockets helped.

Having become my newest friend, the man next to me asked, "What's a white boy like you doin' on this side of the tracks anyhow?"

"Looking for a friend," I said.

"Youse in the wrong place, lookin' for a pro skirt," the older man offered.

"Not that kind of friend," I said. "A fellow sax player."

"Yeah? Who's that?" my new friend asked.

"Grafton Freeman."

"Grafton Freeman?" the smiling men asked. "Who dat?"

"Plays sax over at the Rouge," I said. "Rents a room from Mrs. Harrison."

"I know Grafton," the man next to me said. "Comes here all the time," but before he could continue, he received what I guessed was a swift kick under the table. "Ow!" he exclaimed. "What you go and do that for?" he asked the older man who was seated across from him.

"Best you hop it on out of here," the older man said with a glare. "If you can't keep your worthless trap shut. When's the last time you seen a white boy come in here asking questions? He's the Johns for sure."

"I'm booted," the man said, rubbing his leg.

"I assure you, I'm not the police," I said. "Grafton and I have similar interests."

"Sure, Jack. I believe you," the older man said. "Came in here to lay down the licks is all. I suppose you got a horn in your back pocket."

"Actually, it's in its case in my front room; a Selmer Mark VI with a Vandoren mouthpiece and reed, if you must know. I keep it there, so it won't get out on its own and cause a ruckus."

The old man raised a skeptical brow, but let it pass.

"Speaking of which," I continued, "any of you been to the Rouge yet?"

"That joint's a hoppin'," one of the men said.

"You get a look at those girls they dun hired?" another asked. "Whewee, they got legs to spare!"

"That place is gonna give every othern' a run for its money, that's fo' sho'," the first man said.

"All you jingle brains do is bash ears," the older man said. "Ain't no way in hell whities gonna' let that place compete with their fine resorts over there on Hiway 91. She'll be out of business within the month, you wait and see."

At just that moment, the front door flew open and in walked a man I'd seen earlier in the day: Booker Percy. He rambled over to the bar and spoke to the old man tending it. I don't know what they said to each other, but it was clear who the subject was when the bartender pointed a finger in my direction. That was twice I'd been the topic of a private discussion. I was beginning to get popular. Percy looked over at me; his face grew dark and the room with it.

TWENTY-FOUR

AS SOON AS my new friend saw Percy, he jumped from his seat, almost knocking over the entire table, and headed straight for the boxer. "You layin' down the hustle?" he asked, not caring who heard him.

"He ask everybody that?" I asked.

The older man clicked his disapproval and shook his head just for emphasis. "That boy spends more time snowed up than he does anything else," he said. "Can't hold down a job neither, but he's always got money for the hop."

Percy didn't even bother to give the man the time of day. He simply pressed his over-sized mitt onto the man's face, stiff-arming him like a linebacker, as he pressed on, ambling toward the table. When he arrived, he stood there, towering above us.

Percy was a rough-looking man—a man to whom life had not been kind. His nose showed the distinct signs of having been broken on more than one occasion. There was a scar above his right eye and a bandage over his left cheek. He sported a thin whisp of hair on his upper lip and needed a good shave. He wore black trousers and a white shirt with no tie. A herringbone tweed newsboy cap sat askew atop his head.

"Got room for one more?" he asked, then flashed an aggravated look toward one of the players. "You're in my seat," he said.

"I don't see your name on it," the man said.

The table fell silent.

"I said get out of my seat," Percy said, and he meant it, but it didn't faze the seat's current occupant. He seemed to settle himself in even further, claiming property he felt rightfully his.

"I got as much right to be here as . . ."

Before the man could finish, Percy grabbed him by the shirt collar and pulled him from the seat, throwing him onto the floor in one swift motion. He then scooped up the cash from the man's spot and threw it at him; coins bounced across the floor. Percy starred at him a moment to get his point across, then turned back to the table and took the now vacant seat, planting his eyes firmly on my corpus masculum. He looked at me so hard, were I a dame, he would've had to buy me dinner.

The old man didn't miss a beat. He finished shuffling, took a long drag of his cigarette, and began dealing.

Percy ignored his cards. "Don't I know you?" he asked me, keeping eye contact.

I said to him, "I doubt it. We don't really travel in the same circles."

The old man finished dealing. The table picked up their cards. All except Percy. He eyed me purposely, squinting tightly as if doing so would somehow give him a better view. He played the part well, giving a performance that would've made John Ford take notice.

"No," he said. "I do know you. Didn't I see you at the Rouge today?"

"I don't see how you could have," I said.

"Yeah, I saw you. You was eating in the restaurant when I was talking to Joe."

"I'm sure you're mistaken," I countered.

He bristled. "You callin' me a liar?"

"I'm calling you mistaken," I said firmly. "Whether that mistake is purposeful or accidental is not for me to say."

The men held their cards and their breath.

Percy's squint got tighter. "Sounds like you're callin' me a liar," he said. "You the kind a' bird that's got the stones to back that up?"

"You asking me if I'm trying to pick a fight with a light heavyweight?" I asked. "I'd have to be daft."

"So I did see you at the Rouge."

"Perhaps you did," I conceded.

"And now here you are, asking after Grafton Freeman."

Finally, we were getting somewhere. "You a friend of Grafton's?" I asked.

"You could say that."

"Would you say it?"

"You tryin' to be smart?"

"I'm trying to find Grafton."

"Why's that?"

"It's personal," I said. "We travel in the same circles."

His face strained as he drew his mouth so rigidly his bottom lip almost completely disappeared. Jowls bulged as his jaw tightened and his eyes fell dead. He clenched his fist and grunted, "What's a flatfoot for the Sands doin' looking for a sax player from the Rouge? What happens there ain't got nuttin' to do with you."

"I knew you was the Johns," the old man said. "Didn't I say he was the Johns?"

I turned to the old man. "I'm not the Johns," I said, then to Percy said, "And I'm not a flatfoot . . . well, not officially. I'm just looking into the matter for a friend is all."

"Your friend got you stickin' your beak where it don't belong, mister."

"Who told you I worked at the Sands?" I asked.

That caught Percy off guard. He got quiet and let his eyes dart quickly to the side before bringing them back to me. "Joe told me," he lied.

"He happen to tell you where Grafton could be found?" I asked.

"You wanna see Grafton?"

"It's what I came for."

He rubbed his unshaven chin slowly, pinching the end between this thumb and forefinger, then said, "I can take you to him. You got a car?"

"I do," I said. "Just outside."

"Good, let's go. We'll take yours."

I stood, put my lid in place, then followed Percy out the front door into the daylight. "I'm over here," I said, pointing to my Roadmaster. I slid behind the wheel and he in the seat next to me.

"Head on down E Street towards Bonanza," he said. "Then take Main over to Charleston."

I did as I was told.

Percy sat uncomfortably in the front; half turned with his back more toward the passenger door than the back of the seat, as if he was worried about being clipped from behind. He rested one large mitt on the dashboard and threw the other over the back of the seat.

"You good friends with Joe Louis?" I asked casually.

"He's helping me," he said. "Gonna make a comeback."

"Is that so?"

"What?" he growled. "You don't think I can do it? Think I lost my nerve?"

"It doesn't matter what I think," I said. "Yours is the only thought that matters."

"Damn straight," he said, as we crossed Fremont. "I can do it too."

"I'm sure you can."

I didn't know much about Percy, never saw him fight. Just that he was up and coming; someone to keep an eye on before it all dissolved into nothing. He quickly went from destroying his opponents in the ring, to not being able to buy a decent hit—not even for a ten spot. Maybe he did lose his nerve, or maybe the mob took it away from him. What did I know? Either way, a comeback didn't seem likely.

"You mind if we make a stop first?" he asked.

"Sure," I said. "Let's make a party of it."

"Don't get sore," he said. "It'll only take a minute. I need to stop at Johnny's real quick like. Got some business to take care of. You don't mind."

"Johnny Tocco's?"

"Yeah, that's the joint. You heard of the place?"

"Louis mentioned it to me."

"You know something about boxing?"

"Something," I said.

Percy seemed to relax a bit. "Been fightin' since I was a kid," he offered. "It was Johnny who took me off the street. Taught me how to hit. Most of the kids he sent 'cross town to the Golden Gloves gym, but not me. Let me workout in the jail—that's what we called it: Johnny's Jail. If you're tough enough to survive there, you're tough enough to make it anywhere."

Percy glanced down at the floorboard. His shoulders slumped slightly as a melancholy seemed to overtake him. "Guess he thought I was tough enough," he said softly.

A nice guy would have let him alone with his thoughts. I'm not a nice guy. "How'd you get that cut on your face?" I asked.

He instinctively brought his hand up to the bandage, then sent me a glare. It was a warning to drop it. I wasn't good with warnings.

"You ever do any time in the can?" I asked.

His face grew stern, and the muscles in his neck tightened. "That's a hell of a thing to ask," he said.

"Just trying to be personable."

"I like you just fine," he said. "Don't make me change my mind."

As we approached Charleston, he sprung up and began rubbing his hands together. "It's over there," he said, pointing a thick finger. "Just pull around. We'll go in the back way."

I pulled in the back and parked the Roadmaster next to a row of cars that looked as haggard as the Old Mongoose in the ninth round with Marciano. We got out and headed to the back door of a non-descript cement-block building. There was nothing to indicate on the outside that a thriving gym functioned within.

That all changed when we opened the door.

TWENTY-FIVE

THE FIRST THING that hit me was the sweaty smell of men, dirty socks, and stale coffee grounds, slapping me in the face like a disdained woman. It was the aroma of a gym. A place where men worked out, serious men, not dogs looking for table scraps. Pugilists, eager for combat, hungry to slam their respective fists into an opponent's gut or kisser.

It wasn't a fancy place. There was only one ring, set up in the center of the main and only workout area. The place wasn't even large enough for showers. Only a bathroom with no door and what appeared to be an office off to the left. Posters of past and upcoming fights plastered one wall.

There were heavy bags, and speed bags, and jump ropes hanging from hooks. Men who weren't hitting bags were boxing shadows, or skipping ropes. Some hung from high bars while trainers slammed medicine balls into their midsections. Others used those same bars to jerk themselves upward ten, fifteen, twenty times.

Filled with strong, sweaty men, the place was easily forty degrees hotter on the inside than the outside, the air a murky gray. It grabbed you by the collar, slapped you twice in the face, then dared you to step inside. It was stiff enough to choke the life out of the average Joe, but not Percy. From the look on his face, he felt right at home.

"You been in a gym before?" he asked, taking a hand to the back of his neck.

"Yeah," I admitted, "I've boxed a little. Nothing to write home about."

"Really? You ever been in the ring?"

"Once or twice."

"Well, I'll be. Come on." He brought me over to a speed bag that wasn't in use. He hit it once, hard, then took hold of the thing to steady it. "Let's see what you got," he said.

Speed bags were showy things. Boxers liked to use them because they looked much harder than they actually were. Unlike other things a boxer hits, the speed bag is struck with the side of the fist, not the front, on a count of three. The key to the thing is rhythm, counting, and not getting ahead of yourself. I squared up to the bag. It'd been a while since I hit one and while I knew it's secret, I was admittedly rusty, and didn't want to look the fool in front of an actual, honest-to-goodness boxer. I stuck my elbows out, balled my hands into fists, and brought them up near my chin.

I hit the bag once, counted to three, then hit it again, moving my fists in a circular motion and keeping them up around my face. I did this several times, switching hands, and going slow while I established a rhythm. As it began to feel comfortable, familiar, I sped up. I could feel the adrenaline course through me and all at once, I was eager to get back in the gym.

"Hey, that's pretty good," Percy said, and I appreciated the comment. Then I watched as he took to the bag himself, making me look the amateur I was. And as he did, a change came over him. The slump in his shoulders was gone. His muscles tightened, and a fire sparked in his eyes as he mastered the rhythm of the bag—one, two, three, one, two, three, one, two, three—switching hands with ease, right, then left, then left, then right—one, two, three, one, two, three, one, two, three.

As Percy danced with the bag, we were approached by a man, thick as a side of beef, in sweatpants and a stained t-shirt. He was too old to be a boxer, but too tough to be anything else.

"You got some nerve coming back here," he growled.

I watched the air empty from Percy. His shoulders slumped as they had outside, and his hands fell to his side, while the bag slowly swung to a halt.

"I brought a guy to show the place," he said, almost as a defense. "Used to box. Name's Rossy."

"Rossi," I corrected him. "Long O."

The man extended his hand. "Johnny Tocco," he said, with his own long O. "This is my place."

"Max Rossi," I said. "Pleased to meet you."

"You a real boxer, or a canvas back like him?" he asked with a jerk of the thumb.

"I dabbled a little," I said. "Mostly at the Brockton Y back home."

Tocco seemed impressed. "Marciano's stomping ground," he said. "You any good?"

"I did all right," I admitted with a certain pride. "I didn't stink out the house, but I wasn't fancy enough to make a go of it either."

"What are you doing with the likes of this palooka?" he asked.

Percy protested. "Aw, c'mon, Johnny. That ain't right."

"It's you that ain't right, Percy," Johnny said, "and you know it. Coming in here like everything's fine and dandy. Like you didn't make a mess of things. Like you didn't take your shot and spit on it. You know how many of these guys would kill to have what you had?"

"I'm makin' a comeback," Percy said, rubbing the back of his neck.

The old fellow let out a hard, dismissive laugh. "Comeback? Hell, you ain't nothin' but a ham and egger. I should have sent you to the Golden Gloves when you first came in here." Then he turned to me. "I'll let him stay on account of you," he said, "but it'll be the last time." Then he left.

Percy went over to the ring and hung all his weight on the bottom rope. I wasn't sure what was going through his head, but I had a pretty good idea. He'd just been scolded by a man he clearly respected and now all his past sins were coming to light. Dancing around in his skull, mocking him, slapping him around a bit.

A colored man with a weathered face approached. He was decked out in the same uniform Johnny Tocco had worn. "Well, I'll be dammed," he said. "That you, Percy?"

Percy turned. His face lit. "Sammy!" he exclaimed, then hugged the man. They slapped each other on the shoulders and said their hellos.

"You lookin' good," Sammy said. "You still hittin' the bag?"

"Whenever I can," Percy said. "I'm gonna make a comeback."

"Is that so?" Sammy asked without judgment.

Percy wrapped his arm around the man's shoulder and presented him to me. "This here's Samuel S. Johnston," he said. "But you call him Sammy. We all do." He slapped the man's back. "Best trainer in the gym."

Sammy smiled. "Johnny's the best trainer," he said, "but I get by." He held out a hand.

"Max Rossi," I said, taking the offering. He had the gnarled hands of a man well acquainted with the ring, coupled with a nice, firm grip.

"Pleased to meet you," he said.

"Rossy used to be a boxer," Percy explained.

"Oh, yeah?"

Percy went over to the wall and removed a pair of sparring mitts. He handed them to Sammy. "Why don't you put on the mitts and see what he's got?"

"Oh, no," I protested, but before I could mount a proper protest, Sammy had already put them on and was facing me.

"Let's see your stance," he said.

"I'm not sure this is a good idea," I said.

"Aw, c'mon," Percy said. "You ain't gonna get an opportunity like this again. Show the man your stance."

I relented and showed the man my stance.

He eyed my hips and feet and nodded. "Not bad," he said. "Not bad at all."

My father would have been pleased.

"Now, let's take some shots," Sammy said, raising the mitts.

I removed my lid, balled my fists, and brought them to the sides of my face. I could feel the energy rushing through my arms.

"Jab," Sammy said.

I jabbed, pressing my fist hard into his mitt.

He grinned and nodded. "Again."

I did as I was told.

Sammy began calling out shots—jab, punch, hook, cross—throwing in an uppercut, every so often, just for good measure. He moved the mitts high and low, right and left, as I aimed for the center, following his moves like some odd ballet.

Before I knew it, I had worked up a fairly decent sweat.

Sammy slammed the mitts together and stepped back. "Not bad," he said. He pulled the mitts off and handed them to Percy, then he moved over to me, taking a stance by my side. "You've got to use your hips more," he said. "When you throw your punch, put your hips into it." He demonstrated. "Like this."

He took a position behind me and placed his hands on my hips. "You try it," he said. As I punched, Sammy worked my hips, extending them farther than was usual for me. "There," he said. "Just like that. Now, let's try it again."

He slid on the mitts and put me through a second round of punches, jabs, and uppercuts. I immediately felt an improvement in my strike, my hits containing quite a bit more power.

"There you go," he said, as I struck the mitt. "That's it. It's all in the hips."

"I told you he was good," Percy chimed in, then added. "We need to get you in the ring."

"Oh, no," I protested. "This lesson has been plenty. Besides, I'm hardly dressed for the part."

Percy didn't hear me or didn't want to hear me. Either way, he called out to the other boxers. "We need a sparring partner," he said.

A particularly large bruiser turned his attention from

the heavy bag. "I got you," he said.

"Look, Percy, I . . ."

"C'mon," he said and threw me a pair of bag gloves. "It'll be fun. You can try out what Sammy taught you for real. It's just for play; no one's gonna get hurt."

Famous last words, I thought. I don't know if it was the smell of the canvas, the gloves, and the ropes, or that Sammy had actually taught me something in five minutes that helped my punch immensely, but I got caught up in the moment, and, even dressed like a shoe salesman, I slipped on the gloves, and climbed into the ring.

"I'll leave you to it," Sammy said, shaking Percy's hand.

The bruiser was already bouncing on his toes, shaking out his arms as I made my way over the ropes. Percy climbed up onto the outside of the ring as well and chose a corner. I hoped it was mine. "Nothing hard," Percy said. "Let's just get our feet wet."

"You got it," the bruiser said, then raised his fists in preparation for combat.

I hadn't seen many fights in my days as a pugilist. It's not that I didn't enjoy the sport. I liked boxing. I enjoyed learning how to hit and the feel of my fists slamming into the canvas of the heavy bag. I didn't even mind the workouts, as punishing as they tended to be, or being hit. What I didn't like, what turned me off from a life with the gloves, was the heavy hand the family played in the whole thing. Matches weren't always decided by who had the most skill or was the better fighter. Like everything else the mob controlled, decisions in boxing had more to do with the cabbage than the carnage. You took a dive when you were told to, or you suffered the consequences. You played the game, or you got out of the kitchen—assuming you had a choice.

I didn't want to be put in that position, so I got out with all my parts and pieces exactly where the good Lord had intended them to be. It wasn't long after that I left the life entirely—much to my father's dismay. It was often hard to be the son of Boston Rossi.

I pulled my fists up to the sides of my head and turned to face my opponent. He nodded, and without the requisite bell, our match began. The purpose of sparring is not to fight, that is, not to beat your partner senseless. You're not trying to win a match, you're trying to develop your skill—learning how to block, strike, jab, bob and weave. Sure, you can practice all that stuff in the gym on the heavy bag, but the bag doesn't strike back, and until some bruiser is coming at you full speed, you don't really know what it's like to use any of those skills.

My bruiser started with a straight jab that I would have easily avoided, had not my foot slipped and I lost my balance. He caught me at the side of the mouth and dropped me hard to the canvas.

"You gotta lose the shoes," Percy said. "Them fancy loafers of yours gonna make you slide around like you was on ice."

He had a point, so I walked to the corner and pulled off the bag gloves, then I removed my shoes and my socks, for the same reason, tucked the socks inside the shoes, and slid them against the corner post, before turning back to my opponent.

When we started up again, he tried the same move, but this time, having the traction I needed, I easily avoided his jab and countered with one of my own, catching him in the old breadbasket. It was like hitting a wall and had about the same effect.

"Nice," Percy said. "You got some moves."

My opponent shook out his arms again, then brought them back up to his face. I followed suit, not wanting to appear difficult. We danced around the ring a bit, throwing easy jabs and hooks that weren't meant to do any damage. We'd made it to the exact center of the ring when suddenly, out of nowhere, the bruiser tried an uppercut; an honest-to-goodness, knock your block off, uppercut.

I leaned back as quickly as I could, the flurry of air from his fist brushing across my face, mere inches from my nose. He followed the blow with a succession of jabs, catching me twice in the shoulder, but missing all the important parts. On the last jab, I stepped to the side and caught him with a hook that sent him back a couple of steps, and, I hoped, made him rethink his choices in life.

"Whew ya! Now we got ourselves a fight!" Percy yelled out.

The bruiser was apparently taking this little exercise a tad more seriously than I was. Percy seemed to be seeing things his way. I was about to call the whole thing off when the bruiser came at me hard, two successive jabs, followed by another uppercut. I blocked the jabs and just as I was pulling my head back, he crawfished, turning the uppercut into a hook that caught me square on the side of the head. Then he threw a cross, and I barely got my hand up in time to protect my face and lessen the impact. Still, it sent me backward, and I wondered who'd let the little birdies into the gym. My legs gave out, and I fell to the canvas.

"You all right?" the Bruiser asked, but I wasn't convinced of his concern for my wellbeing. I should have stayed on the canvas, pulled off the gloves, crawled over to my shoes, slid them on, put my lid in place, and left. That's what a wise man would have done, but not me.

I nodded as I got back up, but it was the wrong thing to do. I saw him glance over at Percy and, as I turned my head, I thought I saw Percy nod as well. That was when things took a turn. The bruiser came at me with a jab and then a hard cross, straight to the face. I raised my gloves, but without the padding of ring gloves, mine did little good to soften the impact. My head jerked back and the little birdies got a bit louder, bringing some of their friends with them.

"Hold on," I managed to say, raising my hands and trying to catch my breath. But the Bruiser didn't listen. He came after me again with an uppercut, but found no purchase, so he switched to a hook at my side. That one worked. Even with my elbow tucked in, I could feel the blow down to my ribs. My stomach went queasy. I felt the same blow two more times as well, one right after the other, and as the hits kept coming, it suddenly came to me that we were no longer sparring. This was a fight. One it was clear I needed to win.

My father had taught me that when an opponent changed the rules, one was no longer obligated to allow those rules to dictate one's actions. In other words, all bets were off, rules be dammed, achieve the objective by whatever means necessary. This time when the bruiser came forward, I blocked his strike and brought my knee up hard into his inner thigh. That caught his attention and when he dropped his hands to take hold of his leg, I ripped off the glove with my teeth, squared myself, then, using what Sammy had just taught me, caught him hard on the chin. I hit him again, and as he stepped back, I hit him one more time just for the icing.

As the bruiser dropped to the canvas, I turned to face Percy, but all I saw was his fist. That's when the birdies really began to sing, and the room went black.

TWENTY-SIX

I WOKE UP, flat on my back, to a moonlit sky and a mouth full of dirt. The bells of Saint Leonard hammered relentlessly in my skull, calling the sinners to Sunday mass. My eyes hadn't quite adjusted to the dark and I couldn't get my bearings. It took me three tries to sit up and two more to get onto my knees. I tried a breath, but sucking in air sent a distinctly sharp pain to my side— one I didn't much care for—so I stuck to short gasps. Who needs to breathe anyway?

A wisp of a wind picked up, swirling around, and encircling me in a cloud of dust. It was then that I understood I was out in the elements. I tried to stand, stumbling with each attempt, finally finding my legs, praying they still worked. You never can tell with legs nowadays, sometimes they have a mind of their own. Luckily, mine seemed willing to oblige.

I stood there for a moment, allowing my body to adjust to its surroundings. The full moon shone overhead, bathing the desert in a cascade of warm, soft light. Stars sparkled high above, reminding those who dared dwell below of their diminutiveness in the overall scheme of things. As far as I could tell, I was out in the middle of nowhere—not a familiar rodent in sight. That didn't surprise me. What did surprise me was that I was still above ground. I pinched myself just to make sure. It's not often a person takes a trip out into the desert and is able to talk about it the next day. Amateurs.

I took a hard step and something crunched underfoot. Something sharp, like a needle, shot into the sole of my piede so deep that I cried out despite myself. Wherever I was, my shoes and socks had not made the trip. I hopped like a fool twice on one foot before falling hard to the ground. Pulling my leg up, I fumbled as best I could in the dark and somehow managed to locate the offending object, along with several of its compadres. I painfully extracted each cactus needle from bare foot, one at a time, and when it was over, collapsed backwards. That was when I realized something wasn't quite right.

My head had landed on something harder than the ground, but softer than a rock. I reached overhead and felt the distinct form of a human leg, one that I hoped was attached to an equally human body. I shot upright and sat there until my breathing returned to some semblance of normal. I was outside, shoeless and lidless, with a sharp pain in my side, a headache the size of Boston Common, and at least one spare leg.

I managed a standing position, though only one of my feet was flat, and hobbled over to the body. There was just enough moonlight to see it was a man, a colored man, a young colored man. Whether he was alive or dead remained to be determined, but I had my suspicions, seeing as how he wasn't moving. His body—fully dressed, shoes and all—was laid out nice as you please, just as if he was on a slab at the morgue. I took hold of his wrist and found nothing but ice in his veins.

The poor sap.

His jacket had a large dark spot surrounding a small hole. I couldn't tell the color, but it wasn't hard to surmise the source. I gingerly lifted the flap of the jacket and fished around in his pockets for any type of identification, not expecting to find any. Much to my surprise, his wallet was right where it was supposed to be, in his inside pocket. I pulled out his identification and had a look. It said Grafton Freeman. Along with it, I found a union card, a photo of what looked like the dancer I had met earlier perched atop a diving board overlooking a pool, and one hundred and sixty-four dollars in small bills. I guess Percy had kept his promise after all.

Tucked inside one of the compartments was a condom, standing at the ready, and a small satchel of folded paper. I slid out the sachet and laid the wallet on Grafton's chest. I didn't think he'd mind. I carefully unfolded the paper. Inside was what looked like a hunk of tobacco. I tried to position the thing in what little light the moon saw fit to bestow, but was unable to determine the color, except that it was dark. I passed the dark substance under my nose but didn't smell any type of tobacco I was familiar with. Strangely enough though, I thought I caught a whiff of ammonia.

It was about that time that I saw it. Lights off in the distance, coming up what was likely a dirt road. Swerving back and forth, up and down, they approached, and as they grew closer, a spotlight turned on. It was either whoever left me here, come back to finish what they'd started, or it was the bluebottles. My money was on the latter.

I had two choices: sit and face the music or make a run for it. The second of the two seemed impractical. After all, how far could a shoeless man get in the dark— with its obvious snares—and even if I did run, where would I go? The desert offered few, if any, places for one to conceal oneself, and since I had no idea where I was, I had even less idea which way to head. People lost in the Mojave have a bad habit of showing up dead—especially ones without water, shoes, or any sense of direction—so I decided to put Grafton's identification and all his effects back where I found them and wait out my fate. I knew a setup when I saw one.

I had just slid Grafton's wallet into his pocket when the moonlight alit onto a shiny object just to my right. It was a gun, a .38. My gun. That little bean shooter and I had been through a lot together and I would've known it anywhere. It was a fine how'd ya do. Frame a guy with his own gat. I'd have thought it clever if I wasn't the framee.

As the vehicle drew closer, I pulled the handkerchief out of my back pocket and wiped the gun down. I wasn't sure if my prints would be on the thing, but it seemed like a sure bet, and I wasn't in the position to take chances. After I wiped it down, I put the thing back where I found it, turned, and sat. I'd have smoked if I had one . . . and if I smoked.

It took five, maybe ten more minutes for the squad car to make its way up the road and another couple for the boys in brown to head on over to me, torches in hand. As they approached, their faces became clear. It was O'Malley, and he'd brought a couple of sheriff deputies with him. It was going to be a right fine party with me as the main course.

I didn't bother to stand.

O'Malley stepped up next to me and hovered. He was dressed in the same gray suit he always wore, one he probably slept in—maybe not.

"Well," O'Malley said, "What've we got here?"

"It's a little hard to see in the dark," I said, "but if you shine that torch of yours my way, I'm sure you'll find it's a dead body."

"You the one who made it dead?"

"No. That distinction belongs to another."

I couldn't see, but I was sure O'Malley sent me a glare. "And you just happened to be here with a corpse, one you didn't make," he said, more than asked.

"I would imagine the circumstances surrounding my being here are about as happenstance as yours," I countered.

"Just cut the fancy talk and tell me what's going on," O'Malley barked.

"Over here," a voice behind me called out.

I turned to look as O'Malley headed over to the source of the voice. The deputy was shining his light onto the ground, focusing it on an object, a .38 snub nose—one that looked suspiciously familiar. I felt an unpleasant tingle creep up my spine.

"Am I gonna find your prints on this gat?" O'Malley asked me.

"Who knows?" I said.

"And the stiff?"

"Grafton Freeman. Blows sax at the Rouge."

"But you didn't make him the stiff."

I didn't answer.

O'Malley walked up to me and shined his light in my face. It stung. He whistled loudly. "Who put you through the ringer?"

"A boxing lesson," I said.

"Some lesson," he countered.

"It went a little south," I admitted.

"And your shoes?" he asked. "They go south too?"

"With the wind," I said.

"Well, I guess we'd better hook you up and take you in."

"I supposed you'd better at that."

TWENTY-SEVEN

O'MALLEY PLACED ME in the box, on the business side of what at one time was likely a perfectly fine wooden table but was now simply a shadow of its former self. I sat in the only chair on my side, hoping it still had enough life left to support me. Two chairs just like it were positioned on the opposite side of the table. This wasn't the first time I'd been in the box. I didn't like it any better now than I did then, especially since this time I was in bracelets, hands behind my back.

I waited for O'Malley to make his presence known, hoping he might bring Queeney with him. It's not that I was especially fond of Lieutenant Connor McQueeney, it's just that I missed his cheery disposition—and his much leveler head.

When he showed, O'Malley came complete with a steaming cup of Joe in one hand, something wrapped in cloth in his other, and a lit cigarette dangling from his lips, but no Queeney. He was also without his lid and his jacket. His tie was loosed and his sleeves rolled up—a man ready for business. "You don't mind if I smoke, do you?" he asked as he took one of the chairs.

"Why should I mind?" I asked. "It's your house."

He took a sip from the cup and rested it on the table, then he produced the item wrapped in cloth. He opened the cloth to reveal a handgun and laid it on the table in front of me.

"Recognize this?" he asked.

"I can't say for sure," I said, "but it looks like a gun."

"Always the wise guy, aren't you?"

"Family trait," I said.

"Let's try that again. This your gun?"

"If the serial number matches, it is," I said, but I knew it was mine.

"You wanna explain what your gun was doing at a crime scene only feet away from its owner?"

"Maybe it was lonely," I said. That got me a quick slap across the beak.

"Do I look like I'm in the mood for jokes?" O'Malley asked.

"I already told you in the car, that gun was reported stolen. As for how it got there, your guess is as good as mine. I don't even know how *I* got there."

"Why don't we take this from the top," O'Malley said. "This got something to do with your previous visit to the station and that darkie we got in custody?"

I didn't like O'Malley. I didn't like him one bit. I didn't like the smug look on his face, the way he drank his Joe, how the cigarette bounced when he spoke, or the cut of his jib. And I especially didn't like taking one on the beak from him. "I told you," I said through clenched teeth. "I don't know how I got there."

"Yet you want me to believe that you just happened

to be found out in the desert, next to a stiff who was killed with your gat?"

"I don't particularly care what you believe," I said. "But if you're foolish enough to think I carried a dead body all the way out to the desert, shoeless, and was stupid enough to leave his identification on him, and even stupider not to bring a getaway vehicle, then I doubt there's much hope for you."

O'Malley eyed me coldly, probably trying to decide if he wanted to take another swipe at me. "What do you mean 'carried a dead body?'"

"I'm no coroner, but that man, cold as a frozen fish, was dead long before you found him and I'd be willing to guess that not only will the coroner confirm that, but he'll tell you Grafton Freeman was bumped off somewhere other than where he lay when you arrived."

"Well, aren't you the smart cookie?"

"Look," I said, leaning forward. "This was nothing but a setup and we both know it. Plenty of people meet their maker in the desert, but all of them get a nice little hole to curl up in. But not Grafton Freeman. No. He's found lying above ground, pretty as you please, with his identification intact just waiting to be found, and, just for fun, the murder weapon by his side. All they needed was a rube to pin it on. That's where I came in, shoeless, so I couldn't make a run for it—even if I were so inclined. I know you're only half a detective, but even you should be able to see that . . . unless, of course, you're in on it."

O'Malley threw his cigarette across the room, grabbed me by the collar as he stood and yanked me up toward him, pulling me off the chair. He gave me another one across the beak and a third to keep it company. "Look here, Jobbie," he said, spittle flying recklessly. "I ain't in it with no nogoodniks. And you best watch your tongue if you want to keep it in your filthy little mouth."

I ran said tongue over my split lip and tasted blood. "Then how did you know to come to that exact location?" I asked. "You just happen to be out on patrol?"

He glared, but didn't answer. Then he pushed me back across the table, so hard I almost fell to the ground.

"We got a tip," he said and took his seat.

The bells were back, this time with a vengeance. "How many people you know cut down someone in the desert, then drop a dime to the hammer and saws to come and nail them? There's more bodies buried out there than in the whole of Granary, yet this one's right out in the open and that doesn't seem strange to you?"

"Maybe you did the deed, took one on the noggin' for it, and then got left with the evidence."

"And I just sat there and waited for Johnny Law?"

O'Malley grinned that grin of his, the one that made you want to slap it off his face. "You were doing just that when we got there," he said.

He had a point.

"Except you and I both know that body was moved," I said. "If someone were going to turn me in for killing Freeman, why wouldn't they have just left us where the deed happened instead of taking us all the way out into the desert?"

"Maybe they was hoping you'd make a run for it, and never be seen again."

"With no shoes?" I asked. "No. They wanted me there when you arrived."

O'Malley reached into the pocket of his shirt and pulled out a pack of smokes rumpled enough to look as if he'd borrowed it from a bum. He gave the pack a quick jerk, forcing the butt end of one up to the top. Then he pulled it out with his lips and rested what was left of the pack on the table. He took a book of matches from his pocket, pulled one out and ran it across the striker, bringing the thing to life, then lit the tip of the cigarette. He sucked in deeply, shook the match, and threw it to the floor, then leaned back in his chair.

"Now," he said, blowing out the smoke, "it's time for you to come clean. Who put the beating on you?"

"I told you. It was a boxing lesson."

"Don't get tough with me, Rossi. I ain't a man to get tough with." He took another drag. "You been askin' a lot of questions over there in Niggertown. Stirring up dust. Stickin' your beak where it don't belong."

"What's it to you?" I asked, throwing caution to the same wind that took my shoes. "I got a right to ask questions, don't I? Maybe I'm just doing the job you should be doing."

O'Malley pulled the cigarette from his mouth and looked at me intently. "If you know what's good for you, Rossi, you'll keep your nose out of this," he said, then emphasized the point by crushing the lit end hard into the table directly in front of me.

That's when the door burst open and Queeney walked in.

TWENTY-EIGHT

"WHAT KIND A con you . . ." As soon as he stepped in the door, Queeney gave me the once over. I must have been a sight because it made him stop in mid-sentence. He whistled loudly. "Beat yourself up again?" he asked.

"I may have had a little help this time," I admitted.

The large man settled himself into the vacant seat, as much of him as could fit on it anyway. "What happened?" he asked.

I looked to O'Malley. "I stuck my beak where somebody thought it didn't belong."

"Don't suppose you're lookin' to press charges."

"Don't suppose I am."

Queeney looked over to O'Malley, scolding him with his eyes, then turned his attention back to me. "This is quite a mess you got yourself into here, Rossi. You really stepped in it this time."

I didn't answer. What was there to say?

Queeney ignored my silence. "It begins with you coming in here asking questions about a murder suspect and ends with you right back in here, only this time you got a nice stiff to keep you company. One Grafton Freeman, who, it just so happens, blows horn at the same place as our little murder suspect." He paused. "Now, you gonna try and tell me these two cases ain't related?"

I gave him sheepish eyes. I may have been able to pass this off as a coincidence to O'Malley, but not Queeney. He was far too good a detective to try that game on.

"Are these really necessary?" I asked, motioning as best I could to the cuffs that bound my arms behind me.

Queeney looked at me for a moment as if he was contemplating the pros and cons of letting me loose, then, apparently deciding I was harmless, motioned for O'Malley to take the cuffs off.

O'Malley protested. "He's a murder suspect," he said. "This is proce . . ."

"I'm well aware of what he is," Queeney said forcefully. "Just take the damn things off."

O'Malley stood, fished in his pocket for the keys, then reluctantly brought them to my back, unhooking the cuffs about as gently as a drunk takes a swig of hooch. I brought my arms forward and rubbed my wrists, trying to get the circulation back.

"Why don't you go and get two more cups of Joe," Queeney said to O'Malley, then added, "Put some thought into it. Take your time and get it right."

"Go light on the sand," I said.

O'Malley glared, then left the room, slamming the door behind him.

Queeney turned his attention back to me. "Time to come clean, Rossi. This whole thing stinks."

"Yeah," I agreed, "And I'm getting the worst of it.

O'Malley's too thick to know or care, but you're different. You gotta know this is a setup."

"All I know is I got another stiff on the slab, one who's been iced with a gat that just happens to belong to Max Rossi. And you with no alibi."

"Only I reported that very gat missing, if you recall."

"So you did. Awful convenient, ain't it?"

"There any prints on it? I asked, then presented my hands. "You wanna check for residue?"

Queeney's eyes hardened. "You know darn right well there aren't any prints on it or you wouldn't have asked. Dark like it was, you should've been able to see that squad car comin' a mile away. You sittin' like the cat what caught the canary when the boys arrived. I figured you had plenty of time to clean the thing before they got there. Probably wiped down your hands too."

I told you Queeney was no fool.

"Now, unless you wanna spend the night in the can, you best start talkin' and talkin' clean. Tip your mitt, Rossi, and do it quick, before I start liking you for both murders."

I wasn't a private dick, so I didn't suffer under any obligation to keep my trap shut due to client confidentiality. Still, it didn't seem right to spill the beans about Garwood's interest in the case, or Theodosia's for that matter. On the other hand, a night in the can wasn't a pleasant prospect either.

"A friend asked me to look into the Jones case."

"You acting as a private dick on this one?"

"I'm not acting as anything," I assured him. "I made a few inquiries and got a few answers is all."

"This friend of yours, he got a name?"

"Well, of course he does. We all got names, don't we?"

Queeney sneered. "This ain't the time for the comedy act, Rossi. Just tell me his name."

"I'd rather not," I said. "At least not until I'm forced to. Let's just go with him being the only person in the world whose mother forgot to bless him with a moniker for now, shall we?"

Queeney didn't nod, but he didn't push it either. "Go on with you," he said. "What's this no name person's interest in the case?"

"He's just worried is all. Afraid a man like Moses Jones won't get a fair shake. From what I've seen so far, can't say I blame him."

"Watch your mouth, Rossi. O'Malley may have his quirks, but he's a decent cop. Does his job and does it right."

"Sure, if your skin's the right shade," I said.

Queeney looked a little like he wanted to agree, but thought better of it. "Your friend, he of the opinion that Moses is innocent?"

"He is, but I assured him a man never knows what another man is or isn't capable of doing; including blipping off a dame."

"But he didn't buy it, did he?"

I shook my head.

"If I were to believe you, and I ain't sayin' I do, how did makin' inquiries get you saddled with a stiff?"

"You know how it is; I thought I'd ask a few questions, make the guy feel better about the whole thing, and then put it to rest."

"But it didn't go down that way."

"No, it didn't. Seems like the more questions I asked, the more the story didn't make sense."

"And you just had to know why, is that it?"

"It's not just that. Something stuck in my craw is all, wiggling around there, getting me all bothered."

Queeney pulled a gasper from the deck in his pocket, then offered me one. I passed. He tore a match from a book and struck it against the book, lit the end, dropped the match on the table, then returned his attention to me. Now I understood why the top of the table looked like a teenager's face.

"That's the saddest story I ever heard," he said.

"It was for Margaret Lee Paige, and likely for Moses Jones as well."

The door opened and in walked O'Malley cradling two cups of Joe. He set one down next to Queeney and pushed the other over to me, hard enough to make the liquid splash over the sides. Did I mention how much I disliked the man?

He took a seat next to Queeney.

Queeney tried his Joe. "So, what was this thing that got you all Jonesed up?" he asked.

"Everything points to a bit of a love triangle between Moses, Margaret Lee Paige, and another man—likely Grafton Freeman, with Paige as the fulcrum point. Far as I can tell, she was likely playing one man against the other."

O'Malley chimed in. "Some gumshoe. This ain't nothin' new." Then to Queeney he asked, "Can't we just skip to the part where we charge him and throw him in the can?"

"Well," I continued, "if you knew this information, then why didn't it bother you that Paige lay dead on the slab?"

"What are you talking about?" O'Malley sniped.

"Bird gets his tailfeathers clipped by another goose over some dolly, he usually goes after the goose, not the dolly."

Queeney flashed O'Malley a look, one you didn't have to be The Great Alexander to understand.

"I needed to find the goose," I said to Queeney. "That led me to a pug by the name of Booker Percy. He hooked me with a line about knowing Grafton's location and being willing to take me to him, but first he wanted to stop at a gym."

"Gym?" Queeney asked.

"Johnny Tocco's over on Charleston," I said. "I used to wear the gloves a bit back home. I guess I just got caught up in the moment, the smell of the canvas and all. The next thing I knew, I was in the ring, fighting for my life. Then it was lights out. I woke up in the desert next to Grafton laid out all business like. That's when O'Malley showed. Look, I wasn't trying to step on any delicate toes, and I certainly wasn't getting anywhere with anything I was asking, and, to tell the truth, I wasn't expecting to. I was just doing a good deed for a friend."

I left out the part about Theo coming to the Sands or her revelation that Moses and Grafton were actually friends. I wasn't sure I believed that last part, and I wasn't willing to tell O'Malley any more than I needed.

"A real boy scout, eh?" O'Malley said.

"Something like that," I said. "For all I know, Moses pulled the trigger."

"What do you mean by that?" Queeney asked.

It was a strange question and I'm sure my face reflected its strangeness. "Pulled the trigger?" I repeated. "You know," I molded my hand into the shape of a gun, pointed the finger at my temple, and dropped the hammer with my thumb, "pulled the trigger. Did the dirty deed. What do you call it?"

It was Queeney's turn to be quiet.

I studied the man for a moment, while I let a few

thoughts take root in my head. As my father could attest, it isn't always fertile ground up there, but every so often, when the stars align, something sticks. Queeney was clearly sending me a clue. Whether he meant to or not, wasn't as clear.

"So where do we stand with this little ditty?" I asked. "A gun of mine killed a man. A gun to which I wasn't affixed at the time."

"So says you," O'Malley stated. "What I got is a dead man, the gat that killed the man, and the man who owns the gat. Sounds like an easy one for me to present to the DA."

"Except for the fact that your dead man was killed at some other location than where he was found and the man who owned the gun—the one who would've had to carry a dead body out into the desert—was foolish enough not to take a getaway vehicle with him, but decided to wait shoeless for the cops to nab him, and, on top of that, was also foolish enough to not simply rid the scene of the murder weapon." I was going to mention the missing prints, but thought better of it.

Queeney rubbed his fingers across the red nubs of hair on his chin. "Someone's trying to put a scare into you," he said. "I don't suppose you know who that might be?"

"I have an idea," I said.

"This Percy character?"

I shook my head. "He's not that clever."

"One you're willing to share?"

"Not just yet."

TWENTY-NINE

I SAT THERE with nothing to keep me company but an empty cup of Joe. A bluebottle had come in with a sense of urgency, one which pulled both Queeney and O'Malley from their respective chairs. Those chairs now sat empty in front of me. I tried to relax, but it's hard to do when looking down the barrel of a murder rap. All I could do was hope that calmer head would prevail. Of course, had I listened to those calmer heads in the first place, I wouldn't be in this predicament.

I adjusted my position in the chair over and over again, searching for just the right spot. The hard wood made my side hurt even more, but, after all, I got what I deserved. All I had intended to do was ask a few questions to satisfy the curiosity of a friend and what had it gotten me? Stern looks, contrary stories, a beat down, my job threatened, and a murder rap. I should have listened to my big toe and turned Garwood down the moment he asked me.

Still, the setup stuck in my craw and the more I thought about it, the angrier I got. I was about to take that anger out on a bunch of innocent furniture when the door suddenly opened and in walked Queeney with a suit I didn't recognize. He was a tall, slender man dressed in a tailored, navy-blue, single-breasted suit with wide lapels and no display handkerchief. His matching tie was held in place against his white shirt with a silver collar pin. A fedora sat askew atop his head. He was a right tidy fellow, but that's not what stood out. It was the color of his skin that caught my attention.

Queeney and the suit took the only two available seats. I turned to face them.

"This is Special Agent James E. Amos," Queeney said. "He's with the Bureau."

I looked hard at Queeney. "You know where I stand," I said. "If you're looking for me to cut a deal . . ."

"Just shut up and listen," Queeney said.

The G-man removed his lid, then put it and his clasped hands on the table in front of him. "I understand you discovered the body of Grafton Freeman," he said, as calmly as you please.

"Discovered?" I asked. "I guess you could put it that way."

"How would you put it?"

I didn't like that question. It sounded too much like a setup to me. One of those questions that if answered, put you in more hot water than you were already in. "That sounds about right," I said.

"I understand you were looking for Mr. Freeman."

"That's right," I said.

"And why was that?"

"His girlfriend told me he was missing."

"Are you a private detective, Mr. Rossi?"

"No," I admitted. "I didn't know you had to be one to ask questions?"

"You don't. So long as you're not getting paid to ask them."

"Look, why don't we cut to the chase Special Agent Amos and you tell me why you're here? You seem like an intelligent man. You must know this was all just a setup."

Special Agent Amos reached into the pocket of his suit coat and produced a satchel of folded paper—one that looked disturbingly familiar. "Know what this is?" he asked.

I shook my head.

"Cut the act, Rossi," Queeney said. "I know you ran the rule through on Freeman. You want to get out of this in one piece, you'd better start spillin' and spillin' it right."

I took a deep breath and let it out through my nose. "All right," I said. "I frisked him. You wake up next to a dead man, you get a little curious about who he is."

"He had this packet on him?" Special Agent Amos asked.

I nodded.

"You didn't put it there?"

"Don't make me get offended," I said.

"This is a packet of opium, Mr. Rossi. It was the evidence we needed to break up an opium ring operating here on the West Side."

The realization hit me like a slider. "Grafton was working for you?"

Special Agent Amos nodded. "The man you knew as Grafton Freeman was an undercover agent with the Bureau of Investigation. He was brought in to help us bust the opium ring. We had him selling marijuana to get noticed."

"I guess it worked."

"Don't get wise," Queeney admonished.

"We figured it would give him a way in. He was on his way to us with the evidence and the information we needed to break the case when he disappeared."

"Well I'll be," I said, not knowing what else to say. Then I remembered Finger's question, asking if I had spoken to a G-Man and it all began to come clear. Somehow, Grafton's cover had been blown, and the mob found out just who he was. And now, here was I, in the hot seat.

"And you think I whacked him?" I asked.

Special Agent Amos shook his head. "No, but we think you know who did."

THIRTY

FOR THE NEXT three hours, I told Special Agent Amos everything I knew about the case. This time they had me over a barrel and I was forced to give up Garwood's name. He was not really a client, so I didn't have any standing to protect him—besides, he's the one who got me into this whole mess. Still, I gave the name reluctantly and wasn't any too happy about it.

While I did tell him most of it all, I didn't tell him about Fingers' part in the whole thing—unsure myself how much of a hand he had in the matter, and when he asked me who had my gat, I pled ignorance. That was a matter I intended to handle myself. There would be time to involve Sal if the need presented itself.

The way the feds saw it, whoever whacked Grafton was also his connection to the opium. What they apparently didn't know was that the man they had locked in their holding cell could've likely given them more information than I ever could. But if they weren't going to catch that, it certainly wasn't my job to catch it for them, so I kept my trap shut.

When I was finished, I was allowed to leave, shoeless and with no lid or coat, my mood as sour as week-old buttermilk.

"Stay local," Queeney warned me before he let me go. "This ain't over yet."

After I was escorted out of the police station, I was left to my own devices to find my way home. My foot and side were both a bit tender, something brought to mind with every step I took. I limped my way about half a block when I got the distinct feeling I was being followed. A slow-moving boiler was crawling up the street behind me, matching me tire-per-step. There was nowhere to run, not that I was in any condition to do so, and being in no mood for games, I decided to wait and let the thing catch up to me.

When it rolled to a stop, I bent down to have a look inside. Behind the wheel was a twenty-something ebony beauty with deep brown eyes and hair to match. Her curls were partially tucked into a newsboy cap and the collar of her blouse was pinned high enough that it rose above the collar of her brown leather jacket. She smiled shrewdly.

"Want a ride?"

"No thanks," I said. "I think I've already been taken for one."

"You sure? How far do you expect to get with no shoes?"

I glanced down at my bare feet. My toes wiggled back at me. "Oh, don't worry," I said. "I haven't far to go." I turned and started to walk away.

She called out: "I hear you're looking for Grafton Freeman."

"*Was* looking for Grafton," I said as I walked. "Found him."

"Oh?" she said, maintaining a position next to me. "Care to share?"

I chuckled, but kept moving.

"You raised quite a stir," she said. "But what did you expect? A white man sticking his nose where it don't belong. You're lucky I came along."

I stopped and gave her my full attention. "Look kitten, I don't know who you are or why you're tailing me, but I've had a long day and all I want to do is go home, take a shower, find my car, and maybe grab some grub."

"I can take you to your car."

"You know where it is?" I asked.

"No, but I'm sure I can help you find it."

"Thanks, but no thanks. I think I'd do better on my own." I said and started once again down the block, keeping a nice, steady limp.

She continued to follow. "How's that worked out for you so far?"

It was a good point, but I'd already gotten some points tonight and I didn't like this one any better than I liked those.

"What's in it for you, sister? What do you shake them down for?"

"It's not like that," she said. "We have a common interest is all."

"Oh? You get beat up today too?"

"No, but I need to find Grafton."

"Try the morgue," I said.

The news brought her and her vehicle to a sudden stop. I followed suit, took a deep breath, and went to her.

She was staring straight ahead, hands on the wheel, as if she seen a ghost. Not as much distraught, as confused.

"You on the up and up?" she asked sincerely.

I assured her I was.

"How?"

"Pill to the chest," I said, leaning on the door. "What's your interest in this, sister?"

"Why don't you just get in and I'll tell you. I don't bite."

I opened the door and climbed into the seat next to her. It wasn't the first stupid decision I'd made that day, and I had a feeling it wouldn't be the last.

"Maybe we should start with names," she said. "Mine's Mosley, Isis Coffey Mosley."

She extended her hand. I took it. It was soft, but firm. "Rossi," I said. "Max Rossi."

"Where can I take you, Max Rossi?"

"Down to Seventh and Bridger," I said. "A little white stucco number with a tiled roof and curved entry."

The car began to move forward. "You own the place?" Mosely asked.

I shook my head. "Renting. Now why don't you tell me about your involvement with Grafton?"

"My involvement isn't so much with Grafton as it is with Moses," she said.

That caught my attention.

"You know Moses?"

She shook her head. "Never met the guy, but I know his girl, Meriday. She hired me to look into the singer's murder."

"Hired?" I asked, incredulously.

Mosely clicked her tongue and shook her head. "I suppose you're one of those eggs who thinks a woman's place is in the home."

"I think no such thing," I assured her. "Women have just as much right to make a fool of themselves as men do."

"Oh, so you think a woman is foolish for working?" she asked, but it sounded more like a statement.

"Perhaps we should start over," I suggested. "What is it that you do for a living?"

"The same thing you do."

"Drink and play poker?"

"What? No. What are you talking about?"

"Never mind," I said, then asked. "What is it you think I do?"

"You're a gumshoe. A private dick."

"Hardly," I said. "I'm the house dick for the Sands, nothing more."

"Then how did you get involved in this?" she asked.

"I'm not involved in this," I assured her.

"Could've fooled me."

As she approached Seventh, I told her to turn and then pointed out the house that was my current abode. She pulled her car into the empty carport, the one where a bright red Roadmaster should have been parked, and kept the engine running.

"Would you like to come in?" I asked.

"Really? You want me to come inside?"

"Of course," I said.

"You want me to come inside? Your house?" she repeated.

"Yes," I said. "Why wouldn't I want you to come inside?"

"Because most white people don't want me anywhere near their house unless I'm wearing a maid's uniform."

"That's ridiculous," I said. "Come in if you want. If not, then wait here. But I'm going to be awhile."

She killed the engine, got out, then followed me to the front door. I retrieved the spare key from its hiding place—don't ask where it was, I won't tell you—and let her in first. She studied me as she passed.

"Where'd you say you was from?" she asked.

"I didn't."

She let that pass while she had a look about the place.

"Meet with your approval?" I asked.

She nodded and continued her inspection. "You sure are the strangest white man I ever knew," she said. "Inviting a colored girl into your home like this."

"I don't bite," I assured her. "You gonna be okay while I take a shower?" I asked.

"I'll manage."

I pointed my guest to the kitchen and instructed her to help herself while I scuddled off to my room, grabbed a change of clothes, and brought them with me to the bathroom. I took my time in the shower, letting the warm water revitalize me while I collected my thoughts. I wondered what the dame in my living room knew about the whole thing. Did she know about Moses' relationship to Margaret, about the fight she and Meriday had in the dressing room, or about the chumminess Theodosia claimed the two men shared? I also wondered if she knew if Grafton shared that same chumminess with Margaret? But most of all, I wondered why Meriday was so keen on pinning this rap on Grafton.

My biggest concern, however, was what to do next. I had received a clear as a bell warning from Fingers to stay out of the whole thing, but did I listen? No, I let a pair of brown eyes talk me into doing something I never should have done. I asked more questions—ones I never should have asked, in a place I never should have been, and then I got questions asked of me. I wondered *how long would it take Fingers to find that out*? If he didn't know already.

When I finished my shower, I dried myself off and had a look at the damage in the mirror. My eye was a deep purple, and my lip had a split in it big enough to build a bridge across. A bruise on my cheek matched the one under my eye, and there was a nice gash on the bridge of my nose. A large and rather purple bruise was beginning to form on my side. If only my mother could see me now.

I slipped on a pair of tan suit pants, buttoned up a cream shirt, and wrapped a tie around my neck like a respectable person. My head was already in a noose, so what could a tie hurt? I placed a display handkerchief in the pocket of my suit coat and brought it, and myself, out into the living room to face the music.

Isis Coffey Mosely was sitting on the couch, legs crossed, a cup in her hand. The strong aroma of coffee floated in the air above her head. It was a surprise to me. I didn't even know I had coffee, let alone a coffee maker. Besides her leather jacket and newsboy cap, she had on what appeared to be a pair of men's pants. The surprises never end.

I took a seat across from her. "Tell me, Miss Mosely, why are you here?"

"I told you, Meriday hired me to look into the singer's murder."

"Isn't that a matter for the bluebottles?"

"Meriday believes they have the wrong man?"

"And what about you? What do you believe?"

She uncrossed her legs and leaned forward. "I believe you're stalling, trying to find out what I know," she paused, "and what I'm willing to tell you."

I smiled despite myself. "What are you willing to tell me?"

"Look, we both have limits here. You're not going to get very far on the west side and me, well, in this town, the color of my skin stops me from going anywhere else. You know how it is. Las Vegas is a town of whities. Sure, we're allowed to work in the casinos—well, the back of the house, anyway. They put us in the kitchens and laundry rooms, as cooks, maids, janitors, and porters. Just so long as we're not seen.

"We light up the marquees, of course. We just can't go into the casino afterward. Did you know that Nat King Cole once tried to enter the same casino he performed in and was stopped at the door by the doorman? 'I don't care if you're Jesus Christ,' the doorman told him: 'You stay out.' Sammy Davis Jr. once took a swim in a 'whites only' swimming pool. The manager drained the pool afterward and had it cleaned."

I didn't doubt what she said, but it was still strange to me. I hadn't grown up that way. In all my time working with and being around my father, he only ever distinguished people in one of two categories: dead or alive. That was how he saw the world. Occupational hazard, I guess. Everyone on either side was on an equal playing field; unless you were a fool—my father didn't suffer fools easily—dead or alive.

"You think it's only the mob who doesn't want us here? You think that's the reason they don't let us in the front door? Boy, you are thick."

"Why don't you enlighten me?"

"Nevada may be out West," Mosley said, "but we might just as well be in the Jim Crow South. You're in the Mississippi of the West, Rossi, with all the rules, customs, and trappings of anywhere in the South. Who do you think built Hiway 91? It wasn't the mob—they just took advantage of a good thing. It was the oilmen. Texas oilmen, to be exact. People like your Jake Freeman opened hotels and casinos, then filled them with their southern buddies who brought with them their southern prejudices. Las Vegas is a backward town. Backward in its attitude toward colored folk and backward in how it views civil rights."

She suddenly changed her manner of speaking, continuing in a thick, mocking accent. "Day don't wants us sooties in the casinos cause day's afraid we'll spook all the decent white folk."

She placed her cup on the table in front of her. "What do you expect to accomplish, Mr. Rossi? Do you think you can just ride in here with your big, fancy car and save us poor ol' colored folk? Is that what you think?"

I didn't answer.

"We can help each other. I can ask questions where you can't and you can go to areas beyond my reach. This could benefit us both."

"Except for one thing," I said. "I'm not a private dick, and this isn't my case."

"Yet you spent most of the night in the can."

It was a fair point.

"How'd you know where to find me?" I asked.

"That goober sitting at the bar, the one you tried to buy a drink for, he's my brother. He saw you leave with Percy."

"You know Percy?"

"Everyone knows Percy," she said. "He's the local dealer."

"Dealer?" I asked about three seconds before it hit me. "Drug dealer?"

"What other kind is there?"

I stood and grabbed my coat. "Let's go," I said, placing my lid into position. "I need my car."

THIRTY-ONE

ISIS MOSELY FOLLOWED me out the door and to her car. Moses was an addict, more than just a hophead. It was likely opium had messed up his career more than once, and whatever happened between him and Margaret Lee Paige, I was willing to bet, opium had something to do with that as well. I hadn't worried much about where he'd gotten the drugs before—it didn't seem to matter— but Moses' opium addiction, Percy's fist in my face, and me waking up next to a stiff offed with my gat was too much of a coincidence.

"You know where Johnny Tocco's is?" I asked.

She nodded.

"Good, take me there."

She started the car, backed out into the street, then headed south. "Why d'you want to go there?"

"It's where this all started. It's where I got this face."

"Your car ain't gonna be there."

"Oh? How's that?"

"Cause if that's where I handed you a beating, I certainly wouldn't leave your car there as evidence."

"Just take me there," I said. I was developing a full head of steam and unwilling to concede her point, no matter how sound it was.

We drove in silence for several blocks before she asked me her next question. "And what happens when we get there? You shining me on?"

"How do you know your client didn't kill Paige?" I asked. "Word on the street is that her man, Moses, was making time with Paige. Did Meriday tell you that little jewel of information when she hired you?"

She paused. "No, but she told me you were a jerk. She nailed that one."

I couldn't argue the point.

"If Meriday did kill Paige, why would she hire me?"

"For show," I said. "She knew you, being colored, would face certain limitations, as you have already so rightly pointed out. Limitations that would hinder your progression in the case. But hiring you, she could still keep a pulse on the goings on."

She thought about that a bit.

As she pulled her boiler into the parking area behind the gym, I felt a pit starting to form in my stomach. It was a pit I knew all too well; the same one that used to show before every fight I ever had. I'd learned to ignore the thing, pretend it wasn't real. It liked to remind me it was.

It didn't stop me.

I charged into the place, looking for Tocco. Isis followed behind. I found him in the far corner, near the heavy bag, showing a gloved boxer how to jab. I walked right up to the man with the intention of turning him on his heels, but when I took hold of his arm, I quickly discovered my mistake. Johnny Tocco was a thick man; ribbons of muscle hid under his sweat clothes. It was like trying to turn a bull.

He looked at my hand, then turned to me, showing his displeasure.

"What goes on?" I demanded.

It took him a second, but the recognition set in. "Let's talk outside," he said.

"Right here's just fine with me," I countered.

My raised voice cast a stillness over the entire gym. Speed bags stopped speeding, jump ropes stopped jumping, and the two heavyweights in the ring turned their attentions away from each other and directed them toward me.

"Let's talk outside," Tocco repeated, a bit more forcefully.

Perhaps he had a point.

I followed the man outside. Isis came with us.

"I'm sorry about what happened," he offered. "I had no idea what Percy was up to. He's banned from my gym. I only let him in because he was with you. I should have stuck to my instincts." He examined my kisser. "I hope he didn't hurt you."

"Hurt me?" I asked. "No, he didn't hurt me. He just set me up for a murder rap is all."

Tocco was confused.

"After he knocked me cold here, he took me to the desert—well, he or someone else—and deposited me next to a right fine stiff. Then he called the police and told them where to find me."

"I had nothing to do with that," Tocco said, forcefully. "I told him to take you to the hospital."

"But you didn't try to revive me, did you?"

"Look, I don't want no part of Percy and all he's into. He's done nothing but throw away his life. He ain't welcome here no how, neither is that other guy. He's out too." Tocco moved to the door. "I'm sorry for what happened to you, but it doesn't involve me."

"What do you mean, 'all he's into?'" I asked.

"I don't know what your deal is with Percy, but it's best you stay away from him. He ain't no good. Do you know what it's like to have a shot at the big time? You have any idea how many kids come into this gym looking to make a name for themselves? Tryin' to escape their lives, seeing boxing as their only way out? For every one kid that makes it, forty or more don't. The one who gets that shot takes a slot—one that ain't now available to anyone else. He has a responsibility to make it, or at least give it his best try. You don't squander them shots. You carry the hopes of every kid in this place on your gloves.

"Booker Percy got that shot and he threw it away. He had a right that could knock you into next week, and he had guts—plenty a guts. But he was a hothead and he let it get the better of him. Then he was nothin'. He threw fights and he let every one of these kids down."

"You knew he threw them?" I asked.

"Of course I knew. Percy didn't just have a great right, he could take a punch like nobody's business. Suddenly he develops a glass jaw? Gets taken out by shots that barely connect? You can't hide that from a trainer."

Tocco's expression suddenly saddened, as if he was paying penance for an egregious sin—one he hadn't committed.

"He get in with the mob?" I asked.

Tocco nodded.

"And drugs?"

"That too," he said, but I could tell it hurt him to say it. Here was a kid, one he had pinned so many hopes and dreams on. Not for himself, but for all the others in the gym who might dream of climbing out of their scornful existence and make something of themselves. How could it not hurt?

"You know where I can find him?" I asked.

Tocco didn't answer. He just shook his head, lowered his gaze, then headed back inside. Percy was lost to the world and Tocco didn't know whether to pity the man or to hate him.

"C'mon," I said to Isis. "I think I know where my car is."

THIRTY-TWO

I HAD A feeling I knew who'd set me up. After all, he had my gun, and this last little bit of information sealed the deal for me. Besides doing New York's bidding, Sal had his hands in prostitution, and now I was sure his mitt was into drugs as well. It was high time Manella and I came to a little understanding—a come to Jesus, so to speak. Unfortunately, that would have to wait. I had a job to finish first.

I told Isis to take me to the Sands. It was where my car would be. The office wasn't the only message I'd been sent. Since I chose not to listen, a stronger one had been ordered, one that put me square in the sights of Detective O'Malley and a murder rap.

When we arrived at the Sands, as expected, my Roadmaster was sitting in my spot, pretty as you please. Isis stopped by the car and I got out. There wasn't a scratch on the thing. In fact, it had been polished, all nice and clean. My lid—the one my grandfather gave me—rested on the front seat. My shoes and socks were on the floorboard and the keys in the ignition.

The message was loud and clear. I was the Sands' man.

I turned to my chauffer. "I appreciate the ride," I said, "but I'm done here."

"What do you mean, you're done?"

"I mean, this case has nothing to do with me. All it's doing is putting my life and my livelihood in danger. Meriday is just as likely to have offed Margaret Lee Paige as Moses."

Isis was not pleased. "Then who killed Grafton?" she asked. "Moses was in the can so he couldn't have done it, and Meriday had no reason to kill him."

"No reason that you know of," I said. "But then again, you didn't know Paige was playing tummy tickle with her man." She probably didn't know Moses was on the pipe either, but I chose not to push that point. "Look, I'm about as useless as a concrete life vest in this whole thing. I'm out of this charade, and if you know what's good for you, you'll be out of it too."

"It's easy for you to give up on this. You're white," she said, forcefully. "But that man in the cell, the one accused of murdering a white woman, isn't. And there isn't a chance in hell he's gonna get a fair shake."

"Don't be a bunny," I said. "Cheese it. Go home and let the bluebottles do their job."

She glared at me. "Stupid Ofay," she said, then hit the gas and sped off. I watched as she skidded out onto the street, then headed off down the highway. I reached into my Roadmaster, pulled the keys from the ignition, and placed them back in my pocket where they belonged. Then I closed the door and headed inside.

The casino was slow, but it was, after all, Monday morning and who gambles on a Monday? That question was answered when I went to the baccarat table. There sat the Texan in another fancy suit, his twenty-gallon atop his head, a cigar in his beak. To his left sat Madame Wu in a bright green silk number, with a high collar. The dress, which traveled the entire length of her body, was ordained with cherry blossoms. Her hair was pulled back and resting to one side of her head was a small, black hat that was almost indistinguishable from her jet black hair. A net fell from the hat, partially covering her porcelain face. Baubles, shaped like miniature fans, hung from her ears.

She was exquisite.

I decided not to approach the table this time, instead choosing to sit at a slot machine a short distance away. I wanted to see what was happening, but not at the table, and not from above. A discrete distance would better serve my purposes. I sat there watching the play for the better part of an hour. The Texan matched Madame Wu's play hand-for-hand. Sometimes she lost, but mostly she won. If she was cheating, I couldn't see it.

I got up and switched my seat to another machine, hoping a change of angle would make a difference. That's when I noticed the porkpie hat—the same one from the night before. The same one whom I played poker with before we both switched to baccarat, though not at the same time. He was still as nervous as ever, still tapping the table, waiting for that bus.

Madame Wu noticed it too. "Could you please stop that?" she asked with disdain. "I find it quite obnoxious. I find *you* quite obnoxious."

The porkpie hat pulled his hand from the table, like a child scolded by a parent.

The dealer started to turn over the cards, but before he did, Madame Wu changed her bet, just as she had the night before, just as she had many times today as well. The dealer allowed the change, but it was to his detriment, as she won the hand. The Texan, who had changed his bet with her, did as well.

The porkpie hat lost.

Almost every time Madame Wu changed hands, she won. What were the odds of that? I wondered. The dealer took the cards and began to shuffle. I have to admit that when playing the Bees, I don't always pay much attention to the dealer's face. But I do watch very closely how they handle the cards, as handling the cards is the most important part of the dealer's job. So as I watched this man stumble through the deal, I glanced up at his cleft chin and realized I'd seen him before.

I rose from my seat and headed to the front desk. I picked up the blower and asked to be connected to surveillance. When the attendant answered, I asked for Charlie.

"That dealer on baccarat," I said when he answered. "He's the same from the other night, isn't he?"

There was silence.

"Charlie?"

"I'm not supposed to speak with you, Mr. Rossi," he said.

"Mr. Rossi?" I asked. "What's going on Charlie?"

"I'm not supposed to speak with you," he repeated.

"Says who?"

"Mr. Abbandandolo."

"Look Charlie, I . . ."

Charlie cut me off. "I have to go, Mr. Rossi."

"Charlie, wait!" I implored. "Just answer one question. Did Madame Wu request the dealer who's on the table now?"

Silence.

I waited.

"Yes," he finally said, and hung up.

I put down the receiver and marched myself up to Fingers' office on the mezzanine loaded for bear. Leona stopped me in my tracks.

"Hold on there, Buster. Where do you think you're going?"

"Is Fing . . . Frank. Is Frank in?"

"Mr. Abbandandolo is not available at the moment. Perhaps you would like to make an appointment, Mr. Rossi."

"You too?" I asked.

She grinned. "Why, Mr. Rossi, whatever do you mean?"

I could tell she was enjoying this little turn of events.

"Perhaps you should check your office," she said, then made a face as if she had misspoken. "Oh wait, you don't have an office, do you?"

I turned and left, heading to the office I had been shown just the day before. Both my name and my title had been removed. Easy come, easy go.

I didn't bother going back to Leona's office. What good would it have done? I needed to see a friendly face and knew just where to find one. I snuck back through the employee's cafeteria to the backstage entrance. Nobody stopped me, but I had learned a long time ago that if you act like you know what you're doing, people will let you do it without hassle.

The afternoon show wouldn't have started yet, so I knew my Virginia would be able to give five or so minutes without issue. I popped my head in and found the seamstress sewing away. She looked up briefly and poked her thumb toward the dressing room door. I tipped my lid, knocked on the door, and waited.

It opened only moments later, and I was greeted by a beautifully tall, black-haired Oriental woman with porcelain skin, one who could have rivaled my Virginia with her legs alone. I thought I knew all the girls in the show, but was embarrassed to admit the name of this one escaped me.

"Is Virginia available?" I asked.

She chuckled. I don't know why.

"Could you please tell her Max is here?"

She chuckled again, only this time, the seamstress joined her. Apparently, there was a secret I wasn't in on. But I didn't have time for secrets, or for games.

"Look, is Virgin . . ."

"It's me, Max."

"Virginia?" I asked, surprised.

She laughed. "Pretty good trick, huh?"

"But . . ."

"Olivia is still ill, and I'm still taking her part."

I was speechless.

She gave me a spin. "Don't ya just love it?"

"Indeed," I said. "If I hadn't seen it with my own eyes."

"It's amazing what makeup can do."

"Isn't it though?" And that's when it hit me; at that very moment. *It's amazing what makeup can do.* "I gotta go, Sugar," I said.

"Go? But you just got here. Is everything okay?"

"No, but it will be," I said, and left as quickly as I came.

THIRTY-THREE

I HEADED STRAIGHT back to the baccarat table just to make sure all the players were still in place. Then I headed over to the front desk and called surveillance.

"Look," I said when Charlie answered, "I know you're not supposed to talk to me, but I have a hunch I know what's going on at that baccarat table. So just listen. I think the jasper in the porkpie hat is signaling Madame Wu to either keep her bet or to change it. I think he's somehow seeing the cards. That dealer is sloppy. It's no coincidence Madame Wu requested him. All I need you to do is keep an eye on the table and have security in the area in case the porkpie bolts. I'm headed back to the table now."

I hung up before Charlie could answer, not wanting to give him a chance to protest. I headed to the cage and found a supervisor—one who hadn't yet been corrupted. I inquired as to Madame's Wu's stake—the five large she'd deposited when she first arrived. He told me she had taken back all of her five grand just last night. It didn't surprise me.

Back at the baccarat table, I nestled into a nearby seat behind a slot machine where I could keep an eye on the porkpie hat. His hand was back on the table and he was tapping away. This time, I focused on his fingers. His tap seemed to be restrained to the first two fingers. The fingers in sync to some unheard rhythm, alternating up and down. Up and down. Up and down.

Then, every so often, the middle finger would raise higher than the first finger, and when it did, the tapping became more irregular—more pronounced. I didn't catch it at first, but then I realized that every time the finger raised, every time the tapping became irregular, Madame Wu switched her bet. It was a signal and the porkpie hat was the signalman.

I turned my attention to the dealer, listing to the tapping as he dealt. He was sloppy with the cards, not protecting them like a good deal dealer ought to. It was the angle at which he held the deck. Most dealers use the mechanic's grip, holding the deck from below with the thumb on the top of the deck, the first finger at the front, and the remaining fingers along the side. With this grip, the front of the deck is slanted downward to help the cards slid off the deck and make the deal smoother.

But this dealer held the deck with the front higher than the back. Instead of sliding out the cards, he pulled each one from the deck, and when he did, he lifted the edge of the card ever so slightly. I watched hand after hand and every time the porkpie's tapping became irregular, it coincided with the dealing of the cards. The porkpie was reading the cards. He knew what was dealt with each hand.

Madam Wu's chastisement had been a ruse to make the tapping seem habitual and annoying. She did it every so often just to keep the ruse going.

I flagged down a cocktail waitress and asked for a shot of whiskey and a glass of water without ice. When it arrived, I handed her a dollar and sent her on her way with a smile. I stood, downed the Whiskey, then made my lid crooked on my head. I held up the glass of water and stumbled over to the baccarat table.

"Hey, whass goin' on here?" I said as I arrived. I turned toward Madame Wu. "Well, you're a looker, ain't ya?"

"You're drunk," she said.

The Texan spoke up. "You oughtta be on your way, Mister. Leave this young lady alone."

"Oh, I don wan nothin'" I slurred. "She's yust pretty s'all. Ain't ya?" I asked.

As I'd hoped, the Texan took hold of my arm. But before he could get too good a grip, I pulled back and as I did, I let the water fly from my glass. It slapped Madam Wu in the face and cascaded down her dress.

She yelled out.

The Texan stood and took a jab at me. I pulled back, allowing the fist to connect, but not with full force. And as I fell backward, I reached out and took hold of Madame Wu's hat, which, as I'd hoped, was attacked to her jet black wig. I fell to the floor, hair in hand, as Madame Wu's makeup started to run down her face.

The porkpie hat bolted, but didn't make it very far before landing in the arms of security. I stood, rubbed my chin, and moved over to Madame Wu. As the water dripped down her cheeks, her once almond-shaped eyes had turned round and her porcelain skin was showing signs of color slightly darker than snow white. Her red hair was pulled up tightly, the way women do before they put on wigs.

"What have you done?" she demanded. The water

took away more than just her makeup, it took away her accent as well.

"Why Madame Wu," I said. "You seem to be . . . melting."

"Now see here," Latisse said, but his protest ceased when security stepped in behind me.

Two officers stepped up to Madame Wu and took hold of her arms. She pulled herself free, straightened her dress, and regained her posture, as well as her accent. She looked directly at me and put out her hand.

"My affects," she said.

I handed her the wig and hat. She ran her fingers through the hair, then slid the thing back onto her head, adjusting the hat into its proper position. She glared at me with distain, then raised her chin, before allowing security to escort her to whatever demise awaited.

The porkpie hat followed, an officer ahold of his arm.

One security officer remained. He followed me over to the baccarat table. The dealer was wide-eyed. "I guess you'd better go to," I said to him.

The pit boss nodded, as the dealer placed the cards solemnly down on the table and left with security. Without missing a beat, the pit boss pulled a dealer from a vacant table and placed her in front of the Texan. Nothing stops the games in Vegas.

I headed to the front desk and picked up the blower. Charlie answered on the first ring.

"How did you know?" he asked.

"Something had stuck in my craw from the moment I saw Madame Wu, but I couldn't put my finger on it. The porkpie hat sealed it for me. We played together on a poker table the night before; one with that same dealer. Then I saw him on the baccarat table with Madame Wu. Porkpie hat was the signalman."

"And the dealer? Is he in on it?"

"I doubt it. I think the porkpie was just looking for a sloppy dealer. Probably been scoping him out for a couple of days before Madame Wu made her appearance. She came in like a whale so as to be less noticeable. Nobody thinks twice when whales win big. She never even touched her stake."

"But how did you know she was in makeup?"

"Lucky guess. I went to the cage and found she had taken out her stake. My guess was she was about to hit and run. When we finally realized we'd been scammed—if we did realize—she'd a been out the door, a redheaded dolly, while all the while we'd've been searching for an Oriental. Pretty decent plan if you think about it."

"Mr. Abbandandolo will be pleased."

"A parting gift," I said and hung up. Then I climbed into my Roadmaster, pointed it to the police department, and waved my goodbye to the Sands. If Fingers didn't want me, I knew someone who did.

THIRTY-FOUR

I PARKED MY car in the spot marked for visitors and headed inside. At the desk sergeant's podium, I asked for the PI paperwork. The balding man in blue gave me the once over, raised an eyebrow, then opened a drawer to this left and pulled out the papers. I passed him my thanks, took the sheets, and scratched the essentials on the lines provided. When I finished, I took myself and the papers upstairs.

At the detective's bureau, I headed straight for Queeney's office. He was there, sitting behind his desk, Paul Bunyan without his Babe. He looked up at me and sighed.

I laid the paperwork on the desk in front of him. "What's this?" he asked.

"I suppose if I'm going to do this, I better do it right." I opened my wallet and laid down fifty berries on top of the papers.

"So you quit the Sands?" He asked.

"Something like that."

That got me a grunt. Queeney slid the paperwork and the cash into the top drawer of his desk, then went back to ignoring me.

"I'd like to see Moses again," I said.

He studied me a moment, then said, "Boy, you just don't give up, do you?"

"Why should I?" I asked. "You think Moses is gonna get a fair shake on his own?"

"Why? Because he's black?"

"That and the fact that O'Malley seems to think he's already got his man."

"Oh, you got something to prove he's wrong?" Queeney asked.

I stayed silent.

"That's what I thought," Queeney said, then went back to ignoring me.

"You know as well as I do that justice isn't blind," I said. "If it were, that kid wouldn't be sitting in a jail cell right now, having taken a beating, and waiting for O'Malley to do his job."

Queeney looked up at me. "Justice ain't blind," he said. "She's as prejudiced as anyone else. We all got some prejudice in us, don't we? Can you really say you aren't prejudiced in some way? You root for the Sox and hate the Yanks, don't cha? Don't we all want to hang out with people who are like us?"

"Sure, but how many coloreds are likely to be on Moses' jury?"

Queeney didn't have an answer for that one. Instead, he pushed his chair back and stood, towering over both me and his desk. He walked to the side, poked his head out the doorway and yelled for O'Malley.

When O'Malley arrived, Queeney introduced me as Las Vegas' newest private dick.

"I thought you were the Sand's man?" O'Malley said.

I didn't answer.

"Let him in to see Jones," Queeney said.

O'Malley sighed deeply. "You want to push the car out into traffic?" he said. "Be my guest." He motioned for me to go ahead of him.

"You two play nice," Queeney admonished, and took his seat.

Once we left Queeney's office, O'Malley took the lead. I followed him to the thick metal door with the little window. He stopped before he hit the buzzer.

"What do you expect to accomplish here, Rossi?" he asked.

"Just tryin' to square the thing," I said.

O'Malley humphed.

"Tell me, O'Malley, why are you so sure Moses did the deed?"

"I told ya, I got a dead body, and I got a witness. What more do I need?"

"You've got a witness, but it doesn't answer," I countered. "She's a drunk."

"And she's a pro skirt, so what? She saw what she saw, didn't she?"

"She witnesses the actual murder?"

O'Malley didn't answer. He just stood there grinning that same grin, the one that always makes me want to slap it off his unshaven mug.

"And the girlfriend? Did you even consider her? Maybe she pulled the trigger."

O'Malley laughed. "You're so far behind on this one,

Rossi, you'd need a two-day head start just to come in last."

O'Maley reached over to the buzzer and gave it a push. The uniform on the other side slid open the window, then seeing O'Malley, pressed the buzzer on his side, opening the door.

"Go say yer goodbyes," O'Malley said. "This one's headed for the chair."

O'Malley turned to leave but stopped when I asked if he had a gasper I could borrow.

"Didn't know you smoked," he said.

"I don't," I admitted. "Just trying it out for a friend."

O'Malley produced a pack of Luckys, pulled one from the foil, and tossed it to me. He followed it with a single wooden match.

As O'Malley walked away, I followed the uniform down the narrow hallway to Moses' cell. It looked the same as it did the last time I was here. Moses, however, did not. He was wrapped up in a thin prison blanket, clutching himself, shaking. He looked up at me with watery eyes, his face ashen, his forehead dotted with sweat.

"What you want?" he asked through trembling lips.

I nodded to the uniform, who left, locking the door behind him.

"I'm layin' down the hustle," I said.

His eyes widened, and he pulled himself upward. "You on the up and up?" he asked.

I shook my head.

His faced turned to anger. "Man, just go on and get yourself outta here," he barked as he slumped back down.

"How long since your last fix?" I asked.

He didn't answer.

I tried another tactic. "Why'd you lie to me?"

"What you talkin'? I don't know you from nobody."

"You saw me two days ago," I said. "Lied to me about your involvement with Margaret Lee Paige. Pretended not to know her outside of the Rouge. But that was all a lie, wasn't it, Moses? You know Miss Paige very well, don't you?"

"I know her some," he said.

"Come now, don't be modest. You and Miss Paige were a thing, weren't you?"

I produced the cigarette O'Malley gave me. Moses studied me for a moment, then snatched the offering. I struck the match on the bars and brought the flame to eager lips. He held the gasper to the flame, then sucked in deeply, filling his lungs with satisfaction. It seemed to revise him—for the moment, anyway. He pulled the thing from his mouth, examined it, and smiled.

"Thanks," he said.

I nodded. "Now, shall we try again?"

Moses took another long, slow drag. "I knew Margaret," he admitted. "We hung around a bit. Played the boogie woogie, if you know what I mean."

I knew what he meant.

The thought brought him a smile.

"And Grafton Freeman? He boogie woogie with Margaret too?" I asked.

His smile left as quickly as it came. "Why you want to know about Grafton?"

"Well, he replaced you, didn't he? When Margaret fired you? Is that why you killed him?"

A look of shock painted Moses' face. "What're you talkin' about, Mister?"

"Grafton Freeman's dead. A pill to the chest. Just like your Margaret. What happened, Moses? You find out she was two-timing you? Is that why you fought? Is that why she replaced you? What'd you do, Moses? Take out Grafton, then turn the gun on Margaret just for fun?"

Moses looked confused. "What you say, Mister? Grafton ain't dead."

"Oh, he's dead all right. Laying on a slab in the morgue, playing toe tag with your Margaret."

Moses' face flushed. "Now looky here," he said forcefully. "I didn't kill no Grafton Freeman."

"But you did kill Margaret, didn't you? Shot her dead."

The fluster turned back to confusion. "Margaret wasn't shot," he said. "She was strangled."

"Say again?"

"Margaret was strangled," he repeated. "I saw her, dead on the floor. Hand marks right around her neck."

"What do mean you saw her?"

Moses took another drag. The ashes at the tip of the cigarette formed a gray snake. It fell to his lap as he pulled the thing from his lips. He didn't seem to care.

"All right," he said. "I was in the bedroom, doing a little flyin', you know. I came out into the main room and there she was, all sprawled out on the floor." He paused as it replayed in his head.

"She was just . . . lyin' there," he finally said. "Her eyes as red as the devil's. Her lips . . ." He turned away, closed his eyes, and tried to squeeze out the memory. "I tried to see if she was breathing," he said, continuing. "I put my ear next to her mouth, but there was . . ." He shook his head. "There was nothing."

A tear streamed down his cheek.

"Did you call the police?" I asked, but I already knew the answer.

Moses looked startled. "What good would it've done? Call the police? A black man in a white woman's apartment?"

"What did you do?"

"Me? I got the hell out of there. Booked it on home." He looked at me intently. "I didn't kill Margaret," he said.

I matched his look. "If not you," I asked, "then who?"

Moses fell silent.

"What did you and Margaret fight about?" I asked.

Moses took the last drag of the smoke, savoring the moment. He burnt it right down to the filter, not wanting to waste a bit of it.

I waited.

He finally spoke. "We just fought is all. Meriday got wind of us and confronted Margaret in their dressing room. She turned wildcat and tried to snatch the hair from her head. Margaret was mad as all get out, and she let me have it."

"That why she fired you?"

He nodded.

"It wasn't the drugs?" I asked.

He told me it wasn't, but I didn't believe him. Moses was three or four days from his last fix and it was showing. That wasn't casual use. The man had a problem—a bad one. One that was seeping out of his pores.

"Margaret do drugs," I asked.

Moses glanced down at the floor. "Just a little juju," he said.

"Opium?"

"No, just the juju."

"Who's your supplier?"

He shook his head.

"Look chum, this isn't the time to get all quiet. Who's your supplier?"

When I didn't get an answer the second time, I went to Moses, took him by the collar, and yanked him up from the bunk. "Who's your supplier?"

Moses swung his head from side to side. "No," he said. "No. I can't tell you. They'll kill me. They'll kill me! THEY'LL KILL ME!"

I took hold of his shirt in one hand and slapped him across the face with the other. "Who's your supplier?" I demanded.

"No!" he cried out.

I brought the back of my hand across his face and then slapped him another.

He shook his head. Tears streamed down his face. I lifted my hand for a third round.

"Percy. It's Booker Percy," he succumbed.

"He give you drugs that night?" I asked.

He looked a man defeated. "Yes," he said. "He gave them to me that night."

I lowered Moses onto the bunk. "Right there in front of Margaret?" I asked.

He shook his head. "I slipped outside to smoke. I'd arranged for Percy to meet me there."

"Why'd she take you back?"

He shrugged. "I don't know. I promised her I'd break it off with Meriday. Stop the opium."

"Some promise," I said. "Guess it didn't last long."

Moses sat there, shoulders hunched, his face covered in the look of the lost. "It never does," he said softly. "She went into the kitchen to make us some eggs. I snuck into the bathroom, took out the pipe, and, well, you know."

"And when you came down?"

"I realized it'd been a while since she'd left and I went out to see what held her up."

"That's when you found her on the floor?"

He nodded. "I swear, she was like that when I came out of the bedroom. I didn't know what to do. I panicked."

"Anybody see you there?"

"Not that I know of."

"What about that nosey neighbor?"

"Who, Evelyn? Hell, she probably wasn't even home yet. She's a pro skirt. Stays out pretty late."

"She a drinker?"

"Yeah, she puts them down. I guess you have to, to do that job. You got another smoke?" he asked.

"I'll get you another if you're straight with me."

"I'll be straight," he said.

"Then you and Grafton? You really hate him?"

He shook his head quietly. "No. Grafton and I are friends. He was always trying to keep me on the straight and narrow. He even refused to play on Margaret's album."

"But you took a poke at him?"

"I did, but it was because I was frustrated is all. Margaret pulled him after me just to make me mad. I guess it worked."

"Margaret liked to make you mad, didn't she?"

He looked up at me, puzzled at first, but I could see it came to him. Still, he didn't answer. I decided to agitate him.

"She flirted with other men, didn't she? Played a little tummy tickle. Who'd she go after? Grafton? Did she like Grafton?"

"I don't know what you mean," he said, his hand beginning to shake.

I stepped closer. "Sure you do," I said, not letting up. "She spread out the honey. Liked to make you jealous. Embarrassed you in front of your bandmates. There's only one thing to do with a woman like that, right, Moses? A woman makes you look foolish, you need to show her the back of your hand, don't you? Don't you?"

"No."

"Don't you, Moses?" I said, then slapped my hands together, right near his ear, hoping it would startle him.

It did the trick.

"Yes!" he belted out. "She liked to flirt. Liked to get me riled up. I had to take her down a peg. I had too!"

"That's what happened, Moses, didn't it? You got into a row with Margaret that got out of hand. You slapped her, but it wasn't enough. She hadn't learned her lesson, so you needed a stronger message. You'd show her. You were the man. You took her by the throat and squeezed," I said, demonstrating with my hands. "You squeezed, didn't you, Moses? She needed a lesson. She needed to know who was boss. She needed to know her place?"

"No," he said.

I stepped even closer. "It's okay, Moses," I continued. "A dame needs to know her place. Margaret needed to know you were the boss. So you showed her that place, didn't you?"

"No."

"Didn't you?"

"No!" Moses cried out. "I couldn't ever do that to her. Not to Margaret. Not while she was . . ."

"Not while she was what?"

Moses slumped down and began to sob. "Pregnant," he said. "Margaret was pregnant."

It was a shot that came out of left field. "How do you know?" I asked.

"She told me."

"When?" I asked. Then I understood. "You didn't promise to go off the dope, did you? You were going to leave Margaret. Leave her because of what she was doing with the other men."

Moses nodded. "Grafton told me to leave her. Told me it wasn't right what I was doing to Meriday. He told me that Margaret was flirting with him and with Booker. I didn't believe him, but then I saw it for myself. What I said about the drugs before was true. She didn't like me doing the chandoo and threatened to leave me if I didn't stop. We got into a fight about the drugs and her flirtations. I gave her the back of my hand and told her I was going to leave. She begged me to stay."

"Said she was pregnant."

Moses nodded.

I called the uniform over. "You ready to beat it?" he asked.

"You smoke?"

"Yeah, I smoke. What's it to ya?"

I pulled out a five and pressed it between the bars. "How about you give me your pack?" I said.

"You gonna give it to that darkie?" he asked.

I bristled. "I'm gonna use it for a seat cushion," I said. "Now give me the pack."

The uniform studied me. He went for the bill. I pulled it back. "Unh-uh," I said. "The pack first."

He handed me the pack.

"And the matches."

"All I got is a Zippo," he protested.

"I'll return it," I said.

He handed me the Zippo and I slipped him the five. When he left, I tossed the pack to Moses. He wasted no time slipping another into his mouth. I flipped the top of the Zippo and pulled the roller with my thumb. Moses sucked in the flame.

"Where do we go from here?" Moses asked. He stared at me in earnest, hoping for an answer to a question that had no answers. Not yet anyway. I tossed the uniform the Zippo, and he opened the bars. The puzzle was beginning to come together, but one piece was still missing, and I was pretty sure I knew just where to find it.

THIRTY-FIVE

I POINTED MY Roadmaster toward the Diplomat Apartments and hit the gas, hoping a plan would come to mind before I got there. When I arrived, I parked, took out the lock pick set I kept in the glove compartment, and headed upstairs.

I knew how to pick a lock almost before I could form a complete sentence—something my father made sure I understood. While most kids were learning their ABC's, I was learning how to manipulate a tumbler to my will. My father devised a practice lock. Well, two really. One was a deadbolt lock and the other a simple old-fashioned doorknob lock. In my father's eyes, these were important skills.

I was willing to bet that while O'Malley and his crew had swept Margaret's apartment, it hadn't yet been cleared by the manager. That would have to wait until the trial—if there was one. I slid the tension wrench into the bottom of the keyway, then scrubbed the pins with the rake until the plug rotated. My father would make me practice this over and over again until I could scrub the pins well enough to rotate the plug on the first try. I guess that's what happens when you grow up in the house of a fixer for the mob.

Once I got past the lock, I slipped inside and stood a moment while my eyes adjusted to the dark. Another part of my training as a youth was crime scene evaluation—though that isn't what we called it. My father taught me the importance of understanding what happened on any scene you came upon. If you couldn't see what happened and determine how it happened, how could you possibly expect to clean it up? It was, in fact, my father who taught me to catch things others did not.

"Any clue unnoticed was a clue that could be used against someone," he would say. In his line of work, it was important to ensure all clues were noticed then made to disappear.

Keeping the lights off, I stepped to the side of the scene and studied what lay before me. There were definite signs of a struggle—ones even O'Malley would have noticed. A lamp lay broken on the floor and the coffee table had been overturned. I moved behind the couch, over to the chair and turned on a lamp that was resting on an end table. Then I reviewed the scene from a different angle, just as my father had taught me.

I turned my attention to the lamp on the floor. It was in several pieces, not as much broken as shattered. It was a small lamp—white porcelain with red roses painted on the front. The end table it likely rested upon was still in position. A matching one was under the lamp I had just turned on. In fact, that lamp was identical to the one that lay broken on the floor. I took hold of it and lifted the thing; it was light, but sturdy. Light enough that a woman could easily lift it, yet sturdy enough to do some damage.

I moved over, crouched down, and examined the pieces. The shards the porcelain created were sharp—razor sharp. As I looked them over, I spotted one that had a definite tinge of color along the edge. A color that came not from the red of the roses. No, this was a color I'd seen many times before. Blood.

There was indeed a struggle—one that had broken a lamp and resulted in a woman's death. But that lamp didn't break from falling off an end table. It had been used as a weapon, and I was willing to bet it was a defensive weapon.

I was still in the crouched position, examining the broken lamp, when the door suddenly flung open.

"What are you doing here?" a female voice demanded.

I looked up and saw Evelyn, bat in hand. She was dressed in high-waisted black and white gingham capri pants with a red halter top-style shirt. Her feet pressed into a matching pair of Mary Janes.

"Trying out for the Sox?" I asked.

It took her a second, but she seemed to recognize me. "Oh, it's you, handsome." She lowered the bat. "How'd you get in here?"

"Same way you did, through the front door."

She gave me a smirk. "Don't try that one on me."

I stood. "You work security for this place?" I asked, motioning to the bat.

She laid the bat against the wall. I moved in closer. Her hair was done up high, held in place with a red kerchief made to look like a bandana. I ran my hand down the side of her cheek. She smiled.

She pursed her lips. "You making love to me?"

"There anything to drink in here?" I asked.

Evelyn motioned toward the kitchen. I found a bottle

of bourbon and a couple of glasses. "Straight okay?" I asked.

She nodded, then sauntered over to me.

"What're you all about?" she asked.

I poured a couple of fingers in each glass, then handed one to her. She took the offering and stepped in closer, placing a hand on my chest.

"This is nice," she said.

I grinned.

She brought the glass to her red lips and drank. I joined her.

"You don't answer a girl, do you?"

"I guess that depends on the girl," I said.

She took another sip, relishing the brown liquid. I took hold of the bottle and poured her a second. Then pretended to pour more into my own glass. She took another swig. I placed a hand on her tight waist and pulled her even closer. She didn't resist.

I set my glass on the counter and gently caressed her cheek. "It's healing nicely," I said. "Not even tender to the touch."

"Hey," she said. "What's all this about?"

She tried to pull away, but I held her close. After a moment, she pressed into me.

"Who took a poke at you?" I asked. "Sal?"

She leaned back and studied me intently. I helped her take another drink. The effect was beginning to show in her eyes.

"You're one of Sal's girls, aren't you?"

"Who are you?" she asked.

"Name's Rossi," I said. "Max Rossi."

"Ummm, the sax player," she said.

"That's right. And your name is Evelyn. You're one of Sal's girls. Isn't that right?"

She took another drink, then laid her head against my chest. "Does it make a difference?" she asked.

"It does to Sal," I said.

Her glass was empty, so I led her over to the kitchen table and sat her down in one of the chairs. I set the glass in front of her and poured a little more.

She smiled.

"Evelyn," I said. "I want you to tell me what happened the night Margaret was killed. You were here, weren't you?"

"The colored boy killed her," she said and took another drink.

"Did you see that?" I asked.

"I want to dance," she said. "Do you want to dance?"

I repeated the question.

"Take me dancing," she said with outstretched arms.

"What did you see?" I asked.

Her face turned sour. "No," she said. "If you won't take me dancing, then I don't think I like you, Mr. Sax Man."

I took hold of her hand and guided her to her feet. Then I slid one hand around her waist and took hold of her other. I began moving her around in small circles. She let loose of my hand and threw her arms around my neck. I placed my free hand against her back, but she moved it down to her hips.

"There's a radio on the counter," she said. "Turn it on."

I danced her over to the counter and turned on the radio. The song was upbeat. Something the kids were listening to nowadays.

"Unh-uh," she said. "Find something slow."

I turned the dial until I found something that met with her approval. She swayed her hips slowly to the beat, and suddenly I was back on the ocean. I danced with her there in a dead woman's apartment, letting the alcohol work its magic, letting the melancholy set in.

"You didn't see Moses kill Margaret, did you?" I finally asked.

She placed her head against my chest. "I don't want to talk about that," she said.

"Aw, but it's my dime. I paid for this dance."

She sighed. "Can't we just dance?"

"Sure," I said. "Dance and talk."

She nestled in closer.

"You didn't see Moses kill Margaret, did you?" I asked again.

"Is that his name?"

"It is," I said. "But you already knew that. He's sitting in a cold jail cell, accused of killing Margaret, but he didn't do it, did he? They beat the tar out of him, you know. He's got a mug of ground beef."

She was quiet. I worried I'd given her too much hooch. We swayed in circles as the next tune replaced the first. After a while, she finally spoke.

"What will happen to him?" she asked.

"He'll get the chair," I said. "No questions asked. They've got a dead body and a witness. It's all they need."

We swayed some more.

"You mean me?" she asked.

"Who else? You're the witness, aren't you? The condemner? You're the reason the kid was arrested and the reason he took the beating he did. You called the police, didn't you?"

She stopped dancing. Her eyes wide. "I had nothing to do with that," she protested.

"Sure you did," I said. "You fingered a colored boy in the murder of a white woman. What did you think was going to happen? They took him and they beat him. They beat him hard, then they threw him in a cell to await his death. He's in there because of you and you alone."

She looked at me with soulful eyes. "They told me to say it."

"Who told you? Sal?"

She nodded.

"So, you are one of Sal's girls?"

"Yes," she said and took her hands from my neck.

"He the one who took a poke at you?" I asked, and removed my own hands from her waist.

She turned away. "No, that was Percy."

"Booker Percy?"

"Yes," she said, wrapping her arms around herself.

"He was here that night, wasn't he?"

"Yes. He met Moses outside and sold him drugs."

"But he didn't leave after Moses went back inside."

She shook her head.

"How did Margaret take to Moses' addiction?"

"She didn't. She hated the stuff. Hated Percy for giving it to him."

I moved over and placed a soft hand on her shoulder. "What did Percy do?"

She looked up at me, then hugged herself even tighter. "I heard a noise in Margaret's apartment. I had just gotten home from . . ." she paused. "I had just gotten home when I saw Percy and Moses outside. I knew what they were doing. A bit later I heard the noise in her apartment, so I went over to see. I thought she and

Moses were having another fight. After all, Moses had just bought drugs after promising Margaret he wouldn't use them. I thought that's what it was."

"But it wasn't, was it?"

She glanced down and shook her head. "Percy was there. He had her by the neck. She was afraid of him, you know. He had made passes at her many times. Would say to her, 'What? I'm not good enough for you?' and 'What's he got that I ain't got,' stuff like that. She was afraid of him. She told Moses never to let him over to the apartment."

"But didn't she flirt with him?"

"Sure, at first. She liked to get Moses riled up, said it heightened the passion. I told her it was a dangerous play, and that's what it became with Percy."

"He had her by the neck," I said.

She moved over to the area where the murder had taken place—seeing it play out in front of her. "He was choking her," she said, raising her hands as if they were around Margaret's neck. "I ran over to him and tried to stop him," she said, acting out her movements, "tried to pull his arms away, but he didn't stop. He pushed me. Pushed me onto the ground. I didn't know what to do."

She knelt down near the lamp. "I picked it up and hit him with it." She looked up at me with hollow eyes. "He let Margaret go and she dropped to the ground. Then he turned on me." Her eyes grew wide. "He chased me into my apartment. I got inside before him, but he kicked in the door."

I went over to her and took her in my arms. She wept. "He beat me and . . ." her whole body shuttered with the memory. "He threatened to kill me if I told anyone," she said. "A little later, Sal came and told me to say it was Moses who killed Margaret." She looked up at me. "I did what they told me to do."

I helped Evelyn to her feet, then took her back to her apartment. I laid her on her couch and covered her with the throw she kept on the back. I waited with her until she fell into a deep slumber. After all, I was the reason for the state she was in.

Once I had her settled, I called Queeney and told him everything that had happened, leaving out where it had occurred. I would have called O'Malley, but I wanted it to be taken seriously, and who knew what O'Malley would do?

"Well, aren't you the smart one? Queeney said. "You determine how the other stiff figures into all of this?"

"To be honest with you, I don't get that one. All I can figure is that Grafton must've somehow knew Moses was innocent and tried to do something about it. Maybe you can get O'Malley to do his job this time."

It was a cheap jab, but I took it anyway.

After I hung up with Queeney, I returned to Margaret's apartment, put the hooch back where I got it, then cleaned the two glasses, and put them away. Before turning off the lamp, I picked up the bat, then headed out, relocking the door behind me. I slid into my Roadmaster and pointed it home, but before I could get there, the beast took a turn, and headed in a way I had not expected. Sometimes my Roadmaster has a mind of its own.

THIRTY-SIX

THE ROADMASTER PARKED itself at the back door of Huey's. It didn't like Sal any more than I did. The burger joint and bar was Sal's hangout. He liked the place because it was out in the middle of nowhere, which made any approaching bluebottles stand out like a neon light in the desert. The place also had two doors, one in the front and one in the back—convenient when a quick escape was imperative.

Most people came in the front door. I had tried that a couple times and found it difficult to sneak my way in unnoticed. This time I didn't want to be seen by Sal's Mountain or his Molehill before I had to, so I chose the back entrance. Sal would be nestled into the booth at the back of the place, meaning his would be the first I encountered upon my entrance.

I got out of my Roadmaster and headed to the back door, wishing I had a nice little .38 snub nose to keep me company. It was probably better that I didn't have it—I might have been tempted to use the thing. But I didn't need it. I had the bat.

As the sun hid itself behind the mountains, I pulled the door open and slipped inside, trying to prevent as much light as I could from sneaking in with me. Just as with Margaret's house, I waited a moment to let my eyes adjust to the darkness. While Huey's was lit inside, that lighting was quite dim, creating what I assumed Huey thought was ambiance. I wasn't sure mobsters needed ambiance, but what did I know?

As I made my way down the narrow hallway to the seating area, I spied the Mountain standing by Sal's booth, his back toward me. I snuck up behind him and swung hard, catching the Mountain by surprise as the bat slammed into the side of his knees. He dropped quickly to the floor. Channeling my inner Ted Williams, I followed up with another strike between the shoulder blades. I should have felt sorry for the big brute, but I didn't. The Molehill jumped up from his seat at Sal's booth, but as he did, I spun the bat and brought the thing up between his legs, dropping him like the proverbial sack of potatoes.

I turned to Sal. "I wouldn't try that if I were you," I said and pushed the bat into his chest before he could reach for his gat.

"What do you think you're doing, Rossi?" Sal barked. "I'm a made man."

"I don't live in your world," I said. "Your rules don't amount to a tinker's dam to me. You wanna play get even? Let's play?"

"What's all this about?"

"You know what it's about."

Sal's eyes hardened. "We tried to tell you respectful, Rossi, but you wouldn't listen. You just had to keep sticking your beak where it didn't belong."

"So you decided to frame me for murder?"

"Got your attention, didn't it?"

"Yeah," I said. "You got my attention, but didn't your mother tell you? It isn't always good to get what you want. You and I are going to come to an understanding before I leave this place, Manella. You're gonna keep your nose out of my business."

"Or what?" Sal asked.

"Or one of us don't walk out that door."

Just at that moment, Sal's eyes shifted to something behind me. I turned quickly to find the Molehill had somehow gotten back to his feet. I pulled the bat back hard, slamming the knob into his gut as he tried to take hold of my shoulder. When I turned back, Sal had managed to produce his gat and was pointing it right at me. As the hammer began to slide backward, I pulled the Molehill's arm toward me and twisted my body, shifting the brute to my position and mine to his.

The gun went off.

The bullet slammed into the Molehill's back.

The gun went off again.

The result was the same.

I let the Molehill fall to the ground, at the same time swinging the bat hard toward Sal. It caught him in the wrist, sending the gun flying into the wall. It bounced onto the seat, then fell under the table.

I pressed the bat a second time into Sal's chest, only this time I used enough force to keep his attention. His eyes went wide. "You're gonna leave me alone," I said forcefully. "I didn't rat about who had my gun. Don't make me change my mind."

I backed up, making sure to step over the Molehill. He was slumped over the Mountain, who was still clutching his knee in agony. I might have kicked him once, I wasn't sure. Before I left, I bent down and picked up Sal's piece. "Now we're even," I said, and left the way I'd come in.

When I got outside, I wiped the bat down and threw it into the dumpster, then I followed it with Sal's gun. This time when I got into my Roadmaster, it headed home.

THIRTY-SEVEN

I THOUGHT ABOUT Grafton Freeman all the way home, wondering how his cover had been blown. I understood Moses, he was a convenient fall guy, the perfect rube to create a scandal. And what a scandal it was—a black man killing a white woman, both coming from the Rouge. I was beginning to get it now. Scare all the white people, make them afraid that if they go to the Rouge, the fate that befell Margaret Lee Paige might just befall them as well. Booker Percy had handed them that scandal on a silver platter.

I thought of Evelyn, lying there on her couch—a woman who had lost her innocence a long time ago. I always wondered what made someone become a happy lady. What had happened in her life to make that choice the only option left? I wondered what would happen to her when Sal found out what she'd done, and hoped Queeney would help her get out of town when it was all said and done.

I wondered, too, if Queeney would find Percy before Manella did. I wondered even more if I cared. I was pretty sure Percy had killed Grafton, and I was even more sure that Manella had made him pull the trigger. Percy didn't seem smart enough to think of any of that on his own. How Grafton came to his end, however, was still a mystery. What I did know was that Manella wouldn't want Percy sitting solo in a jail cell pondering his fate.

I pulled the Roadmaster into the carport, locked the door, and headed inside. What I wanted to do was play the Bees while drinking enough manhattans that none of what had happened mattered any longer, then spend the evening in the arms of a long-legged Copa Girl. But that was no longer an option. My favorite spot had turned sour.

I took out my key and readied it to unlock my front door, when I noticed someone had beaten me to the punch. The door was ajar. The strike shattered. I reached instinctively into my jacket for my gat, before remembering it wasn't there—probably should have kept hold of that bat.

The door creaked eerily as I pushed it open— something I hadn't noticed it doing before. The living room was dark, and I could feel his presence even as I entered. I tried to scan the room while keeping the door positioned as a shield, but something was buzzing in my head and my eyes seemed unwilling to focus.

"C'mon in, Rossi," the voice said.

As I took a step forward, a light came on. Percy was standing by the chair. Isis Mosley was in front of him, his hand was wrapped around her neck.

"Shut the door."

I did as I was told. This time, when I looked back, I noticed Isis was holding a gun in her right hand. Her arm was to her side.

"We got two nosey snoops," Percy said. "Askin' too many questions."

"What're you worried about, Percy?" I asked. "Afraid the cops might find out it was you who killed Margaret Lee Paige and Grafton Freeman?"

"They got their man," Percy said.

"They've got a man," I conceded, "just not the right one."

Percy had that look on his face. The one boxers get right before they step into the ring—the one that readies them for battle.

"Why'd you do it?" I asked. "Why'd you kill her?"

"Shut your beak and get your hands where I can see them."

I opened my palms and raised them shoulder level. I shot a glance at Isis. One of her hands clung to Percey's forearm, the other to the gun she was holding. She was trying to be brave, but her lips were trembling, her face pallid.

"Just what's your plan here?" I asked.

"Somebody broke into your house," Percey said. "You caught up with her, and the two of you got into a rumpus. She shot you, but not before you strangled her to death."

Isis' eyes went wide.

"That's the stupidest plan I've ever heard," I said, and took a step forward. "You think the police are going to believe this little thing busted down my door?" Isis suddenly looked offended. I continued. "And how would I possibly be able to strangle her after she shot me?"

Percy swallowed hard. "You, um, strangled her before she shot you."

I took another step. "She shot me after she was dead?"

Percy rubbed his chin. "It don't matter what happened," Percy said. "She's black, you're white. They'll buy it."

Isis raised to her toes as Percy's grip tightened.

"Just like they bought Moses killing Margaret?" I asked.

"Yeah, just like that."

"Only, they didn't," I said.

Percy loosened his grip slightly, enough for Isis to stand back on her own two flat feet. "What are you going on about?" he asked.

"The jig is up, Percy. The police know all about what happened at Margaret's house. They know it was you who choked the life right out of her. That's how you got that cut on your face."

Percy instinctively pulled his free hand up to his cheek.

"In fact, they're probably out looking for you this very minute."

The boxer's mouth opened, but nothing came out.

I took another step closer, and as I did, I glanced at Isis to get her attention. When I had it, I put my eyes on the gun, then on his foot. She nodded.

"Who told you?" Percy demanded.

"Grafton," I said. "Just before you killed him."

Percy's face flushed red. "He deserved to be killed. Pretending he was friendly and all, when all the time he was a G-Man. I took care of that, didn't I?"

The bang caught me off guard. It caught Percy that way as well. He let go of Isis and reached for the gun, taking hold of both it and Isis' hand in his oversized mitt. As she tried to pull away, I rushed the man, catching him in the chin with a right hook. He stumbled backward and might have fallen if the chair hadn't been there.

I swung a second time, but his boxing instincts kicked in and he easily blocked the punch. Then he took hold of Isis' arm and twisted until she let loose of the gun. She took a step backward just in time to receive a backhand that sent her over the coffee table and onto the floor.

I turned and swung again, putting all my weight behind the punch, just as Sammy had taught me. It connected on Percy's cheek, twisting his head. The gun dropped to the floor and took a hard bounce. I would have gone for the thing, but Percy came back at me with a hard right that just barely missed my nose. Seeing the opening, I went to work on his midsection, hitting his brick wall of a stomach so hard my knuckles ached.

Percy slammed his fist into my side. It knocked the breath out of me. Then he took a jab, coming in fast and hot with his right, catching me smack dab in the beak. Blood began to spew, and I stumbled backward before falling to the floor. I'd been hit many times, but nothing that hard. My face flushed, and all sounds seemed to disappear.

I pulled myself out of my jacket as quickly as I could, just as Percy took hold of my neck with both hands. He squeezed tight. I grabbed his wrists as he began to pull me to my feet. On the way upward, I jammed my fist into the big man's inner thigh. He cried out and let go of me. I dropped back to my knees. The room was getting darker with each second and I knew I had but one shot. I drew my fist back and launched myself upward with the only might I had left. I threw my fist in front of me, slamming it hard into Percy's chin. He stumbled backward and tried to catch his balance. Then his head jerked forward, and he dropped hard to the floor.

That's when the room went black.

THIRTY-EIGHT

I JOLTED AWAKE, surrounded by a ring of bluebottles, to the burn of ammonia stinging the inside of my nose. It wasn't the best way to wake up, but it did the job. I recognized one of the men above me immediately. Mainly because he was larger than all the rest.

"Look at you," Queeney said. "You just can't help yourself, can you?"

"Where's the fun in that?" I countered.

A medic asked me if I wanted to try standing. "Sure, why not?" I told him, but my legs refused to cooperate, so I settled for resting against a nearby wall.

"You really stepped in it this time," Queeney continued, "tryin' to take on a guy like Percy. What were you possibly thinkin'?"

"I beat him, didn't I?"

Another voice jumped in; it was O'Malley. "Yeah, you beat him all right," he said. "You and sap poison."

255

The room was beginning to spin and having nothing to hold on to, I closed my eyes and pressed hard against the wall, fighting against the urge to vomit all over O'Malley's shoes—not that I would have minded, I just didn't particularly enjoy vomiting. It took a while, but things finally began to settle.

I cocked my head toward O'Malley and tried to focus. "What are you talking about?"

"That one over there hit him hard with a sap," Queeney said, motioning toward the couch.

I squinted enough to make out the form of Isis Mosely sitting on my couch, her forearms pressed into her lap. A bluebottle stood above her, racking a pen across a notebook as she spoke.

"She gonna be all right?" I asked.

Queeney nodded. "She took a hard one across the kisser, but still managed to get the drop on him when it counted."

"And Percy?"

"We checked his elbows," O'Malley offered. "He's on his way to the cooler."

"He killed Grafton," I offered.

Queeney nodded. "That's what Mosely said. You ready to give us a statement?"

I tried again to stand, but it didn't take. "Can I do it from here?"

Queeney turned to O'Malley, "Take his statement," he said.

O'Malley pulled out his notebook. "Spill it," he said.

I told him everything I knew while he scribbled it down. I told him about Moses' drug addiction and everything he told me in the jail cell. About Percy being his supplier and about Margaret's flirtations with Percy turning sour. I told him about Evelyn's involvement—

though I was pretty sure he already knew that part—and Moses' friendship with Grafton, despite how it appeared.

"What I can't figure is how Percy found out Grafton was a G-Man," I said.

"Amos solved that one," Queeney said. "Said he found the guy who squealed it to Manella. He recognized Grafton from a courtroom he'd seen him in."

"And you think Manella ordered the hit?" I asked.

"What do you think?" Queeney said, then asked. "You sure you don't want to tell me who had your gat?"

I don't know why I didn't tell Queeney that Sal had my piece. It's not that I liked Sal or his minions. It's not that I cared what happened to him. He probably wouldn't see jailtime anyway. He'd either pay off witnesses—or bump them off.

"You know perfectly well what happened to your gat," O'Malley said, hovering above me, "and we both know you're covering for your pals."

If I could've gotten up, I would have given O'Malley one right in the kisser. Instead, I chose simply to ignore him.

He persisted. "So you sayin' you don't know who took your gat or how it got lost? You expect us to believe that?"

"Believe what you like," I said. "All I know is I wasn't treatin' it well, and it ran away from home. Must've fallen in with the wrong crowd."

Queeney looked at me hard. He knew I was lying, but what could he do? Of course, he could have thrown me in the can for a day or two, but he knew as well as I did he had nothing to hold me on and would eventually have to release me. My father taught me when to talk and when to keep my trap shut—even if it meant a couple of days in the can. This was one of those times. I guess it was because lessons from my father ran deep.

I tried changing the subject. "I guess you solved three murders today."

Queeney looked at me queerly. "What d'ya mean three?"

"Grafton, Margaret, and the baby?"

"What baby?" O'Malley asked.

It was my turn to look queer. "Margaret's baby. The one she was pregnant with."

"How hard did Percy hit you?" O'Malley asked. "Margaret Lee Paige wasn't pregnant."

It took three men and a crane to lift my jaw off the ground.

THIRTY-NINE

IT WAS SEVERAL hours before O'Malley and his crew left me in peace. Pictures were taken, prints were dusted, and O'Malley searched areas of the house he had no business searching, just for fun. But I didn't mind. I knew how to hide what needed to be hidden.

By the time they all left, I was able to stand, but as I sucked in air, I was pretty sure Percy had left me with at least one broken rib. I went into the bathroom and had a look at myself in the mirror. Queeney had tried to get me to go with the medics to the hospital, but what good would that have done? I knew how to take care of myself. Besides, I was allergic to hospitals.

Having refused medical assistance, Queeney admonished me to at least have my nose looked at, so I thought I should oblige. The man in the mirror looked nothing like the current occupant of the house on Seventh Street. His eyes were blackened and his nose was favoring one side of his face. It was definitely broken and needed to be set. I probably should have gone to the hospital like Queeney suggested, but who was I to listen to reason?

I pulled off my belt, doubled it over, and placed it between my teeth. Then I positioned a hand on either side of my nose, bit down hard on the belt, and snapped it back into place. Tears streamed downward, but no one was there to see it, so it didn't matter. When I got the thing back to some resemblance of normal, I pulled a piece of medical tape over the top of my nose to help keep it in place.

I had gone the rounds with a light heavyweight, and I imagine he fared better than I had. If only the Mountain could see me now.

My stomach was filled with blood, and my clothes were covered with the same. I pulled off both my shirt and pants and placed them, along with my suit coat, across the tub. I removed my undershirt as gingerly as possible and laid it there as well. Thanks to my father, I knew how to remove blood from just about anything, but that would have to wait. I needed to set my ribs, so I wrapped more tape around my body, just below my chest. That would have to do.

I made myself a cup of Joe, and downed it along with several saltines, hoping it would settle my stomach. Afterward, I climbed into bed.

I slept like a man who'd been run over by a truck, one that backed over him again just for good measure. When I did sleep, I dreamt I was a punching bag for Marciano who, when he was finished, turned me over to Louis, each man pounding against my midsection without a care in the world. Mostly I tossed and turned, thinking about Moses and Margaret Lee Paige, and what having a mulatto baby would've meant to them. Especially with what Isis had told me about Las Vegas. It might have been career ending for both of them.

It was nearing 7am when my phone joined in the conspiracy to keep me from sleeping. I picked up the receiver and made a groggy hello. Leona was on the other end.

"Mr. Abbandandolo would like to see you. Can you be in the office by eight?"

"What on Earth does he want to see me for?" I asked, more than a little surprised at the request.

"I'm sure I don't know," she said. "Shall I tell him to expect you?"

"Sure. Why not?"

I hung up the phone and somehow managed to drag myself out of bed. The healing waters of the shower refreshed me enough to continue to ready myself for whatever Fingers had in mind. I lathered up and took the razor to my face—as well as one can with broken ribs— then assessed the damage in the mirror. My eyes were still a deep black, but at least I was clean shaven.

I dressed in my best blue suit and periwinkle shirt. I found a tie that looked like it might match and wrapped it around my neck. Then I tucked a display handkerchief into the pocket of my suit before placing my lid atop my head. If I was going to get fired, I was darn sure going to look good doing it.

My Roadmaster was right where I'd left it the night before. I charged it up and headed it south toward the Sands. I took my time getting there, figuring Fingers could wait to can me until I was good and ready to be canned. When I did arrive, I parked in my usual spot out of spite more than convenience.

It took a bit more effort than I expected to climb the stairs, but I managed to get to the mezzanine in one piece. As I made my way to Fingers' office, I passed what was once my humble hole in the wall and forced myself not to look at the door that once bore my name.

Leona, as expected, was at her desk. She looked up. "You're late," she announced.

I wasn't surprised.

She picked up the horn that connected her office to Fingers' and announced my arrival. Then she said, "Mr. Abbandandolo will see you now."

I walked into Finger's office, a place I'd been in many times before, and each time it came with an eerie uneasiness. When he saw me, he stood from behind his desk and offered me one of the chairs that faced him. I accepted the offering and slowly slid myself onto the seat.

"Heard you had some trouble last night," he said, as he removed a new stogie from the box on his desk. I watched as he snipped off the end.

"A bit," I said.

He placed the Cuban into his mouth—I knew it was a Cuban because that's all he ever smoked—and brought a flame to the end.

"Want to get to it?" I said.

Fingers eyed me over his cigar. "Get to what?" he asked.

"Get to canning me."

"Why would I want to do that?" he asked.

I'm sure my face betrayed my confusion. "Well," I said. "I was under the impression you already had."

Fingers took a deep drag, then blew out the smoke in a cloud above him. "And what gave you that impression?" he asked.

"You took my name off the door," I said.

"Did I?"

"Well, somebody did."

"Maybe those black eyes are affecting your vision."

I stood and walked right out of Fingers' office and went to look at the door in question. There it was, in letters as fine as you please.

Max Rossi

House Detective

"What's the meaning of this?" I asked when I got back to his office. "And don't give me any crap about not having fired me."

Fingers placed the stogie in the Sands ashtray to his right and leaned forward. "I asked you not to keep on the same track you were on, didn't I?"

"You did, but there were extenuating circumstances. A man's life was at risk."

"A ditsoon's life."

"It's still a life," I said. "And as it turns out, the man was innocent. But I know that doesn't matter to you. I know why you wanted me to stop the investigation. You'll still get your scandal."

"Maybe," he said. "We'll see."

"So I still got a job here, then?"

Fingers nodded slowly. "You still got a job. That work you did on baccarat saved you. You were right about her plans. We found a complete change of clothes in her suite, along with the five large and another nice tidy sum in a small suitcase."

"She was planning her escape."

"Looks that way."

"And the dealer?"

"I canned him, but it doesn't look like he was involved. You were right there as well. She picked him because of his sloppiness."

"What's going to happen to her?"

Fingers didn't answer. He just picked up the Cuban and sucked on the end. "I'm still not entirely sure this whole thing is going to work out with you, but I'm willing to give it another try."

"I'm not a lacky," I said. "And I'm not going to stop doing what I believe is right just because you tell me to. Even if you do try to frame me for murder."

"That was Manella's idea," he said.

"Yeah, but you didn't stop him, did you?"

"No, I suppose I didn't."

"Is what happened with Manella going to be a problem?" I asked.

Fingers smiled. "He deserves what he gets, the pompous pain in the ass." He turned somber. "You know his man is still in the hospital."

"He gonna make it?"

Fingers shrugged. "It's touch and go."

"It was him or me."

"I know. Still, you better watch your back around Manella. I can't guarantee anything. You're not in the family, so I can't guarantee your safety." He paused and took another slow drag before continuing. "Now, if that were to change . . ."

He let the sentence hang.

"No thanks," I said.

Fingers opened the drawer to his desk, pulled out an envelope, and pushed it across the desk to me.

"What's this?" I asked.

"I know you gambled on your own money. This is just a little reimbursement."

I picked up the envelope and peaked inside. It was a bit more than a little reimbursement. I wasn't sure how to take it.

"I may have to testify," I said.

"Yeah, so? What does that have to do with anything?"

"So, this isn't a payoff?"

"I told you, it's a reimbursement. If you don't want it, push it on back. It makes no difference to me."

I stood, slid the envelope into the pocket of my coat, then left to get better acquainted with my new office.

EPILOGUE

HE THOUGHT HE was going to die in there. In a cell. All alone. He had experienced withdrawals before—when he had tried to get clean—but never in a jail cell. One time when he was arrested he watched another man go through it all: the nausea, the muscle cramps and aches, the vomiting and diarrhea. The sweats. It was an ugly thing to watch, even uglier to go through.

When they released him, it was as if his life had been saved, as if his prayers had been answered. He didn't want to die in prison. Not like that. He swore he'd change his wicked ways. But then he was invited to the party at the Rouge. Garwood Van had thrown the party. Rented the suite on the top floor and everything.

It had been a great gathering, musicians, singers, dancers, performers, everyone. And as musicians are prone to do, they broke out their instruments and the party turned into one big jam session, filled with music and song.

He had stepped outside onto the balcony to get some air and smoke himself a jade. He'd been offered the drug multiple times the entire night and finally relented. It felt good to take it in—to breathe in the smoke and let it take him away. Away from the party.

Away from the truth.

Meriday had not come, but he really couldn't blame her. He'd done her wrong, and she'd deserved better. Theo hadn't come either. Grafton was dead, and she blamed him. She was probably right.

As he took another drag, his thoughts turned to Margaret. Poor Margaret. *Why*, he wondered, *did she have to go and get herself pregnant*? They were just having fun. Just foolin' around. It didn't mean anything. He'd never had a white woman and she, well, she'd never been with a colored man. It was taboo. It was dangerous. It was fun. It was . . . stimulating.

But then she went and got herself pregnant.

A man peeked his head out the sliding glass door. "Moses," he said, "get yourself on in here and blow that axe of yours. These cats are all hyped up, ready for that crazy beat."

"Give me a minute," he said. "I'll be there in a bit."

The man poked his head back inside.

His thoughts returned to Margaret. He took another drag.

She was alive, you know, a voice said. *Alive when you came out of that room.*

He didn't want to hear it. "I did what had to be done," he said.

Sure you did, man. Sure you did.

"She wouldn't take care of it. What was I to do? I had the doctor, found someone who'd take care of things like that, but she wouldn't hear of it. What were we supposed to do with a mixed baby? You think we could have lived anywhere? Think they would have left us alone?"

You didn't have to do it. You could have called the police.

"And tell them what? That I found this white girl half strangled to death, lyin' on the floor? They'd of hung me for sure."

And what about Booker?

"What about Booker?"

He's gonna take your place on the gallows.

"I can't help that none. He's done a lot of bad things in his life. Besides, he did kill Grafton."

Because of you.

He had no answer for that.

"There he is," a woman said, stepping out onto the balcony. She signaled, drink in hand, for others to follow. They did, pouring out the sliding doors and quickly filling the balcony. Moses stepped backward to make room for the oncoming throng of people, then stepped back again.

But they kept coming, laughing and singing as they came. Unaware of their size. Pressing into the small space. Before he knew it, he was backed up against the railing. He looked down at the darkness below, bodies pressing against him.

"Back up!" he called out, but he couldn't be heard over the noise—the singing and the music.

"BACK UP!" he called out a second time, but it was no use. They pressed against him even harder. He took hold of the railing. "BACK UP!" he yelled, his heart pounding. "BACK UP!"

It was the last thing he said before his body was forced over the railing and he fell in the darkness to the cold, hard ground below.

ABOUT THE AUTOR

Paul W. Papa is an award-winning author, having won the prestigious Next Generation Indie Book Award with his book *Maximum Rossi*, and the Will Rogers Medallion Award with his book *Desert Dust*. Paul is also a two-time finalist for the International Book Awards and a three-time finalist for the Best Book Awards, both from American Book Fest, as well as a finalist for the Indies Today Award.

He is a full-time writer and ghostwriter of both fiction and nonfiction who has lived in Las Vegas for more than thirty years. It was there that he developed a fascination with the area and all its wonders while working for nearly fifteen years at several Las Vegas casinos. Something which inspired his book, Maximum Rossi. In his role as a security supervisor, Paul was the person who actually shut and locked the doors of the Sands Hotel and Casino for the final time. He eventually became a hotel investigator for a major Strip casino, during which time he developed a love for writing stories about uncommon events.

When not at his keyboard, Paul can be found watching a classic crime noir film, investigating some old building, or sitting in a local diner eating a club sandwich and hunting down his next story.

Night Mayer

Keep reading for a sneak preview of paraqnormal noir. It was a case **P. M. Mayer** never should have taken--a rich developer found dead in his trailer, the victim of a self-inflicted gunshot wound. But when a fancy man in a fancy suit strolls into your bar, tells you his partner would never have done the Dutch act, then lays five Cs on the table, it isn't scratch you can just walk away from. Now it's up to P. M. Mayer to dig deeper and find out who--or what--really sent the man to the big sleep. Only to do that, he must head down a dark road and face an ancient creature so gruesome, so terrifying, that the mere mention of its name is forbidden.

PRELUDE

A SHADOW CREPT steadily across the desk, covering the blueprints and obscuring the notes R. J. Hawthorne was making. "What are you doing here?" he asked with a bit of a huff. He wasn't expecting visitors, nor did he care to have any. He stopped making notes, but didn't look up. "You must have an appointment. You can make one tomorrow. I do not see anyone after hours. Now please leave."

The shadow did not move.

It had been one thing after another since they announced the project. Protesters, mostly from the local tribe of Paiutes, doing everything they could to block the resort development that he and his partner, William James Pierce, had started. It was prime real estate 25 miles outside of Las Vegas in the foothills of the Spring Mountain Escarpment. A place where water was plentiful and the temperature much cooler than its desert neighbor to the east.

The partners had a vision. People coming from all over to vacation at the base of the picturesque mountains, bathed in rich reds, blues, browns, and oranges. A modern dude ranch, complete with horseback riding, herds of cattle, and nights by the campfire. Of course, this dude ranch also had a pool, a spa, and a blue-ribbon chef. Some people would come to Las Vegas to gamble. Others to escape the drudgery of their daily lives. Still others would need something a bit more lasting—a permanent escape from the ones they once loved. Nevada's liberal divorce laws would make that possible.

He waited, not wanting to look up for fear that if he did, it would encourage the person to engage him in conversation. It was late and all he wanted was to finish his notes on the revisions, then head for a good meal and an even better nightcap. But the shadow stood its ground. He laid his pencil purposely on his desk and let out a second huff. It was clear this person was not going to leave unless he addressed him specifically. "What do you want?" he asked and looked up.

He was met with an inexplicable sight. At first he thought it was a Paiute dressed in some kind of ceremonial garb. It happened quite often. The protests turning into makeshift powwows with dancing and drums beating incessantly. But this was no Paiute. In fact, he wasn't even sure the thing in front of him was a man at all.

Though it stood on two feet, those feet were nothing human. Thick hair cascaded downward from just below the knees to the claws protruding from beastlike toes. The hands, like the feet, were covered in thick, brownish-gray fur. Fingers, ending in sharp claws, were held at the ready. The beast loomed over him. Its head had the shape of a wolf . . . no, a coyote, grotesquely blended with that of a human—pointed ears and saliva dripping from yellow-stained fangs.

Hawthorne shoved his chair back hard and scrambled for the revolver he kept in the bottom drawer of his desk. With a trembling hand, he took hold of the .38 and pointed it at the beast. The creature made a guttural growl, but did not move.

"I'm not afraid to use this thing," he said, as firm as he could muster.

The creature took a step closer, then another.

He pulled the trigger. The echo bounced off the walls in the small office. He'd hit the creature in the chest, but it had no effect. He fired again and again, but nothing happened; nothing stopped it from drawing closer. Its yellow, bewitching eyes—more human than creature— bored into him.

Several seconds passed before he realized the gun was clicking with each pull of the trigger. The creature glared at him, meeting his eyes with its own. He wanted to look away, but he couldn't. Something compelled him, controlled him. The creature took one final step, only inches away from him now, its furious breath defiling his cheek. The putrid stench filled his nostrils and worked its way into his lungs.

He dropped the gun.

It was the eyes. They captured him, peered inside him. Deep inside. Piercing and then stripping away a hidden veil. Though the creature was still in front of him, something had changed. Something dreadful. It was now inside of him as well. It overtook his mind and controlled his limbs.

He sat back down in his chair. picked up the revolver, and laid it on his desk. Then he calmly opened the top drawer and took out a piece of blank paper. He wrote the date at the top, then wrote more. Much more. When he finished, he positioned the paper at the corner of the desk. Then he picked up the revolver, opened the cylinder, and emptied the shells. They bounced from his desk and fell to the floor. He filled the weapon with six new bullets, fresh from the same drawer where he had gotten the .38. He brought the gun to his head—his eyes wide and his mouth agape.

If anyone had been around, they would have heard the echo cascading throughout the canyons and would have come running. But there was no one to hear. No one at all. So the sound faded into the mountains and vanished.

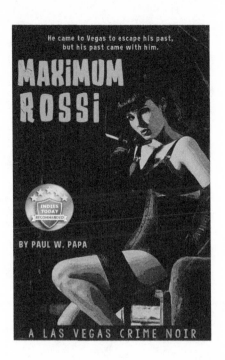

PRAISE FOR MAXIMUM ROSSI

"To find a modern pastiche of the noir/hardboiled novels of the 40s and 50s this good is quite rare. This is a really decent homage to the age of Chandler and Hammett, and it's a pleasure to read." - **Booksplainer**

"A wildly pleasurable and perfectly written gritty crime drama." - **Indies Today**

"This is an excellent hard-boiled mystery: cleverly written, smoothly paced, and with a protagonist who's compelling enough to sustain a series." - **Publisher's Weekly**

"A companionable mob tale, enjoyable unserious and dramatically immersive." - **Kirkus Reviews**

DON'T MISS OUT!

To keep up with Max's adventures and all of Paul's book, sign up for his noir newsletter at:

https://paulwpapa.com

To find out inside facts and tidbits about the Sands, Las Vegas, and Rossi's world, join *The Adventures of Max Rossi* Facebook group.

You can find out more about Paul W. Papa on his Facebook page at:

www.facebook.com/PaulWPapa/

or on his website at:

www.paulwpapa.com

If you enjoyed this book, **please leave a review** on Amazon, Barnes & Noble, Apple Books, Google Play, Kobo, or Goodreads.

Reviews help authors get noticed. If you do write a review, please let Paul know at paul@stacgroupllc.com so he can show his gratitude.

Books by Paul W. Papa

Fiction

Maximum Rossi

Rossi's Gamble

Rossi's Risk

Night Mayer

Non-Fiction

Desert Dust: One Man's Passion to Uncover the True Story Behind an Iconic American Photograph

Haunted Las Vegas: Famous Phantoms, Creepy Casinos, and Gambling Ghosts

Discovering Vintage Las Vegas: A Guide to the City's Timeless Shops, Restaurants, Casinos, & More